ON TREACHEROUS GROUND

BY EARL MURRAY
FROM TOM DOHERTY ASSOCIATES

Flaming Sky
Free Flows the River
Gabriella
Ghosts of the Old West
High Freedom
In the Arms of the Sky
On Treacherous Ground
The River at Sundown
Savage Whisper
Song of the Wovoka
Spirit of the Moon
Thunder in the Dawn
Whisper on the Water

SECRET STORIES OF THE WEST

A TOM DOHERTY ASSOCIATES BOOK
NEW YORK

ON TREACHEROUS GROUND

EARL MURRAY

This is a work of fiction. All the characters and events portrayed in these stories are either fictitious or are used fictitiously.

ON TREACHEROUS GROUND

This book is printed on acid-free paper.

Design by Heidi Eriksen

A Forge Book
Published by Tom Doherty Associates, LLC
175 Fifth Avenue
New York, NY 10010

www.tor.com

ISBN 0-312-86922-3

First Edition: April 2002

Printed in the United States of America

0 9 8 7 6 5 4 3 2 1

TO JOHN NEWMAN.

THANKS FOR ALL YOUR HELP.

CONTENTS

HIGH ON WINDY WATER

The day began with a stream of gray that swam down off the peaks and lodged over the valley. This meant certain showers in the afternoon. Good for the grass, a very precious commodity in these parts.

Dan Miller trailed a strong chestnut gelding behind him laden with salt blocks, loaded into crate boxes on each side of the horse's back. The cattle ranged way up to the base of the peaks this time of year and there was no easy way to salt the high country. Not even a four-wheeler could get within miles of this area. This method worked as well as any.

Dan had grown up in the mountains. He knew the high country in these parts better than any other living soul.

A group of men rode behind him, led by a young

real estate agent named Ken Watson, a whippersnapper with tight-fitting designer jeans and the latest in hair oil. With Watson were three executives from Wild at Heart, a company within a company that provided scenic retreats and summer excursions for discriminating clients.

Dan rode Jasper, a horse that thought like a mule. The others had been mounted on stock dude horses from the main ranch, handpicked by Dan so that they would make fairly good time, but with no surprises. No one wanted a rodeo.

Dan had also seen to it that they each had a slicker against thunderstorms and a collection of sandwiches and candy bars.

"We all really appreciate this, Dan," Watson had said back at the ranch. "You'll be happy to know that should the deal come through, there'll be no changes here. You'll always be doing what you've done. Promise."

Dan told Watson he wasn't worried about losing his job. He was glad for the company, others to share his thoughts with and to enjoy this wild land where change was creeping up the slopes like snakes on their way to den.

Marks and Preston and Gillman, all senior executives from Wild at Heart's corporate location in Phoenix, had come to tour the best of the best, the most scenic of the scenic that huge money could buy. All agreed that all business aside, the ride was going to be something worth remembering.

Gillman had brought his girlfriend, Jackie, sweet and friendly, but with few questions or comments.

As they rode, the three ranch dogs broke ahead. One of them, little more than a pup, kept pace easily. They zigzagged up and along the hills, sniffing and poking like small furry detectives through the grass and shrubs and flowers. Their breed was mixed but the Blue Heeler stood out in all of them. Cow dogs with a flair for the mountains and the adventure that abounded in every draw. They brought strays and stubborn heifers from brushy draws and steep ravines. In cow country there was no substitute for a good dog.

They hurried on ahead and lost themselves for a time, somewhere in the vastness that lay in every direction.

It was early yet and from somewhere in the haze the sun broke through and spilled gold on the tops of the lodgepole pines. Normally, Dan would be concentrating on just dropping the salt. Today, he would be giving a tour and some of the history of the ranch and the area. The places they wanted to see the most hadn't changed in three millennia. So today, with the guests along, the going would be more deliberate and geared toward a good time. The executives wanted to see the best parts of the ranch and its vast array of contrasting terrain: thick-timbered flats interspersed with grassy parks, and slopes that rolled with sweeping forest and rocky gorges that would carry an echo forever.

A hard day's ride wouldn't bring twenty percent of this spread into view. But today would be enough to allow for a good feel of the place—enough for a lot of money to change hands.

Dan felt sure these guys were already sold. This was just a lark, a good way to get out and call it last-minute bargaining.

As they neared the first salt lick, the trees along the cliffs darkened to a soft, deep green from the early sunlight. Overhead, four ravens winged their way lazily across the sky, croaking in gravelly voices. The grass swayed in the breath of a sudden breeze, and a Franklin's grouse hopped onto a log and stared at them with one eye.

"What a funny-looking chicken," Jackie commented.

"Is it hunting season?" Gillman asked.

"No," Dan replied.

"Why isn't it scared?" Marks asked. He ranked as the senior executive of the three men.

The bird jumped from the log and wandered

through the grass and flowers, in absolutely no rush.

Dan swung his leg down from the saddle. "That's their nature," he said. "Not a care in the world."

He ambled to the pack horse. While his guests watched he took the salt blocks from the crate boxes on either side of the horse and let them drop to the ground. One came to rest near a low rosebush whose scarlet blossoms were nestled against the black and stony earth.

Dan placed the block in a worn wooden trough. He needed to even the load on the horse and grooved the second block with a double-bit ax. He cursed when he slammed the blade into it and got two uneven halves.

"Damned if I didn't botch that one," he commented while placing a half into each box. He didn't want to be accused of having a bad way with salt blocks; he usually cracked them down the middle.

The dogs arrived, almost on cue, to sniff the salt blocks and look up at Dan accusingly.

"Damn you dogs," he said. "Don't you laugh at me."

A short ways farther, the group stopped to stretch their legs. The guests had each ridden, but on rare occasion, so they had some cramps to look forward to. Ahead, the trails they would follow curved past high lakes where cutthroat trout skimmed for flies, along the base of jagged peaks tipped with old snow.

Dan thought of the times he would have stayed back up in this country and likely never come out, had he not been married and expected back home at the end of the day. It was good to come out into the valley and talk with folks hereabouts, but there was something special about the silence of the back country, something that left a man with a special kind of peace.

Watson approached him. "We'll see some elk, won't we?"

"Maybe," Dan replied. "Can't promise it, though."

"It would be worth a lot. They could see the game in real life. It would maybe sweeten the deal."

Dan turned the column of riders toward a grassy pass between two towering cliffs. The timber on top was lanky and close. Twisted and uneven tops and branches spoke of harsh winter blasts that stripped new growth in the bud.

The gray sage meadows were vast and splashed with the blue of lupine and the gold of balsamroot. Whitebark pine had seen fit to take up residence wherever they pleased, their big, twisted trunks bent away from the weather.

The sun was now a round ball of light bringing a clear line between the sky and the peaks just behind. Near the tops of the mountains, the north slopes held patches of stubborn snow and the white banks gleamed like heavy pearl. A few of the riders brought their cameras out while Dan removed his dusty dark hat and rolled a forearm across his brow.

"Ever see a bear up here?" Watson asked. "A grizzly?"

Dan grunted. "Believe me, we don't want to see a grizzly."

"You hear that?" Watson shouted to the others. "We might see a grizzly."

They rode up and looked in all directions.

"Where's the bear?" Marks asked.

"He went over the hill," Watson said, pointing. Might as well make a game of it, if nothing was really going to show.

"What hill?" Marks asked.

"Maybe we'll see him later," Watson said.

Dan stared at him. "Let's hope we don't see him again. He'll eat the horses first and then every one of you."

They all laughed nervously, except Watson.

"Take a joke. Would you lighten up?" Dan said. He reached over and slammed a fist into Watson's shoulder. Again, everyone laughed but Watson.

The trail went over the pass and on through a maze of trees and grass. At one salt drop Dan plugged one crate on the pack horse's back with a rock to balance the weight with the last block of salt on the other side.

A camera went off and Dan growled. "Hey, don't take that picture. I don't want people wondering why I put rocks in my pack."

He led them ever deeper into the backcountry, through a maze of heavy timber. Finally, the trees broke into a grassy park. At the edge of the trees was a canvas tent, complete with cast-iron stove and cots and a patterned rug, old and worn clear down to the stitching—a dusty remnant of civilization meant to give the tenant's feet the impression of a bedroom.

Like all line camps, it served its purpose as home away from home, and afforded some shelter against the high country wind and darkness.

"This old tent has quite a history," Dan told them as they dismounted. "See that zigzag sew pattern along the side? That's what a hungry grizzly can do."

The men studied the tent while the dogs scrounged for lost scraps of food. Jackie dropped to one knee and the youngest dog rushed over for affection.

Watson pulled Dan aside.

"Aren't you overdoing the bear thing?"

"You're the one who started it, cowboy."

Watson frowned. "You don't understand, do you?"

"You're damned straight I do."

He walked over to where the executives had taken to snooping inside the tent. Inside, he pulled a holstered .357 Magnum from a duffel bag.

"What's that for?" Marks asked.

"I don't know yet," Dan replied. "I hope nothing."

Not far from the tent were the remains of what used to be the preferred line quarters. At the edge of the meadow lay charred logs and melted metal, once a cabin used by anyone needing shelter for the night.

Dan had used the cabin for many years and had never worried about who borrowed it. Then one morning, while eating breakfast down below, he had seen smoke. After calling the Forest Service, he had rushed down to discover the remains of an old drugstore cowboy from town, faceup in the ashes.

"Snuffed out with a match and a batch of gasoline," Dan told them now.

The mystery was who and why. Dan continued with the story, suggesting that a group of antisocial woodsmen might be the culprits.

"Those kind are hard to deal with," he said. "They can think what they want, but they had no business doing that to an old man."

For a moment the group was silent. Then Preston spoke up.

"What about the law? Sheriffs and deputies?"

"Too far back here to do much good," Dan replied, shrugging. "Things happen."

"So, no one was brought to justice for this?" Gillman put in.

"Not so far," Dan told him. "I've got my own ideas, though, and someday I'm going to spend some time down in the Jack Creek Saloon and learn just who it was that did this. Then I'm going to look them up and tell them just how much I hate living up here in a tent."

Lunch was a leisurely half hour under the pines where a stock corral had been built by a grazing association. The heat had built up throughout the morning and the flies had found the horses. As the group prepared to mount up once again, Dan noticed his horse was throwing its head in frustration. There was a big fly biting hard somewhere.

"Where's he at?" Dan asked the horse. "Show me where he's at."

The horse cocked its head as if trying to reach under its chest and Dan brushed and slapped until things with the fly were settled. Then he was once again in the saddle and ready to lead the guests.

The dogs returned after having gone ahead. They appeared, cocking their heads to say, "What's holding you all up?"

A short ways along, Watson called to Dan.

"We turning back soon?"

"We'll wind around," Dan replied. "We're a ways yet from the prettiest part of the ranch."

It was past midday, and the heat had grown intense. The flies were a nightmare: deerflies and horseflies that swarmed in masses and lay wicked striped wings to rest along the backs of the horses. And along the soft belly parts where tails and hooves and thrashing noses couldn't reach.

They stopped more frequently to stretch cramped muscles. Thunderheads rolled across the valley, shedding streaks of heavy water. They untied their slickers and nestled them over their backs and across their saddles, waiting for the storm to hit.

Soon spatters of moisture popped on their slickers. They rode through a mixture of sunlight and water, the light dancing in the trees while droplets of rain sifted through the branches. They eased through deadfall timber and crossed open parklands where elk had bedded the night before, leaving the grass in smooth hummocks.

"We should have been here earlier," Dan said.

The main storm rushed across the valley to circle around and come down off the peaks at their backs. Soon the sun was gone, smothered by the boiling clouds overhead. But still the forest wasn't dark. Instead it took on a deep green glow that seemed to radiate through the misty air. The flies had disappeared, causing the horses to rejoice. Each snort from their nostrils was a small blast of steam, and the rain and sweat from their backs rose into the shadows of the lodgepoles like fine smoke.

They were in the open when the storm struck with full force: loud claps of thunder and a blinding rush of water. A crack overhead froze the horses momentarily and two of them crow-hopped, tossing Marks and Gillman into the wet grass.

Dan frowned down at them from his saddle. "You two okay?"

Marks got up and wiped his muddy hands. "So much for a peaceful ride."

Gillman still lay on his back, allowing the rain to stream into his face. Jackie moaned and leaned over him.

"Bob, you okay?"

Marks pushed her aside.

"Bob, you need to get up. You hear me?"

Dan dismounted. So did Preston.

"Give him some room," Dan commanded.

Gillman rose up to his elbow and shook his head. "What happened?"

"Take your time," Dan said.

Jackie held his head against her breast. "Thank God."

Marks leaned down into his face.

"We still have the prettiest part of the ranch to see, Bob," he said. "Ready to go?"

Dan led them down a steep trail and into a rocky creek where three deer bounded into the aspens. Cameras clicked, flashing the deer in their haste to escape, their creamy tan back ends with their white flag tails flying.

Dan hurried them on. They had little time to enjoy the view. The rain had turned into a downpour and the trail was quickly deteriorating.

The rocks and black soil quickly churned mud under the shod hooves of the horses. What Dan called the Stepladder, a steep trail with no mercy, was rapidly becoming impassible. Had the group of riders been any larger, it would have been difficult for those toward the back even to get themselves out—let alone their horses.

Finally the end of the storm passed in a rush of cool air and birdsong. The trees seemed to come alive: leaves bursting with green produced a steady drip of moisture. The sun was again warm, and the clouds drifted apart, leaving only the wet on the grass to prove that the storms had come and gone.

The three dogs were gone again, and Jackie said she heard barking in the distance. Dan told her they had likely found something to yap at, and would be along shortly.

At the edge of a clearing, Dan pointed out a weathered corral once used by horse thieves. High up and secluded, this location made it easy for them to bring in stolen stock and herd by the light of the moon.

"They say there was a shootout up here," Dan went on. "They say there's graves around here, but I don't know."

Just past the corrals they came to a hidden park surrounded by aspens and rock. Dan suggested candy bars and everyone dismounted.

The dogs were there, sniffing the area with a lot of energy.

"It looks to me like you had yourself a party up

here, Dan," Gillman suggested. He lifted an aluminum beer can out of the trampled grass.

"That's not my brand," Dan said. "Let me see it." He studied the can with a frown. "Damn."

Jackie, who was playing with the pup, let out a shriek. Everyone hurried to where she pointed down into the grass. In separate pieces lay sections of an automatic rifle.

"What's this all about, Dan?" Marks asked.

Dan turned a circle, looking around the area.

"Dan," Watson said, "can you answer Mr. Marks?"

"No, I can't," Dan replied. "Not to his liking, anyway."

"Nor to mine, either, I suppose," Watson said.

Dan grunted. "Probably not."

"Is this some kind of camp where killers live?" Jackie asked. "Why would they be up here?"

"Let's just leave everything in place," Dan said. "I'll get ahold of someone when we get back to the ranch."

The trail finally wound out into the open once again, and Dan led the riders in the last descent toward the foothills and the ranch below. He could feel Watson's eyes boring into his back.

The others were talking about the day and looking back over their shoulders toward the peaks that rose up behind. But they weren't discussing the pristine beauty.

As they crossed an alfalfa field on the last stretch to the ranch buildings, Dan wondered if it would ever get dry enough to cut it and put it up. Haying was a catch-22 proposition: you had to get it put up at the right time to have good hay, but you had to have water to make it in the first place.

Marks and Preston and Gillman, along with Jackie, told Dan thanks in clipped voices. They wouldn't be staying for the barbecue that Watson had suggested, so the caterers went home.

Dan put the horses up and talked to them. They buried their noses in oats while he commended them for their day's work and warned them there was more to come in the next few days. Stray cattle had to be located and moved to pasture. Business as usual, no matter what.

Watson walked into the barn stiffly.

"No worries about losing your job now, huh?"

"Wasn't worried before. I told you that."

"Dan, did you set all that up? The beer cans and the gun?"

"I'm going to tell you this just once, Mr. Watson. I don't leave my weapons out in the rain."

"Then who did?"

"Go back up and maybe you'll learn."

Watson turned and left. His SUV spun gravel on its way out of the yard.

Dan hauled the saddles and bridles to the tack shed. He had put in half a lifetime on horseback in this country and it would be good to grow old in the saddle. He hoped this country wouldn't get too far away from what had made it so great in the first place.

A lot was going on, though, and times were changing. There were men with automatic rifles ranging the country now, back in the hills. Maybe these who had left their calling card behind had just been passing through. No way to tell yet.

He hoped so. Just let the world go by at its own pace and leave things as they are high on Windy Water.

UNTOLD HONOR

With the last rays of the sun, a flock of geese winged their way over the covered wagons and stopped for the night along the Crazy Woman fork of the Powder River. With the rain and mud of the past three days had come hard traveling and the worry that the clouds would soon bring snow.

Lieutenant Sheldon Price held the same concern. But now there seemed to be something more pressing he would have to contend with.

He peered from a high hill to where a ring of fire in the distance twinkled against the darkening land. To the west, the jagged peaks of the Bighorn Mountains outlined the crimson twilight.

"Are you telling me those are burning wagons?" Price was saying.

Bird Tail, a Crow Indian scout, pointed. "Can't you see the smoke rising from the flames? And, look, the Sioux are dragging people with ropes behind their horses." In addition to the Crow language, he spoke English, French, and some Lakota Sioux as well, making him invaluable as a scout.

Price strained to see what Bird Tail was pointing at. "Are you sure?"

"How can you not see what's happening there?"

"It's almost too dark to make out anything."

"The flames you can see clearly. If you can't see the Sioux, surely you can see the smoke rising."

"I wish I hadn't lost my telescope," Price said. He had lost it with an entire pack of goods the previous week, crossing the rain-swollen North Platte River. "I guess I'll have to take your word for it."

Bird Tail nodded. "So now you don't want to go any farther into Sioux lands. Right?"

"I didn't say that," Price told him. "My orders are to press forward to Fort Reno, pick up reenforcements, and escort the wagons on to Fort Phil Kearny."

"But you said that you will have no extra Bluecoats to help you take the wagon on from Reno. That many of them have left."

"I had no idea so many had deserted," Price said. "But that doesn't change my orders."

“Do you think that you and your small number of Bluecoats can fight the Sioux and win?”

“We’ll do what we have to,” Price told him. “And you agreed to stay through until Fort Phil Kearny.”

“Your people at the Laramie fort said the Sioux were hunting buffalo in the Black Hills,” Bird Tail argued. “I shouldn’t have believed them.”

“We’re all in this together, like it or not,” Price pointed out.

Sees-the-Horse, the other Crow scout with Bird Tail, had been sitting his horse with them, silent until now. He said something in Crow and Bird Tail laughed and slapped his leg.

“What did he say?” Price demanded. “What’s so funny?”

“He says that maybe you’re too eager to impress the woman in the red dress,” Bird Tail replied, “the one you told me was like taking a baby from a cradle. Sees-the-Horse says that when he saw her, she didn’t look like a baby to him.”

Price frowned. One of the civilians, a young woman named Maggie Finnerty, had been trying to seduce him ever since leaving Fort Laramie. He had told Bird Tail that she couldn’t be more than sixteen or seventeen and that it would be like robbing a cradle. Bird Tail had said that his people didn’t make cradles that big.

"What are you going to do when the red-dress woman is taken by a Sioux warrior?" Bird Tail asked. "You should do what we say and save her from that."

"That won't happen," Price insisted. "The Sioux won't get anybody."

"I'll bet the Sioux won't call her a baby," Bird Tail said. He repeated it for Sees-the-Horse in Crow and the two laughed.

Price pointed into the distance. "Maybe you two are just making that up," he suggested. "Maybe that's just a grass fire down there, and not burning wagons."

Bird Tail turned sober. "A grass fire? After all this rain, a grass fire?"

"You have a point," Price said.

Bird Tail looked to the west. "Maybe you should tell the wagon people to ride their horses and let us lead them across those mountains. We would be in Shoshone lands then and would be safe. And their silly gold wouldn't be that far away."

"I told you, my orders are to report to Fort Kearny," Price said. "You and Sees-the-Horse both shook my hand, and we smoked the pipe. You'll stay with me, I think."

Bird Tail grunted. "It would be much better to take all the horses and cross the mountains. Even with snow, the travel would be much faster."

"Even if it were an option, these people would never agree to that," Price explained. "All they own in the world is in their wagons."

Sees-the-Horse asked Bird Tail what they were arguing about. Bird Tail related their conversation and Sees-the-Horse shook his head.

Bird Tail turned to Price. "He says that the wagon people are foolish to die for a few belongings that mean nothing. And that you are foolish to die for the red-dress woman."

Price bristled. "You aren't listening. I told you, I have my orders. I'm going back to camp."

"Not yet," Bird Tail requested. "We will smoke and pray."

The three sat together at the summit of the hill. Sees-the-Horse carefully unwrapped a pipe from a cut of tanned elkskin. It was small, of the type taken on hunting trips and war parties. A band of beaded rawhide adorned the stem, and the bowl of red clay had been formed into the shape of a hawk's head, complete with four feathers tipped with horse hair.

Sees-the-Horse took a pinch of tobacco from another beaded bag, holding it between his thumb and first two fingers. Singing in Crow, he raised the tobacco to the sky, then stuffed it into the pipe, and after lighting it, offered it to the four directions, and to the earth and sky.

Price had witnessed the scouts praying each sunrise and sunset without fail. Though most of the emigrants, clutching Bibles tightly, thought of them as heathens, Price had a different view, and he was glad to have them guiding the train.

They had been at Fort Laramie and available to scout only because they had left a hunting party earlier in the summer to trade for some goods at the fort, and had been left behind.

Bird Tail took the pipe from Sees-the-Horse and smoked, praying in Crow. When he was finished, he offered the pipe to Price.

Price accepted and said his own prayers before smoking. He had prayed with them at Fort Laramie and again just after leaving Fort Reno. He had known the trip to Fort Phil Kearny would be a challenge, but he hadn't realized how difficult things would become.

Price puffed hard on the pipe, asking God, the Creator, whom the Crow called First Maker, to help everyone reach Fort Kearny safely. He thought of the things he had done wrong in his life and wondered how much they would weigh against him now.

When he was finished, he handed the pipe back to Bird Tail, thanking him.

"I'm going back to camp with Sees-the-Horse," Bird Tail said. "You should stay here for a time. Take another look at the burning wagons and listen to the wind. Hear what it tells you."

Price watched the two scouts descend the hill, melting into the shadows. They would go to their camp and, when morning came, wait for him to give them their orders. Though Price had invited them, they never went near the emigrants, who showed fear and distrust. They were content to ride out each morning ahead of the wagons, looking for signs of the Sioux.

Tomorrow would certainly be an interesting day.

Price peered into the last shades of twilight, thinking of the road ahead, and what they would find. The scouts were never wrong about what they observed.

He wished he'd never accepted the assignment to Fort Laramie. This was his first experience escorting wagons through Indian hunting grounds. He had survived two gunshot wounds fighting for the North and had learned the ways of war, but he had no idea how hard it would be trying to keep civilians calm while watching for an enemy that blended so well with the land.

An attack by a Sioux war party seemed imminent. If they survived to reach Fort Kearny, there would be another problem for the emigrants to face. Despite the Indians, a lot of hard country lay between there and the gold fields. Montana Territory, the Promised Land, would take a month's journey to reach, even with open weather.

Since leaving Fort Laramie there had been nothing but rain and mud bogs for the people to fight. Conditions would not be getting better. Nights of heavy frost and biting winds that slid down off the mountains promised an early snow.

Many complained that they had left too late for the gold fields, and that the smart thing to do would have been to lay over at Fort Laramie until spring. But the majority ruled.

Price had been given orders to lead two companies of cavalry and a pack string of provisions to Fort Reno, and then take the wagons on to Fort Phil Kearny. Though he had complained, his commanding officer had dismissed him with a stern reminder not to fail.

One of the commanding officers at Fort Kearny had relatives among the emigrants. Price had been told that Maggie Finnerty was one of those relatives, and that the officer expected her at the fort, safe and sound. The thoughts of such a commander couldn't be all that clear, and certainly questionable from a sane man's perspective. You don't send a relative into the jaws of death.

Now Price's uncertain future lay with his two companies of cavalry and a wagon train of emigrants, caught in the middle of Sioux hunting grounds. Everything he had worked for his entire professional life would come down to one day's actions and decisions. His entire military career depended on getting Maggie Finnerty past a war party of angry Sioux and safely to Fort Phil Kearny.

Lieutenant Price watched the last rays of twilight fade, and descended the hill. The air was crisp, and another heavy frost was moving in. His command had pitched their tents in neat white rows, along the bottom not far from the wagons. Some sat around fires, playing cards or working on rifles or equipment, while others curried mud from their horses' coats. All were on edge.

Price checked with the sergeant of each company, going over the rolls. Desertion was a problem, though not many wished to take their chances in open country with the Sioux. Telling them about the burning wagons would surely dissuade even the most determined from leaving.

Still, a private named Riley Cooney had been listed as missing. The sergeant, a stout Irishman named Malone, reported that Cooney had told him he was leaving. When Malone had begun yelling, Cooney had put his pistol to his own head, saying, "Leave me alone. I've been picked to die, anyway, and I don't care if I live any longer."

Malone told Price that Cooney had then disappeared among the wagons, and was thought to be wandering among the emigrants. Price had never encountered this problem before. He had been told to threaten would-be deserters with a firing squad, but there was nothing in the manual on how to handle suicidal troopers.

He entered the circle of wagons, passing children playing tag around the fires and women who busied themselves with the evening meal. Groups of men paced back and forth, arguing whether or not to stay the winter at Fort Kearny or press ahead to the gold fields.

Price had decided that after he had found Cooney and had talked him into staying, he would inform the wagon master about the burning wagons and call a meeting. He couldn't hold the news from them.

In his search for Cooney, the lieutenant passed the Finnerty wagon. Maggie, who owned a number of tight red dresses, called from the back of the wagon, smiling.

"Good evening, Lientenant. How nice to see you." Her long red hair hung over her shoulders, flowing freely between the curves of her breasts. During the day, she wore her hair up in a bun, covered with a bonnet, looking much like the other ladies. But when darkness approached, it seemed she turned into a far different, and much older, woman.

"Good evening, Miss Finnerty," Price said, helping her down from the wagon. "You're looking very nice this evening."

"Oh, *Miss* Finnerty, is it?" she said. "Why must we be so formal?"

Price cleared his throat. "I'm looking for one of my soldiers. He's quite young, and possibly acting a bit lost. Have you seen him, by chance?"

Maggie motioned toward the other side of the circle. "There's a soldier over at the wagon master's camp, a young one." She stepped closer. "But you don't have to go and talk to him right now, do you?"

"Sorry, I haven't a lot of time," Price said. "Thank you for your help, though."

"Lieutenant, do I have the plague or something?"

"Miss Finnerty, you have to understand my position. I'm flattered, but I don't see spending time with you as proper."

Maggie smiled and ran her fingers through her long red hair. "Are you worried about my aunt? I'm old enough to make my own decisions. I think we should take a walk."

"That's out of the question, Miss Finnerty. Besides, I'm going to announce that everyone is to stay with the wagons tonight, in camp. No going for water until morning."

Maggie Finnerty's eyes widened. "What is it? Are there Indians nearby?"

"No reason to become alarmed, Miss Finnerty. Just a precaution."

"This is the first evening you've made any restrictions, Lieutenant."

"Please abide by them."

"Maybe there's nothing really wrong," Maggie ventured. "Maybe you just don't want to be with me? That's it, isn't it, Lieutenant?"

"Miss Finnerty, there's no need for this."

Maggie Finnerty smiled. "Have it your way, Lieutenant. Too bad. I was so looking forward to getting to know you better. I've been looking for a strong man, a leader. Perhaps you're not the man I'm looking for."

"Have a good evening, Miss Finnerty," Price said.

He spotted the disappearing Private Cooney resting near a fire, sipping a cup of coffee. Sitting with Cooney was the wagon master, an old buckskinner named Burnham Tiggs, once a mountain man, who had agreed to take the wagons from Fort Laramie on, to be paid in gold at the end of the journey.

"Mind if I join you two?" Price asked.

"It's a free country," Tiggs said, sliding over to make room. He moved a Spencer repeating rifle with him and strained coffee through his heavy gray beard.

Price sat down, taking a tin cup filled with coffee from Tiggs. Cooney stared into the fire.

"So, Lieutenant," Tiggs said, "do you figure to take young Cooney, here, and give him a good strapping?"

"What for?" Price asked.

Tiggs laughed. "You came over here to take the boy back to your ranks. Don't tell me you didn't."

"I came to ask him why he wants to leave," Price said.

Cooney looked up. "Because I don't care to die in this silly damned uniform," he said. "Somebody else died in it and I don't care to be next." He pointed to a neat round hole in the coat, near the top button. The fabric around the hole and down the front was darkly stained.

"You're not the only one with a topcoat like that," Price pointed out. "You know good and well these uniforms came from the Rebellion."

"Couldn't the army at least clean them up?" Cooney asked.

"Don't you know how to wash clothes?" Price asked.

Cooney looked into the fire. "I suppose I do."

"Then go down to the creek right now and wash it," Price insisted. "If you don't want to come back, then don't. But you know what you'll face out there."

"You're just saying that so I won't leave."

"Ask the scouts."

Cooney stared at Price. "You have your ways of handling deserters, don't you?"

"Just telling you the truth," Price said.

Cooney smiled. "I don't believe you. I think I'll go anyway."

"You'd best hurry, then," Tiggs put in. "And don't let them catch you, or they'll use you for sport. The best you can hope for is to be tied between two horses and get ripped in half."

Cooney's eyes widened. "What are you talking about?"

"Or maybe they'll tie you down, cut you open, and stuff you full of that pad cactus that grows out here," Tiggs continued. "I've seen that firsthand. Your belly swells up like a keg barrel and you can't even scream, because they've got you gagged with wet rawhide that shrinks and rips the corners of your mouth clean back to your ears."

Cooney looked back to Price, whose face held no expression.

Tiggs put a big hand on Cooney's shoulder and shook him. "Are you listening, boy?"

Cooney began to tremble.

"I've seen and heard of things done by soldiers to them as well," Tiggs added. "It goes back and forth and none of it's pretty."

After a moment, Price asked, "What have you decided, Private Cooney?"

"I guess dying with the men is better than dying alone, and in a manner like that," Cooney replied.

"We're strong enough to keep them back," Price said.

Cooney continued to tremble.

"We're all afraid," Price told him.

"And there's nothing wrong with that," Tiggs put in. "We just have to stay together, that's all. We have to support one another. We can't lose our heads."

Cooney finished his coffee and rose to his feet. He left without a word, disappearing past the wagons and into the shadows, toward the cavalry tents.

Price asked Tiggs, "Why did he come to you in the first place?"

"He said he wanted me to take the spell off him. He said that uniform has hexed him. He'd heard I'd lived among the Crow and that I'd learned some medicine from them. I told him that I didn't have any medicine, that he should talk to Sees-the-Horse. But he's afraid of those Crow, the same as he is the Sioux."

"I hope he can hold himself together," Price said. "If he does something foolish, it could demoralize the other troopers."

"If them Sioux decide to come at us, we'll need more than bravery," Tiggs pointed out. "Times have changed since I first came to the mountains. Way back, I trapped among Blackfeet and got by Utes on the Bonneville. There were 'Patches and Commanches down south, just as bad. Back then a man could save his hair by maybe a trick, or by standing up to them with gall in his eyes. No more. That's all gone. These Sioux want their hunting grounds back. No parley. No tricks. These Sioux are out to kill, and that's the whole of it."

"Do you suppose they'll pick any particular place along the trail to attack?" Price asked.

Tiggs set his coffee cup down. "They might be thinking this is as good a place as any." He pointed to the ground. "Lean over and listen close."

Price put his ear to the ground. He felt a vibration, a throbbing from the distance—the sound of drums.

"They'll be going all night," Tiggs continued. "Come dawn, we'd best look out."

"You're certain?"

"As certain as a man can be about these things." He shook his head. "If I had a lick of sense left in my old brain, I'd have found a woman and a blanket and holed up back at Laramie for the winter."

"You've faced odds worse than this, haven't you?" Price asked.

"Maybe, but I've never been more clenched up in my gut."

"We'll make it through," Price said. "You've got to help me by holding everyone together. I'll take care of the soldiers; you take care of the civilians."

Tiggs studied Price. "I have to tell you, young feller, you're not the usual upstart commander. Most men in charge would have had that young Cooney whipped half to death for example. You've got more sense. Why are you a Blue Boy?"

"There are a number of reasons I came out here," Price began. He stopped his story at the sound of a gunshot.

At the far end of the camp, a middle-aged emigrant man lay doubled over on the ground, his rifle next to him, still smoking.

"It discharged when he was cleaning it," another man said.

Tiggs looked at the wound and stood up. "It's bad," he told Price.

"What's his name?" Price asked.

"Jacob Mason," Tiggs replied. "Only good thing about it, he's traveling alone. No wife or kids."

Three of the men laid the wounded man on a blanket near one of the fires. Camp women gathered with wet clothes. There was no doctor, yet no one doubted the wound would prove fatal.

The sun broke into an open sky, the first for nearly a week. But there was no celebration. No one had slept well and some hadn't slept at all. Though it was a Tuesday, many were singing hymns.

Jacob Mason lay unconscious on the blanket, drenched in blood and sweat. He seemed to be taking a long time to die.

He would sit up occasionally and laugh in delirium, scaring those nearby. The women had stopped mopping his brow and everyone kept away, awaiting the inevitable.

Tiggs busied himself getting ready for another sure thing—the arrival of the Sioux. Upon camping the previous night, he had ordered the wagons circled as close to the creek as possible. They were located on an open, grassy flat covered with scattered stands of sagebrush and greasewood. Though he had never been a wagon master before, he had decided to place the wagons as close to the water as possible. If attacked, the Indians would have difficulty surrounding them.

The sun rose higher, with no sign of the Sioux. Tiggs assured Price they would come, and soon. Price had readied his soldiers well before dawn and Tiggs had organized the emigrant men so that those with repeating rifles were spread out. Everyone waited.

Cooney, since his discussion with Price and Tiggs the previous night, had said nothing to anyone. His expression seemed impassive as he stood in formation with the other troopers, awaiting orders.

Bird Tail and Sees-the-Horse remained in their camp, preparing for war. They stood before a fire, their arms raised to the sky, their voices singing in prayer. Between songs, they took turns painting one another.

Price considered his battle plan. He realized that the Sioux might try and lure him on a chase. Tiggs had warned him that warring Indians were adept at setting traps. In the past, overeager commanders had led large groups of soldiers to their deaths by following small groups of warriors into ambushes set by larger forces in waiting.

Price decided that under no circumstances would he leave the emigrants. Depending on the Sioux position, he would place his command in skirmish lines and try to deter their advances toward the wagons. Should they come with a large force, he would mount his men and form lines perpendicular to the creek, leaving the wagons open to allow firing at the Indians by the emigrant men. Then, with his cavalry, he would attack the Sioux from both sides.

As the sun rose higher, Price considered that the drums during the previous night had served some other purpose than war. Then a column of warriors appeared on the bluffs to the east. They rode down onto the flat, within two hundred yards of the wagons, and lined up their ponies.

They were stripped to breechcloths and covered with paint from head to foot. Each had his own individual designs and sets of colors, most with combinations of red and black and white stripes or jagged lines along their legs and upper bodies, and bars across their cheeks and foreheads. A few were painted in solid white or yellow, and nearly every horse had paint markings of various kinds.

Some of them rode back and forth, waving bows and lances, screaming war cries. A few of them had repeating rifles, which they had lined with feathers and scalps. Bird Tail and Sees-the-Horse rode past the wagons, screaming their own war cries, nearly naked and heavily painted. They rode out from the wagons and galloped their ponies back and forth in front of the Sioux, screaming and waving their weapons.

The emigrants collected to watch the Indians, marveling at the show. It appeared as if the Crow scouts might attack on their own. Tiggs assured Price that Indian custom dictated taunts before battle, before the real fighting began. The emigrant men checked their firearms and placed boxes of ammunition near the wagon wheels, from where they would be shooting.

A number of women had joined their husbands, holding rifles ready to fire. Tiggs took position between two wagons, his Spencer repeating rifle across his arm.

"Let 'em come ahead!" he shouted. "They'll get theirs, and plenty of it."

Price ordered his soldiers into two skirmish lines facing the Sioux, with every fourth man holding the reins of four horses. If for any reason the horses were needed, those on the skirmish lines could mount quickly.

Cooney gripped the reins of four horses tightly, staring out at the screaming Indians, his face still impassive. He appeared relaxed, awaiting a certain fate.

Then he turned as Jacob Mason approached him with a vacant look in his eyes. Cooney had heard about the shooting accident. Everyone had.

"What are you doing out here?" Cooney asked.

"I'm done for," Mason said in a raspy voice. "Too late. I'm bleeding inside." He coughed. "I can feel it."

Cooney had trouble coming up with anything to say.

"Won't do you no good to be out here," he finally said.

"I aim to die out in the open, like that soldier did who you know."

"What soldier?"

Mason put a trembling finger in the hole in Cooney's uniform. "The one whose coat you're wearing."

Cooney frowned and stepped back. "I never knew him."

Mason collapsed on the ground. He held a strange look on his face.

"You know him. You've seen him in your dreams."

Cooney's mouth dropped. "How did you know that?"

"Funny what a man knows when he's about to die."

Bird Tail and Sees-the-Horse continued to parade in front of the Sioux lines, moving closer to them with each pass of their ponies. Price called the scouts back to him, asking, "Do you two intend to fight them alone?"

"Maybe one of them will come forward and challenge me," Bird Tail explained. "If one of them will fight me for glory, then the others will be satisfied if I'm killed. And they will have to leave us alone if I win the fight. That will be the agreement."

Price stared. "You don't intend to give up your life, do you?"

"Of course not," Bird Tail replied. "I will kill the one that meets my challenge—if any of them will. But I think they would rather burn the wagons and kill everyone, if they can do that. They want to send a message to you and all wagon people who would invade their lands."

The Sioux began to move forward in a large group. Four of the warriors in front slid to the side of their ponies and rode back and forth in front of the wagons, coming closer with each pass. Four more followed, and then another four.

"I believe you're right," Price said to Bird Tail, as the Sioux drew ever closer. He raised his saber. "At the ready!" he yelled. The troopers leveled their rifles.

Two Sioux warriors broke from the line and rode recklessly straight toward the wagons.

"Hold!" Price yelled. "Hold!"

The two warriors were nearly to the wagons when

Cooney suddenly burst in front of the skirmish line, mounted and riding a borrowed horse.

"Private Cooney, get back here!" Price shouted. "That's an order!"

Cooney paid no attention. He rode toward the Sioux, taunting them in the same manner he had seen the Crow scouts doing.

"Come and get me if you want!" he screamed. "Look at me! I'm already dead!"

The Sioux weren't the only ones who stared in shock. Private Cooney was smeared from head to foot in fresh blood—Jacob Mason's blood.

The Sioux warriors reined in their ponies. Bird Tail began making sign language, interpreting for the warriors the words Cooney was screaming at them.

Cooney continued to yell, motioning for the warriors to come forward and see what a dead man, still alive, felt like to the touch. Bird Tail translated, "Look at the hole in his front, and see all the blood. He is a spirit who will go with whomever tries to touch him. He will scream in the night outside your lodges. Come and get him."

The Sioux all began to point as Cooney continued toward them, raging at the top of his lungs. They turned their ponies and rode away, with the blood-covered soldier riding after them. After a distance, Cooney turned the horse around.

Cheers rose from the emigrants. Tiggs yelled for them to stay behind cover until the Sioux were gone for good. Bird Tail dismounted and stood before Price.

"Is he truly dead?

"He's just as alive as you and me," Price replied. "I don't know what possessed him to do that, though."

"When we smoked the pipe back at the Laramie fort, you didn't tell me there was a crazy spirit among your Bluecoats."

"I just told you, he isn't a spirit."

"That's not what his eyes say."

Price stared out at Cooney, who was riding back toward the wagons, laughing hysterically.

"He is certainly a crazy person, possessed by a spirit we don't want to be around," Bird Tail said.

"Very well," Price said. "Go across the mountains and back to your people. I won't hold you to your promise."

Bird Tail extended his hand. "I'm glad you understand." He and Sees-the-Horse returned to their camp and quickly prepared for departure.

Price kept his men in skirmish lines, in case the Sioux changed their mind and returned. Based on the

Crow scouts' reaction, though, he knew there was no longer reason to worry about a battle. Tiggs agreed.

"Scared them as bad as I've ever seen a war party get scared," Tiggs said. "They watch for signs and won't take chances losing anyone, if they can help it."

Cooney rode up to Price and suddenly stopped laughing. He collapsed off the horse.

Tiggs was there to catch his fall. Price dismounted and helped Tiggs to lay Cooney flat. He opened glassy eyes, appearing disoriented.

"What, is the fight over?" he asked. "Am I still alive?"

"You're still alive, boy!" Tiggs said. "And a hero to boot. You run them Sioux off all by your lonesome."

Cooney sat up. "Where's my rifle? I don't remember shooting."

"You need some rest is all," Price said. "But first you need a bath in the creek."

Price and Tiggs escorted Cooney back, while the emigrants cheered and waved hats and bonnets. Tiggs told Price that once word got among the Sioux about the blood-covered spirit among the wagon people, they wouldn't have a thing to worry about.

"Just have him ride out in front," Tiggs suggested to Price. "They'll stay away, a long ways away."

They buried Jacob Mason within the circle of

wagons and then had the soil trampled by horses and mules. There was a mixture of relief and shock among the emigrants as the wagons pulled out.

Price noticed Maggie Finnerty watching Private Cooney closely as he rode past with the column. It appeared that she might have found the hero she had been looking for.

Even if Cooney never really remembered all that had happened, he would be recognized when they reached Fort Kearny. He would have a badge of honor to put on his uniform, to cover the hole that had somehow driven him to the strangest act of courage anyone had likely ever seen along the Bozeman Trail.

SACRED STONE

Laiya Medicine Wolf huddled on the top of the boxcar while her heart pounded in the dark like a hammer on bone. She blew on her hands and struggled against the chill that enveloped her. The stolen red silk dress she wore felt like a thin coating of ice water, quickly sapping the remaining warmth from her body.

Men walked slowly and deliberately below her, shining their beams of light into the supporting beams of steel underneath the cars themselves. They were moving along the tracks from both directions now, shouting among themselves and worrying that she had somehow gotten away, or that there was a mistake in the transmission that a woman in an evening dress, wanted by authorities, was even in the vicinity of the train.

She had climbed out of the boxcar and onto the top just in time. The trip from Miles City would have killed her, had she not found the deserted coat of a transient in one corner.

She held her breath. They were below her now, converging and talking and asking themselves if they had come out into the storm for nothing. No one seemed to know for sure if there was any use in further detaining the dozen or so hobos they had thrown into a group during their search. None of them were women.

Laiya waited while they talked and finally left, their flashlights probing in all directions through the rain. The cold numbed her mind and body as she worked her way down off the boxcar. She jumped from the last rung and felt her ankle give.

She pulled herself to her feet and caught her breath. She tore the blond wig from her head and tossed it into a heap. She had looked into the mirror a number of times and never once did she think to herself that she looked like a white woman. But it had been close enough.

No one at the big banquet held jointly by the railroad and the mining company had paid much attention to her. Eagle Valley, a quiet little place of serene beauty, had been placed on display—the place of her childhood and a holy place to her people. They wanted to tear it up for the coal underneath.

A big model of the land that would be mined had been laid out along one side of the room. They hadn't noticed her walking quickly toward the layout while a big railroad executive talked about great things for the people of the area. They did notice, though, when she tossed the cup filled with gasoline on the display and set it afire.

Getting away in the smoke and confusion hadn't been that difficult. The shock of it all had held most of them in place long enough for her to get out the door and into the rainy darkness.

Then a cop rushing along the road in his cruiser had noticed her in the Miles City train yard. But the train was pulling out and she had been able to catch it. She had realized they would no doubt alert the little city of Forsyth, the next stop along the rail line, that there could be a fugitive on the way, so the search had been expected.

She leaned back against the cold steel of the boxcar and tousled her matted hair to let it breathe. It was drenched with rain, plastered against her head.

The lights of Forsyth across the tracks were

blotches of blurred white and red. Somewhere in the haze, she hoped, was warmth and her old friend, Teasy Schendine.

She stumbled through the lobby of the Joseph Hotel and over to the night clerk. The bus stopped here and a small crowd was sitting around snoozing or reading. Some stared, but most paid no attention. The lobby was attached to the bar and the sound of a jukebox and laughing was loud enough that Laiya had to raise her voice a little.

"Does Teasy Schendine still live upstairs?"

The clerk, a heavy, toothless woman in a faded dress, studied Laiya a moment.

"Listen," she said, "you ain't about to move in with them, are you? There's already three living in that one-bedroom place."

"No," Laiya replied.

The clerk continued to study her. She looked over toward a young blond woman close to twenty.

"Marcy, did you finish the laundry?"

"I will, Ma! Geez!" The young woman was skinny and drunk, and cracked her gum.

The clerk turned back to Laiya. "Where'd you get a dress like that?"

"Teasy Schendine?" Laiya said. "I'm not moving in. Just visiting."

"Upstairs, second door on the left," the woman

said. She continued to look at the dress. "What did you spill on the front of it?"

"Somebody else spilled it."

The big woman grunted. "We offer laundry service free of charge to visitors first time in." She raised her eyebrows slightly.

Laiya smiled. "That would be nice. This is my best dress."

The woman smiled back. "I'll send Marcy up for it."

Laiya ascended the stairs while the woman at the desk watched her intently. Rock music was blaring from the inside of the second door on the left. She rapped and heard the thud of feet on the other side.

"Who's there?" It was Teasy's voice.

"Laiya Medicine Wolf. Remember me?"

"Who?"

"Laiya. You know, from school at Labre."

The door cracked open. "Laiya! Son of a bitch! Long time."

Teasy hadn't gotten any smaller with age. Her round face bubbled with delight. She hugged Laiya with the strength of a mother bear and hauled her through the door.

The room smelled heavily of pot and booze. The crowd inside, mixed Indian and white, male and female, moved away from the windows. They had been ready. Two stories wasn't that far to jump to escape a bust.

Laiya picked an empty corner and collapsed. Teasy pushed a beer into her face and she took it.

Teasy yelled over the music. "I saw you are limping? You get in a fight or something?"

"Nah, I jumped off a train."

Teasy shook her head. "Not a good way to go. Why don't you drive?"

"I will from now on."

"So what are you doing these days, Laiya?" She pointed at the dress. "You must be on good times."

"No good times," Laiya said. "I wanted to get back down home tonight."

"The party's here, Laiya." Teasy smiled. "Is that what you wear all the time?"

"No," Laiya replied. "It's not even mine."

"Did you puke up?"

"No, a guy spilled wine on it."

Teasy smiled. "Oh."

"Somebody will be coming up after it before long," Laiya added.

Teasy frowned. "Who?"

"I think the daughter of the woman at the desk. The blond one."

Teasy's frown deepened. "It's her dress?"

"No, but she's going to wash it for me."

"Bullshit. She'll just steal it."

"It's okay. I'm tired of it."

"You're tired of it?"

"I'll explain later." She set the beer down. "Got any coffee?"

"It's too early for that. Everyone wants to party," Teasy said. "But you can make some. There's a can with some coffee left on the counter and a pot under the sink."

Laiya worked her way through dirty dishes, packages of rolls and donuts, and a collection of snack cracker boxes to find the coffee. The music blared in the background. She measured it into a deeply blackened pot. Meanwhile, Teasy found some faded jeans and a shirt that belonged to a roommate.

Laiya had no sooner changed clothes and poured her coffee than the clerk's daughter appeared at the door. She popped her gum and pretended to be friendly.

"You got the dress ready for me to wash?"

"Right here. . . ."

"I'll have it to you first thing in the morning," she promised.

Laiya smiled back. "Be careful with it. That's my best dress."

Laiya closed the door and Teasy still couldn't understand.

"Maybe somebody's looking for whoever has it," Laiya explained. "There was a big fire at a railroad banquet tonight and somebody wearing that dress started it."

"That Eagle Valley thing in Miles City?"

"That's the one."

Teasy laughed. "A fire?"

"A bad one."

"What did you do?"

"Burned their table with Eagle Valley on it."

"Geez! You're a renegade, Laiya. An *outlaw*!"

"I just don't want them to destroy Eagle Valley. It's all I've got in this world."

"It's a special place," Teasy agreed. "Oh, are the cops going to be looking for you?"

"They already are."

"Will they come here?"

Laiya shrugged. "They might."

Teasy laughed again. "Want to meet some guys?"

"Not tonight, Teasy."

"Okay, then I'd better get everybody out, if the cops are coming."

Teasy announced that a bust was pending and everyone panicked.

"Not yet!" she yelled. "They aren't here yet. Take it easy!"

Some of the party crowd had already taken the

fire escape out the back way. Others crowded past Laiya and Teasy through the front door.

"I guess you know how to end a party, huh?" Laiya said.

"Ah, they'll be back," Teasy said. "So, when are the cops coming?"

"I didn't say they were," Laiya pointed out. "I said they *might* come."

Teasy shrugged and turned off the music. Laiya headed into a bedroom and collapsed on a double bed along one wall. Soon she thought she felt Teasy prop a pillow under her head and cover her with a blanket.

A loud knock at the door roused Laiya from sleep. She slid off the bed and under it, clear to the wall. She heard the woman from downstairs yelling from the doorway, and the rest of the conversation.

"That little Indian woman came up here. She did, I tell you."

"I'm not that little, Officer Cop," Teasy said. "Do you think?"

"Not you, Teasy!" the lady bawled. "What's the matter with you?"

The cop asked the lady to quiet down and held the dress out for Teasy to look at.

"Is it yours?"

Teasy said, "Do you think I could fit into that dress?"

Again, the woman spoke up and the cop silenced her. "Can I come in and look around?" he asked.

"Help yourself," Teasy said.

The cop said to the woman, "You stay at the door."

"I've got a right!" she said.

"Not this time," the cop said.

Laiya heard him walking around the apartment, stopping at the entrance to the bedroom. Then his footsteps echoed away and back to the door.

"It weren't my daughter!" the woman yelled. She was still yelling as the cop closed the door and ushered her downstairs.

Teasy walked into the bedroom and knelt down, peering underneath at Laiya.

"Guess what, Laiya?" she said. "You really are an outlaw."

Teasy had just finished her third beer and was anxious to get going before the sun got too high in the sky. Today was moving day. Had to get out before the lady from downstairs got back from the Cop Shop.

Laiya studied the local paper. The *Forsyth Inde-*

pendent reported the apprehension of a young blond woman in a burgundy evening gown who was being held by authorities in connection with the incident at the railroad banquet in Miles City.

From the newspaper article, it seemed like a real confused issue. Meanwhile, Teasy's old television was on, reporting local news during a break in a morning talk show. There was the blonde from downstairs, the night clerk's daughter at the Joseph Hotel, screaming as she was taken into custody.

Laiya told Teasy that the newspaper said that authorities in Miles City seemed unwilling to believe that an Indian woman could possibly match any of the descriptions they had on the suspect in the case. A blond Native American wasn't totally unusual, but not the norm, and certainly not at a gala event attended by wealthy mining and railroad dignitaries.

Laiya put down the paper and began helping Teasy gather her things for the move.

"She wanted that dress so bad for her daughter," she told Teasy with a laugh. "So she's so mad at me?"

"Not a good way to go," Teasy replied. "Maybe if she had washed that dress like she said she was going to, they would have been easier on her."

"Maybe," Laiya said. "And if she had spit out that gum."

"Yeah," Teasy agreed. "Who spilled the drink on you?"

"I didn't see him very well," Laiya said. "I kept my head down."

"Good thing," Teasy said. "He might have asked you out."

"I'm not going out with anyone," Laiya said. "I just want to get home."

"It will be good for you to get back down to Indian Country," Teasy agreed.

Teasy had decided she would try the reservation again herself. After all, she was now without an apartment. The lady would no doubt be back to kick her out. Teasy toyed with the idea of flattening the woman on the spot, but she didn't want more police as long as Laiya was there. It would not be good to have something bad happen to Laiya. She had forgotten how much fun the little person could be.

Laiya and Teasy worked together for a half an hour to get packed. No sense taking most of the stuff. The old TV was nearly shot anyway.

Teasy was adept at filling plastic garbage bags with goods that Laiya threw to her from various parts of the apartment. Then Teasy would shove them out the window and watch them thud into the alley below.

"Those bags are strong," she said. "I'm glad they make that kind."

While they worked, Laiya's mind drifted to her childhood. Her mother had used to dress her in shiny blue dresses, just like the one she was holding.

"That belongs to Cassy, one of my roommates," she said. "Her sister's girl was here for a few days. She must have left it." Teasy laughed. "You're little, Laiya, but it's still too small for you."

Laiya had been at her aunt's home, wearing the same kind of dress, the day the phone call came. Her mother and father had been struck at a railroad crossing, from behind, their car knocked into the path of an oncoming train.

She had learned soon afterward that a semi truck had lost control and had run into them from behind. They had likely died before even being hit by the train.

To complicate things, at the time she was still bobbled by a broken arm she had sustained the week before. The emotional and physical pain had made her believe she had done something very wrong, a feeling she had carried throughout her life.

"We'd better hurry," Laiya said. "I don't want to

be seen around here. And they don't like outlaws like you, either."

Teasy chuckled. She picked up the paper again. "Yeah, you're America's Most Wanted. What did you do, burn down the town over there?"

"I should have." She threw a pile of clothes to Teasy, who let them fall as she continued to read.

"Part of it, though. For sure," Teasy said.

"I guess so."

Teasy studied the story. It said the room burned where they had set up a model of the new mine and buildings for everyone to see. The guests had all run screaming from the big dinner party.

" 'A disaster brought on by a mysterious woman, who vanished into the night,' " she quoted from the paper. "That was you, huh?"

"No, that was the woman's daughter downstairs."

Teasy cackled. "But you're more dangerous. I'll be an outlaw, too. We'll be Thelma and Louise."

Teasy went back to the newspaper. She and Laiya could both read very well. Three of their teachers, while in the third, fifth, and sixth grades, had insisted that all their students journal for an hour every morning, both in the Cheyenne as well as the English language.

"You really want to get rid of that mine idea,

don't you?" Teasy said. "Because of the medicine in your family, huh?"

"That mine is supposed to go in at Eagle Valley, where my grandfathers held their sacred sun dances," Laiya said. Her eyes were filled with tears. "I don't want that."

Laiya had gone there as a child with her father, many times. A small man with a bad limp, he nevertheless walked all over and never hesitated to take Laiya to special places he wanted her to see, so that she might learn about her people and herself.

He had instructed her about the images on the surface of some large sandstone rocks that faced the rising sun. She always thought of her father when she recalled touching the images and feeling something within her, something that was a part of her, that was connected to those big rocks with the drawings and carvings.

She had kept it up over the years, even though it brought painful memories. She recalled having been there one time when her father had a friend with him, a large white man whom he called his brother. Her mother never approved of that friendship and they quarreled because of it.

While growing up, the feelings at Eagle Valley had been mixed. It was a sacred place, a part of her very soul, and it was there, when she visited that place, that she always wished her father and mother could have lived longer.

She needed to get back there now, in the worst way. It had been far too long since she had last touched the stone.

Teasy tossed the paper onto the counter and began packing clothes.

"Do you like being an outlaw?" she asked.

"Teasy, we've got to hurry."

"How did you get into that big dinner thing?" Then her eyes got big. "Oh, sure! That fancy dress."

Laiya smiled. "And a blond wig."

Teasy snickered. "You're stylish. Let's go."

Laiya followed Teasy down the metal stairway along the back fire escape. They loaded the bags into Teasy's 1972 blue Caprice, with one gray fender primed for painting that had never been painted. Soon they had the backseat crammed with bulging garbage bags.

Laiya wanted to go back for a selection from the stale and partially eaten donuts and rolls, but decided her hunger could wait. Besides, the toilet was still overflowing from something lodged somewhere deep within its plumbing. The big, bad woman clerk wouldn't like what she saw when she got back up there, so it was time now to leave.

Teasy knew where gas was the cheapest. They went on from there to where beer was on sale, then left a trail of blue-black smoke across the morning sky as they got onto the interstate.

"Maybe you should have put some oil in when you got gas," Laiya informed her.

Teasy put her finger on the glass over a gauge to the left of the speedometer.

"A red light comes on here when it needs oil. I watch that. Things are okay."

Four miles out of town, Teasy pointed to a young Indian woman walking on the shoulder of the highway, toward town.

"That's Darcy," she said. "Darcy Riding Horse."

"Is she one of your roommates?" Laiya asked.

"Yeah. She left with the pow-wow bunch, she and Cassy. I told her not to go." She went past the woman and started into a U-turn. "I wondered how far she would get before this happened."

Teasy stopped the car. The woman was much younger than Laiya, probably no older than fifteen, with long black hair that glistened like sleek velvet. Her jeans and tennis shoes were both amply filled with holes.

"Get in, Darcy," Teasy instructed. "I'm going to have to talk to you again, I see."

"Don't talk to me, Teasy. Just drive. Okay?"

All three were up front and the windows were rolled down, letting in spring air filled with sunshine and meadowlark song. Laiya was in the middle and Darcy Rising Horse was leaning against the door on the passenger side, looking out the window with tears in her eyes. Teasy reached across Laiya with a beer and Darcy pushed it away.

"You are just going to have to stay down to Lame Deer this time, Darcy," Teasy was advising. "I don't live in Forsyth any longer."

Darcy was silent, staring into the distance.

"You hear me, Darcy?"

"Yeah, I don't care."

"Darcy, listen to me. Johnny Crowe is no good for you. Tell him not to come after you again."

Darcy refused to speak and Teasy reminded her that the beer wasn't going to last forever. She also reminded Laiya, who finally gave in and took one.

Teasy turned to Darcy. "You're riding with two outlaws."

"I already knew that," Darcy said.

"No, really."

Darcy frowned. "Just drive."

Their journey took them south and into Colstrip

for more beer. Surface mining was in full operation on both sides of the road. Huge draglines pulled coal from underground seams that ran through the heart of these plains. Massive piles of dirt, the spoils of the mining operation, rose like small gray mountains above the pits. Giant mechanical vehicles traveled in all directions through clouds of swirling dust.

The three didn't bother to look. Even Darcy averted her eyes toward the road straight ahead.

"Why can't things be like the old people talk about?" Laiya asked.

"Those were medicine days," Teasy said. "Great medicine in those times."

Darcy rubbed tear streaks from her face and popped the top on a beer.

"What happened?" Laiya asked. "Why did it all change? It's not just the whites."

"I know," Teasy said. "It's not just them. Some of them have good hearts."

Darcy then said, "But they're not Indian. That's what my grandma says."

"No, they're not," Laiya agreed. "But even some of our own people aren't Indian, either."

They followed the highway along the Rosebud. Teasy and Laiya drank and Darcy began to cry again.

Lame Deer was sleepy when they let Darcy off at a gas station. She was still crying and Laiya got out to comfort her. She laid her head on Laiya's shoulder for a while, then sat down on the curb.

"I'm going to buy her a hamburger," Laiya told Teasy. "She's too skinny."

"You got some money?" Teasy rustled in her pants pocket.

"I've got enough," Laiya said.

Teasy announced that she would drive up to Jimtown and wait for Laiya to buy Darcy the burger.

"If you wanted to hit that place, why didn't we stop before we hit town?" Laiya asked.

"I didn't want to then."

"Don't do that, Teasy," Laiya pleaded. "At least let me go with you."

"Okay," she said. "See to Darcy, then. I'll wait here."

Laiya turned to rejoin Darcy, but she was standing at the window of a pickup truck that had just stopped. She quickly got in and the pickup sped away.

"Johnny Crowe's brother," Teasy told Laiya. "He's just as bad. Sometimes worse."

Jimtown was just north of Lame Deer, a little bar with a reputation that kept even the Mafia away. People had lived it up and died in that bar, and no one could readily predict what might take place at any given moment. Alcohol on the reservation was prohibited, so Jimtown was always busy.

At one time a pile of beer cans loomed so large in the back that on sunny days airline pilots coming up from Denver to Billings could steer by their reflection. When the bounty on aluminum was announced, the pile vanished in the dust of old pickup trucks.

Teasy sat in the parking lot while Laiya waited for her to turn the engine off. Instead, she gunned her car out onto the highway.

"Why didn't you stop?" Laiya asked.

"We'll come back. First, I want to show you something."

"What, Teasy? What do you want to show me?" Laiya's stomach began to churn. She remembered from their school days what all could take place when her friend got that look in her eye.

"My car can do those kinds of tricks you see on TV," she said. "You know, like when they jump the bridges and sail over the hills." She had just opened another beer and her face was one big smile, her eyes swimming like marbles in dark syrup.

"No, Teasy," Laiya said, "that's all fake. They make that up in Hollywood. And it's done by professional drivers who are trained to be crazy."

Teasy laughed. "Didn't you know that I'm a professional driver?"

"Teasy, turn this around and take me over to Ashland."

"Is that where you live these days?"

"Yes. Take me there."

They were approaching a curve in the highway, a sharp curve that was hard to negotiate under ordinary circumstances.

"Teasy, slow down!"

"Laiya, take it easy! I'm a professional."

Teasy braked the car hard and a garbage bag filled with clothes tumbled from the back into the front seat. The others bounced around in the back like large beach balls and Teasy started laughing.

The car slid off the edge of the road and caromed up and over an approach, sending it into a sideways skid through the wet grass. It finally came to rest up out of the ditch and partway through a barbed-wire fence.

A cow stood directly near the left front fender, staring through the windshield at Laiya.

She groaned and rubbed the top of her head. Dust from the upholstery clouded the air inside the car. Teasy's clothes were everywhere, having popped from the garbage bags like stuffing from an old couch.

Teasy laughed. "I think the beers got spilled."

Laiya couldn't open the door on her side because of a fence post. The cow had walked over closer and was now looking in her window.

"Hurry and get out, Teasy," Laiya ordered. "My head hurts."

"Why didn't you hold on when we went up in the air?"

"We shouldn't have gone into the air, Teasy! Now let me out."

Teasy got out and walked around the car, removing broken barbed wire from across the windshield and around the tailpipe.

"Not a good way to go," she commented as she observed where the fence post on Laiya's side had dented in the door. The left rear fender looked like somebody had decided to do a buffing with a can of black mud, and the barbed wire had done a masterful job of scratching zigzag designs along the hood and top. The paint was so faded, though, that one good rain would melt everything together again.

Laiya was standing a ways away noticing how the wheels had left wide, skidding tracks through the ditch. She took a deep breath and raised her eyes to the Creator, giving thanks for the good fortune of avoiding death or even serious injury. Teasy got back into her car and started it up. It ran as smooth as it ever had, scaring the cow away from the right side.

Teasy stuck her head out the window.

"Get in! Let's go!"

"Get it up on the highway," Laiya said.

Teasy jammed the car into reverse; the car whined and slid out and away from the ruptured fence. She then ground the gears into forward and stepped on the gas. Mud flew from under the rear wheels like burned and distorted marshmallows.

She slid her way along the ditch with the fishtailing Caprice until she caught enough gravel to work her way back up onto the road. Blue smoke filled the sky like a homecoming bonfire, and the car backfired as she made a sharp turn in the highway. As she swung around, Laiya noticed the right front tire had gone flat.

"Let's go," Teasy repeated.

Laiya stood at the top of the ditch and pointed to the tire. "We'd better fix that flat."

Teasy tried to lean out of the car to see it. Then she settled back in and said, "I don't have another tire."

"You shouldn't drive it like that," Laiya said.

Teasy shrugged. "It'll still go."

"You'll ruin the whole thing down there."

"It wasn't very good, anyway."

Laiya shrugged and got in. "It's your car."

They traveled a lot slower than before, which Laiya was grateful for. She had sobered up considerably and was anxious to get over to Ashland. Teasy was lamenting the loss of her last beer and stepped on the accelerator. The rim quickly chewed the tire away and the metal grated against the pavement like an ax on a grindstone.

Jimtown came into view and Teasy cheered. She turned into the lot, through the layers of broken glass and cans, churning through the sea of bottle caps, and pulled to a stop. She pointed to the keys in the ignition.

"Just don't leave the keys in it when you get to Ashland. This is my only car."

"I'll just walk," Laiya said.

"Why don't you want to drive it?"

"What if the wheel falls off?"

Teasy shrugged. "Then you can walk."

"I'll see you later," Laiya said.

She got out of the car and saw that Teasy was holding her head, sobbing.

Laiya came to the driver's side window.

"What's wrong, Teasy?"

"I just hate it all."

"I know," Laiya agreed. "I do, too."

Laiya cut across the ditch and onto the road. She still had a headache from hitting the top of the car when they flew over that approach, but the warm sun felt good and the air was fresh. Her thoughts went to the little valley with the sandstone rocks and she couldn't remember how long it had actually been since she had last prayed there.

Pangs of guilt worked at her; she shouldn't have been gone so long. Perhaps she shouldn't have started the fire at the banquet. It had cost her time and a good deal of pain and humiliation. Lucky thing there was Teasy.

Laiya turned her head back and looked west, across Rosebud Creek, the wooded stream that ran like uncoiled rope through the valley. On a grassy bench stood the Deer Medicine Rocks, a favorite worship place for those who had always stayed with the old ways and for those who were going back. She wished her own Eagle Valley were somewhere nearby and not in the path of the railroad and mining plans.

She wanted to turn off the highway and begin walking east, toward her own little valley where the rocks stood quietly waiting for her. She longed to hear once again the soft voices of those who had passed before her. But it was too far to walk to the Custer Forest.

A four-wheel-drive pickup came up behind her

and slowed. She turned to see a middle-aged Indian woman with her head out the window. Laiya didn't know her name, but had talked to the woman at one of the sun dances, a few years back.

The pickup stopped and the woman opened the door.

"You can ride into town with us."

A white man, middle-aged, with a railroad cap and a week's growth of beard, was behind the wheel. He was burly, and worked on a large plug of tobacco. Laiya heard him say something to the woman and then she got out to let Laiya in the middle.

Laiya hesitated.

"It's okay," the woman assured her.

Laiya got in and the man was grinning. He had a slide-type window that opened back into a pickup box. He reached through and pulled a bottle of beer from a cooler. Laiya said she wasn't interested but he opened it for her anyway and thrust it between her legs.

Tobacco juice oozed from the corners of his mouth and he turned his head toward the window to spit. Laiya pulled the beer from between her legs and held it.

She turned to the woman to speak. Now that she was closer, she noticed the remnants of a black eye and dark marks, like fingerprints, along her neck.

Suddenly the man made a U-turn in the middle of the road and headed back to the north, away from town. The woman leaned over Laiya and asked him where he was going.

"I forgot something," he mumbled, and took a long drink from his bottle of beer.

"Just let me out," Laiya said.

"I won't be long," the man insisted. He was spitting out the window. He turned to Laiya and smiled. "Better drink that beer before it gets warm."

"I really don't want it," Laiya told him.

"Look, I know damn well you've been drinking. I saw you come out of Jimtown." He pulled off on a country road that took them up through pine-clad hills and off into a deserted pasture. He stopped the pickup and grabbed Laiya's arm.

"Get out!" he yelled over to the woman.

"What are you doing?" the woman asked.

"You heard me, I told you to get out! Now open the door and do it."

"Don't leave," Laiya pleaded with the woman.

"Get out!" he yelled again at the woman, holding Laiya tight with one hand and doubling the other into a fist.

"I'd better go," the woman told Laiya, opening the door.

Laiya tried to wrench herself away from the man's

grasp, but he was too strong. He continued to hold her while he took off in the pickup. Only when he had raced up to high speed did he release her.

"Jump if you want to," he told her.

Laiya took a deep breath and began to drink the beer. The man slowed the truck and looked at her.

"You don't seem so scared now."

"I didn't want to make it look like I wanted to be with you, now did I?"

Laiya took another swallow. He slowed the truck and put his hand on Laiya's thigh.

"It would be easier if you stopped," she said.

He came to a stop where two hills dropped off into a little bottom, isolated and quiet. Laiya took off his cap for him while he shut off the engine. He smiled just as she slammed the beer bottle into his face.

The bottle shattered, spewing beer in a frothy gush. Laiya followed through with another blow and the glass carved across his nose and face like the claws of a large cat. He brought his hands to his face with a gasp and jerked back, slamming his head against the cab. His fingers welled with blood and he began to choke with shock and pain.

Laiya burst out the other door and rushed madly for the safety of the pines along a hillside. She looked back only when she had gotten herself a good distance away. He was walking in circles beside his pickup, his head tilted over to one side as if he didn't want all his blood to drain out at once.

He was cursing. He wouldn't die, Laiya knew, but he would surely be smarter now about who he picked up off the road.

She never looked at him after that, but continued on over the hill and off into the silence of the spring morning. She shivered and let the tears run as she walked. Lame Deer was over the hills to the south, but she was going east. She would have to make good time, for the day was half over and it was a long walk to the Custer Forest.

Laiya crossed hills and bottoms and gravel roads, and climbed through barbed-wire fences. In the twilight, exhaustion set in. Her clothes were soaked with sweat and the cool air of the forest made her shiver.

She settled against a large pine, its bark soothing and the ground a friend. She peered into a meadow below and let her mind drift at the night sights and sounds.

What wandering shadows, these owls that coasted along the treetops, making their hooting sounds as they found dark perches within the pines. How did those deer learn to dance so well and pick up their feet so that they covered the ground like tumbleweeds bouncing in the wind? It was so beautiful, this glint of light on the stillness of the forest, mixing with the rushing breezes and filling the night with talk.

When the sun came up, Laiya found a slab of sandstone rock facing south and curled herself into a ball. It was sheltered from the wind by an overhanging ledge, yet open to the rays of the sun. She had scared a small buck from his bed and there was still warmth where he had lain.

All was lost to her now so that the blanket of sleep could ease the pain in her muscles and revive her for the rest of her journey. Foremost in her mind was Eagle Valley. She felt the need to be there and derive the comfort she had always known from the beauty and tranquility. Guilt bore heavy on her, though, for bad things had happened to her for having been gone from there for so long. She would be walking yet were it not for the numbness in her feet.

While she slept, small, striped chipmunks darted about her and chewed on everything they picked up. Bustling chickadees sang of their happiness now that nesting time had come again. The warmth of mid-spring flowed through the forest, bringing with it the light hearts of the life forms there.

Joining the sea of daisies and lupine were stalks of wild flax, whose delicate blue petals faced the eastern light, and the cheery blanket flowers, nodding into the morning and looking like sunflowers splashed with red. Overhead, the hunters of the sky began their journeys on the thermal air currents. Their hearts were strong and they could see far across the land and, many of Laiya's people said, into the distance so that the future showed before them.

Through Laiya's mind a golden eagle now flew, screeching and soaring on wings that spread a shadow across the rock on which she slept. She could feel him and see within his eyes an anger that told her he was not pleased.

His shadow came across again and she felt herself rising to meet him, pulling herself up onto his broad back so that the valley below spread before her like an eternal map, colored and distinct and alive. She saw the roads that had been carved across the lands so that things could be taken and not replaced. She saw great clusters of dwellings on the bottoms, where the best and most fertile soils had formed. It was always here that the dwellings were erected, where it was flat and easy to get to, and where bluegrass lawns flourished.

The lands where crops grew best were being gobbled up by houses and businesses. And on the shallow, rocky slopes, where only native grasses are the best crop, there were few dwellings. Most was open rangeland where livestock had been placed and forced to live in groups too large for the land to support. The tall, lush grasses were gone, replaced by shorter species and by various plants that were extremely unpalatable. A trick of the Mother Earth to try and keep her precious topsoil covered.

But the Mother could not stop what was happening. Much of this steep, rocky upland had been used for farming and the land cried out in pain and agony. The skin had been torn away by plows, and ugly, open wounds allowed the rains to rush through and carry the lifegiving fertile humus down the slope and away forever.

The eagle circled over the land, with Laiya clinging to the edge of the broad wings, her knees locked across the strong back. Since it was spring, the streams and rivers were running full. Their color was dark and they choked from the soil that they carried off.

Laiya could see the foaming action along the banks, whose edges were being cut down ever deeper by the swift current as it pressed ever faster through channels ruined by roads and tinkering machines. It was a strange parody of life that she saw, an administration of death by means of life. Though the key to existence had come down from the sky in the form of rainwater, these storms, due to mishandling of the natural resources, were also tearing away the outer layers of the land so that the summer winds could kill it.

The eagle carried her on and Laiya recognized the land directly below her. She knew it from the high pine ridge of the forest that stood above the little stream and bottom she knew as Eagle Valley.

But it had all changed. The large grouping of white rocks along one side was not there, nor was the stream, or even the pines that edged down from the slopes. It was all gone and in its place were ugly dwellings made of steel. A railroad track ran through the middle of it all.

Laiya screamed in rage and suddenly lost her balance. The eagle turned in flight and she found herself hurtling through the air, sprawling and churning through empty space. Everything was spinning around her and the colors became blurred and runny, like a rainbow-colored top, an endless sea of streaked images.

She bolted from sleep. Her lungs felt like they had been crushed by a blow from a fist. Finally air came and she struggled to her knees. Tears flowed from her eyes and an ugly kind of sickness enveloped her.

She rose to her feet, scaring away a small lizard who slipped into a crevice among the rocks and poked his head out to watch her. She had to sit down to let her head clear, and to allow the nausea to subside. The lizard skittered out and turned his head slightly to study her with tiny black eyes. Laiya nodded to him as she rose again.

It was nearing midday and the air was warm. Insects droned among the flowers and the calls of birds mixed with little gusts of wind. She was afraid to look upward, but finally did and saw no eagle circling. She looked in all directions and wondered to herself about the dream.

"I can never again forget to pray!" she told herself.

Laiya limped down the hill and across the meadow. Her feet were swollen badly and the blisters stung like sharp burns. Her injured ankle had swollen once again, but all she could think of was Eagle Valley.

She had no more time left to do anything but pray, and she would do that most fervently, for as long as it took. It was all she had left. With the small amount of money she still had left she would go into Ashland and buy some food and maybe a few blankets. Then she would go to Eagle Valley and she would stay there and pray to the Creator, and the ancestors, and all the powers, until she found an answer.

Later in the day she reached Ashland. Her grandmother and her remaining relatives lived a good distance to the south, in the isolated hills and badlands just north of the Wyoming state line. She didn't particularly care for life in Ashland, but put up with it so that she could be nearer to Eagle Valley.

Ashland bordered the Tongue River, the reservation line, and was little more than a few bars and a couple of general stores. Most of the Northern Cheyenne people who used the post office here made their homes across the river, on the reservation. Laiya had no car and lived close to her job. She worked part-time at a small motel, cleaning rooms, mostly during the summer months when the tourists stopped for the night.

She walked up a dusty side street to her small apartment and found the lock had been changed. She knocked on the office door. The landlady, a widow named Mrs. Bishop, was gruff as usual, a woman up in years who claimed to be of pioneer stock. She always complained when her government check didn't get there on time and told the renters she had no tolerance for people who didn't pull their own weight.

"Laiya," she said, "you were behind on your rent

and I thought you had left. Your things are in the laundry room."

What was left of her things was scattered across a dirty little corner where a broken-down washing machine rested at an angle. Mrs. Bishop followed her in and pretended to be sweeping the floor. Laiya salvaged an old shirt with a rip down the front where the buttons used to be and a mismatched pair of socks. All her jeans were gone and any other wearable clothing had found other wearers.

"I had some money in a pillowcase, inside a closet," Laiya said to the landlady. "What happened to it?"

The landlady kept her eyes averted. "There was no money that I saw."

"Seventy-five dollars!" Laiya blurted. "It was there when I left."

"I don't want trouble, Laiya. Don't make me call the police."

"You're forgetting, Mrs. Bishop, that I know Don Red Horn. He will listen to me."

"Don Red Horn left for South Dakota."

"He'll listen when he gets back, Mrs. Bishop. And he knows a reporter at a paper in Billings. That reporter always wants to write about how you people treat us."

"You can't prove anything, Laiya."

"No, but maybe the reporter could. You want him snooping around?"

"What do you want, Laiya?"

"I want my apartment back, for one month."

"One month!"

"Then I'll be gone for good."

"I'll need more than seventy-five dollars, then."

"Consider the clothes you threw in here as payment for the rest of it, Mrs. Bishop. Either that or face the Billings paper. Which do you want?"

"One month and no more, Laiya."

Laiya went to the St. Labre Misson, something she wouldn't ordinarily do, and received some jeans and a coat and some blankets. She took some beef jerky and potato chips in a grocery sack. She had to reach Eagle Valley as soon as possible and begin her praying.

Mid-afternoon found her there, in hopes of seeing an answer to saving her sacred place. The wind was rustling the tops of the pines and the sky in the west was dark. More rain was on its way. Soon rumbling began in the distance as thunder rolled out from the ceiling of puffy gray across the valley. She wrapped herself in a blanket.

Within her mind was another sound: it was the

rumble big machines make when they are moving earth. Like the ones around Colstrip. She closed her eyes and tried to rid her mind of the vision, the metal monsters chewing through the greening bunchgrass, the fragrant flowers, stripping away the life of the land itself. When the vision would not leave she fell to her knees, lifted her face to the sky, and screamed.

"Is everything all right, ma'am? Are you hurt?"

Laiya turned and rose quickly. She scattered her tears with quick blinks. He was tall and had a complexion that spoke of the outdoors. She wondered how he could have come up on her without her hearing him.

"Nothing is wrong," Laiya told him. "I was just calling to the spirits is all."

The man studied her. He looked to be not much older than her, and solidly built. He had a kind face but Laiya was in no mood to try and read his heart.

"You don't understand. You are not Indian," she said. She noticed that he had a camera around his neck.

"No, I'm not," he said. "Is that a bad thing?"

"Here, in this place, it is." She studied him. "Who are you, and why are you here?"

"My name is Tom Burns. I'm an archeologist. I work for a consulting firm."

"What are you here for?"

"To study the area and look for artifacts."

"You steal arrowheads. That's what you do."

"I make a note of them. And teepee rings. Anything from the past that might need to be preserved."

"You mean, you take it away to a museum, don't you?"

"No, I mean I want it left alone, the way it is." He looked around. "Where's your vehicle?"

"I don't own one."

He looked at her closely. "Have we met before?"

"No."

He turned his eyes to the rocks at the edge of the valley. Laiya wanted to tell him to stop it, that they were hers and no one else should look upon them unless there was reverence in their eyes.

But she said something else instead.

"Take a good look at those rocks, Mr. Tom Burns, Archeologist. They are old and sacred. They have seen many sun dances in this valley, and many stories from days gone by are told on them."

"You mean drawings, carvings?"

"Yes."

He was very interested and asked her to show him. While they walked he slipped the camera from around his neck.

"You ever been to Miles City?" he asked.

"My family lives in the hills, not in the city," she replied.

"I'm not a foreigner here," he said. "I came here hunting once with my dad, when I was a small boy. Spring turkey hunting. It's been a long time, but I remember those rocks."

There were memories in his eyes that he did not want to dwell on, something that spoke of having lost a part of life.

"What is it?" she asked.

"Nothing."

"This is a place where you cannot lie."

"My father wanted to show me something on the rocks," he finally said. "But he had a heart attack just as we got here. His heart was always weak."

"Oh, I'm sorry," Laiya said. "That must have been hard for you. So young."

"It was. I didn't know what to do. Then an Indian man drove up. He was a friend of my father's and he knew how to handle it."

"A friend?"

"Yes, my father had meant to meet him here. He said he was late because he had to take his daughter to the doctor to fix a broken arm."

Laiya thought for a moment. "What was his name?"

"I believe it was Frank."

Laiya's mouth fell open. "A short man, with a limp."

"That's him. How did you know?"

"He was my father. He and my mother died in a car accident a week after that. I wasn't that old yet and I helped bury him with a cast on my arm."

They both stood in shock. Tom Burns was the first to speak.

"My father talked about your father a lot. He said that Frank was like a brother to him, after they'd fought together in 'Nam. He said Frank wanted to adopt him as a Cheyenne brother and that when the day came for him to cross over, Frank would likely go with him."

Laiya covered her face and wept. The memory of her father and how he had wanted her to stay with the old ways overwhelmed her. She had missed him a lot over the years and had never been able to show it to anyone.

She introduced herself finally and they turned again toward the sandstone rocks nearby. The storm moved overhead and a gust of wind whipped through Laiya's long black hair.

At the rocks, Tom Burns took pictures of drawings carved in the face of the rock: running horses with warriors brandishing weapons, pictures of bears with arrows sticking out of them, and the sun and lightning bolts, all made by men who had usually stood on the backs of their horses and worked, telling their stories in jagged lines.

He studied the rocks carefully, while Laiya stood silently nearby. Flashes of lightning popped from the clouds. With each burst of white, the figures became outlined and filled with life. He had once seen something similar in a church, through a stained-glass window.

"Are you afraid?" Laiya asked.

"Not in the least."

Laiya smiled. "That's good."

"There's a lot of information here that needs to be documented," Tom said. "Lots of study done and, if possible, this area needs to be excluded from any mining or disturbance of any kind."

She thought it too good to be true. "You can save this place?"

"I believe so," he replied. "I know some people who will want to do some stories about the rocks, for magazines and newspapers."

"I don't know if I want to do that. Or to have a lot of people out here."

"You have to make a choice, Laiya," he said.

"You're either going to have to share this place and save it, or keep it to yourself and lose it. Which do you prefer?"

Laiya climbed up to a rock face where she was able to reach some of the drawings. She closed her eyes and placed her hands on them, allowing her feelings to absorb what was there, as she had done so many times as a child. After a moment she climbed down to where Tom Burns was waiting.

"You're right," she said. "They are to share, Tom, not to hold on tightly to. That will only cost me dearly in the end. The ancestors want it that way."

Tom beamed. "That's great," he said. "They will be protected, I can assure you of that."

The rain started and they found a rock ledge for shelter. Laiya handed him one of her blankets and they nestled together, sharing body heat.

They looked out across to where the sunlight was filtering through the edge of the storm. A huge double rainbow had formed across the sky.

"Very good luck," Tom said.

Laiya nodded. "Very."

"You know," Tom commented, "maybe that little woman in the blond wig who burned the display down the other night will get her wish after all."

Laiya smiled broadly. "Maybe she will, at that."

A STRANGER IN MADIO'S

My life has, for the most part, always been cactus and mesquite. I grew up in the dust of the Texas panhandle and never got it out of my blood, or my lungs. I'd made a run up along the Rockies a few years back, but came back to where the sun stays pretty close to the top of the sky.

I was born just before the war with Mexico and saw another big change come after the South gave it all up. I got into rangering but turned in my badge after a bullet clipped my ribs on its way into my best friend's head. I'd seen a lot of blood by then and had watched too many good men get covered over with Texas soil. I wanted no more of it.

But trouble has a way of following a man whose life has always been troubled. I decided that if the world wouldn't leave me alone, I'd at least get paid to carry two or three guns around all the time.

Someone always needed a hired regulator to see to his worries. The big ranches starting up always had thief problems, and I found plenty of work training selected cowhands to shoot straight. I charged enough so that the ranchers wouldn't want to keep me for long, but made it so they always thought it money well spent. They didn't have me full-time to pay but had some trained men who could enforce the ranch rules.

My wanderings took me all over Texas and Oklahoma, and finally down into the country around Uvalde—a brush-choked world filled with wild cattle. With everyone gone during the Rebellion, the area had come alive with longhorns. Now the war was over and the beef market was growing faster than they could get cattle to the railheads. After the first herds had made the trip up, nobody on the border could talk of anything but trailing steers to Abilene.

I spent two weeks with a trail boss named Larson, watching his growing herd, while he popped the brush with his *vaqueros* gathering steers for a drive north. He wanted to try going past the Kansas railheads and on north, to where the range "waited with open arms," he said. The gold fields had attracted a lot of people and they wanted beef on their tables.

In the few hours that the hands had before the sun fell every evening, I worked with them in handling their revolvers, those that even carried one. A lot of them didn't. Saw no need for one, really.

We had one incident with a small bunch of border thieves. They lost six of theirs, and one of our hands took a bullet in the arm. A better-than-average exchange for a night raid.

Larson offered me a much-more-than-decent wage to ride with him up the trail, to scout ahead for signs of trouble and generally keep the herd safe. I took him up on it and he paid me for the work I'd already done for him, plus a bonus.

The night before we were to leave I headed into town with the other hands. My idea was to make an effort at doubling my money in a poker game. And everyone knew that the biggest stakes in the border country were on the tables at Madio's.

With the falling sun at my back, I stepped through the doors, hoping to make a good night of it. I saw that a table just inside the door was covered with weapons of every sort. I shrugged and laid my Colt Army .36 down on the pile.

Old Logan Madio, who served as bartender, also owned the place. He seemed under a lot of pressure.

"No, you keep your pistol," he said.

"Fine," I said, which allowed him a smile.

It was one of the poker games going on that bothered him. I could tell by his eyes that he saw trouble gathering with the smoke in the room.

"You might need to help me, here," he told me, "if you're of a mind to, that is."

"I don't want to get into anything extraordinary this evening," I said. "I don't feel like it would suit me."

One thing you learn in the trouble business is to pick your days and not let the trouble pick them for you. A very good way to lose it all.

"Just stay for a little while," he pleaded. "Maybe if they all see that you're here, things will settle out some."

But Logan knew that trouble was certain, anyway, and so did I. There wasn't much he hadn't seen, and he always said he'd be smart to get out of the liquor business.

"I'll stake you to a hundred in chips," he said.

"A hundred?"

"Can't go higher."

"That's enough."

Logan handed me a drink, and I strolled over to the biggest table and stood back to watch. There were a few Mexican *vaqueros* and a few strangers who might well have drifted in looking for work. None of these men seemed out of place.

The reason for the uneasiness was plain: his name was Jack Tonn. He meant trouble, sober or drunk, and it was usually the latter. Besides being big, he was mean and belligerent. Nobody would hire him for a drive, not if they were sane.

The word was that Tonn spent a lot of time with a gang of bandits thieving along the border. He kept up appearances by running a dry-goods store as a front. Since no one frequented his business, everyone knew he had to be making his money in other ways.

I learned from one of the onlookers that he had been winning steadily until a newcomer entered the game. Now Tonn was drumming his fingers against the green felt of the table and staring across at a small stranger who showed hardly any face under a floppy brown hat. A wrinkled cotton shirt and trousers fit like a tent, so you were looking at a nose, a chin, and the tips of eight fingers that toyed with the vast majority of the chips.

Jack Tonn didn't like to lose. I stared at the stranger for a time while Tonn began to get mean, tossing out words like "half-pint" and "sawed-off." The stranger, with a mouth full of tobacco, spoke only to bet or call someone's hand, in a voice that was as raspy as the board floor of the saloon.

After pulling in the payoff for a large win, the stranger said, "I'm cashing in."

The room was silent. All eyes went to Tonn, who said, "No rush, little man. The game's just started."

"It's over for me," the stranger said calmly, pushing the pile of chips over in front of Harry Jones, who was dealing for the house.

Harry's eyes flashed from the chips to Tonn as he began to figure the stranger's winnings.

Tonn threw back a shot of whiskey and slammed the glass against the table. "No, little man, you ain't leaving yet!" He poured himself another shot of whiskey and put his hands on the chips to stop Harry Jones from counting.

The rest of the table started getting fidgety and began to look for things to do with their hands. The stranger reached over and took a wad of bills from in front of Harry, slick as a cat.

Tonn jumped up from his seat and reached over the table to grab the stranger. Whiskey splattered and men scattered like frightened birds. The stranger took Tonn's arm and twisted it back into a hammerlock, leaving the big man sprawled across the table, growling in pain.

"I said, I'm cashing in," the stranger insisted.

Tonn tried to force himself up. The stranger slammed an open hand into the back of the big man's head, ramming his nose down into the table.

While Tonn slid sideways to the floor, bellowing,

the stranger stuffed the money into a cotton shirt that billowed like a tent, while watching the big man intently from under that huge hat.

I stood back with the others and watched as Tonn came off the table and wiped a smear of blood from his nose. His eyes were watery from pain and drink and he was killing mad.

He broke a whiskey bottle against the edge of the table and came toward the stranger, waving the jagged edge in little circles. He bellowed and, with surprising quickness, swung the bottle at the stranger. The stranger almost ducked it, but the blow came crossways and sent the floppy hat to the floor.

That's when all that long red hair fell out.

She frowned at first and then her eyes got wide with anger.

Tonn was standing upright and was as surprised as anyone else. He took a small boot to the groin that doubled him over like a spent sack of flour. The broken bottle clunked off the table and bounced to the floor, followed by Tonn, who sounded like a barrel of salt pork when he hit.

I was closest to her and I guess the shock of seeing her held my feet fast to the floor. I hadn't time to gasp before she had plucked my pistol from its holster and began to herd us into a corner like a group of steers.

"I don't care to use this," she told everyone. "But I'll make it known I've killed more than once." She didn't have to convince me. She had the hammer cocked and her hand was steady as oak wood as she backed out the door and disappeared into the darkness.

Tonn was still groveling on the floor while everyone else searched through the pile of weapons on the front table. One brave soul peeked his head through the saloon door. The blast of my pistol in the hands of the woman sounded from the street and he jerked back inside, holding his breath, splinters torn from the doorway poking from his cheek.

We waited for a time, until we heard the sound of a horse leaving town in a hurry. Some of the men went out the back and I led the way through the front doors. There was some commotion already as the street was filling from the other saloons to see what the shooting was about. There was shouting and talk about going after her, a thief who had pulled a fast one on an innocent bunch playing poker.

I called for quiet and mentioned that everyone's dear friend, Jack Tonn, had caused the entire problem. He had pushed too far once again and had lost this time. The fact of the matter was, I had lost again myself. She got my pistol first and as luck would have it, my horse was the one she picked to make her exit from town.

I stood in the street deciding what I should do when Amillio Vasquez, one of Watson's horse wranglers I had gotten to know pretty well, approached me from the steps of a nearby saloon.

"Señor Windham? Frank Windham?"

"It's me, Amillio."

He laughed. "This night is a strange one for you, no?"

"I was worried about it from the beginning," I told him.

"Do you feel like going after her?"

"I could use my horse and pistol back. But I don't feel my luck is going to improve any."

"Ah, but it is not every day that a woman makes off with your horse and gun, both."

Madio walked up and asked if I'd lead a posse. I told him it didn't matter much because there were already a lot of men following Jack Tonn out.

"He offered five hundred dollars to any man who would bring her to him," Madio told me.

"I'll ride on my own," I said.

Vasquez loaned me a horse and an extra pistol from his saddlebag on the condition he get a chance to meet this woman. I told him I could make no guarantees about anything and he nodded, asking if he could ride with me.

Ten minutes out, Vasquez and I broke from the main trail. I saw no sense in staying close to a number of noisy riders with Jack Tonn among them. Vasquez accused me of having things set up with her for a midnight fling in the stickers, but I knew where I wanted to go and how I wanted to go about it.

Before long he made the suggestion that we split up.

"We'll stay close enough to shout, don't you think?" he suggested.

Fifteen minutes turned into a half an hour. I took my time and just listened for sounds in the *ramadero* but all I was ever able to hear was the posse. By now they were in smaller groups going in all directions, thinking that to cover the entire radius around town would give them better odds.

They would shout and occasionally shoot at shadows, letting anyone with average hearing know where they were.

The main reason I had chosen to be alone is I had a hunch I was going to find her, and she would likely be afoot when I did. I had named my horse Grasshopper. He received the name early on in age when it became apparent that he felt the need to make unannounced jumps with people on him.

You never knew when it was going to happen. Grasshopper never bucked when you first got mounted. He was sly. He would wait until you were comfortable and then do a series of strong crow hops. This usually occurred ten to fifteen minutes into the ride.

I'll have to admit there were times when I was daydreaming, or otherwise lax in mental attention, and he dumped me. But it was just always that one spurt, ten to fifteen minutes after settling into the saddle. Whether or not he threw his rider, he didn't care. He just had to erupt, and then he was satisfied.

He had never gotten over it, even in the five years since I won him in a poker game in San Antonio. He had likely learned the trick as a green yearling being broke to ride. No doubt it had worked a number of times and he felt it was always worth trying.

Soon, the posse's noise had drifted into the distance, and I hadn't heard anything from Vasquez. They were all scattering everywhere.

I had a feeling that she had intended to go north. She didn't look like a border sort to me, but more like someone who was headed as far away from this area as possible. South took you farther into trouble.

Ten minutes later I found Grasshopper beside the trail, trying to rub his bridle off against one of his front legs. I got down off Vasquez's horse and tied him up. The night had become suddenly quiet, except for the click of a pistol being cocked.

"Listen, I'm not here to hurt you," I offered cautiously.

"Damn straight you're not," she said. "I want to see your hands. High."

She moved quickly out of the brush and stopped in front of me, noticeably favoring one leg. Something like that can happen when you get bucked off a horse.

I said a long Thank You under my breath to Grasshopper, still working to scrape the bridle off. She held my pistol steady while she studied me. The moon had risen nearly full and the light painted one side of her face a soft white.

"Now I have two horses," she said. "And another pistol."

"No," I said. "We can work this out."

"No, we can't. Why aren't you with the others?"

"I know my horse," I replied. "Now I'm going to go over and get him, before he rubs his bridle off."

"You stay where you are."

"Shoot me," I challenged. "See how fast Jack Tonn gets over here."

I walked over and took the reins and led Grasshopper back.

"You're really pushing your luck," she told me.

"I'm leaving the country, headed back up north eventually," I explained. "This horse of mine is real trail-wise. He's been in snow and cold and around warring Indians. Besides, he doesn't even care for you."

"Maybe I need a horse that can make it through the snow and past Indians," she said. "Your horse sounds about right. And he'll get used to me."

"No, he won't get used to you. I'll find you one that will suit you."

"What about the one you rode out here on?"

"He's a brush-popper. Likes the mesquite. Never been north as far as I know." I thought a moment. "But maybe he'll suit you until you can buy another one somewhere."

"You aren't even going to try and take me back to Unvalde, are you?" she said.

"I don't care about that," I said. "It seems to me that you'd want to get a long ways from Jack Tonn."

She laughed. "A woman gets the best of a man out here and he's got to save face any way he can."

She limped toward me and sat down in the trail. She groaned as she worked her legs into a cross-legged position, placing my pistol on the ground beside her. She pulled bills from inside her loose cotton shirt.

"Let me buy the other horse then," she said.

I sat down beside her. "You went to a lot of trouble just to get your leg hurt."

"I accomplished what I wanted to."

"Why even gamble with someone like Jack Tonn?"

"Because he was in Madio's." She sat very still, looking out into the night. She seemed upset.

"What do you mean by that?" I asked.

She didn't answer. She turned her attention to her injured leg.

"There's a doctor in town," I told her.

"Don't need one," she said. "I'll pay you for the horse and be gone."

"He's not mine, so I'll need a real good price."

"You'll take what I give you."

After a moment, I asked, "Where are you headed?"

She stopped counting money and rubbed her leg. "Not interested in being social, at all."

There came the sound of approaching horses, and I heard Vasquez calling my name. I stood up and answered, and she struggled to her feet with the pistol pressed close against my ribs.

"That was so very foolish! Now, put your hands

on top of your head and pray that I don't jerk my finger."

"Easy! They aren't going to do anything rash."

"You had better get them headed back to town or things are going to get very messy, I can promise you that."

Four riders came into view and looked at one another when they saw me standing with my hands piled on top of my hat. Vasquez was among them and he started to laugh.

"This just isn't your day, is it, Señor Windham?"

"I've got things under control here," I said. "Is your horse for sale?"

He grunted. "Do I have a choice?"

"No, but the price is fair." I told the woman to give him fifty dollars.

"I'll do the bargaining," she growled. "Thirty is a good price. For your horse, not his."

Vasquez continued to smile. "Can I be of any more service?"

"I'll see you and the others back at Madio's."

"If you say so," Vasquez said.

"You sure?" one of the others asked.

Vasquez answered quickly. "He is certain. He knows about these things, you can trust in that."

———

Even though the night was warm, the muzzle of my Colt pistol felt cold pressed tightly against my stomach. She had moved around to the front of me.

"Our business is done," she said. "You'll just give me the *vaquero*'s horse and you can settle up with him when you get back to town."

"And my pistol?"

"I'll keep them, Mr. Windham."

"I don't know your name, ma'am."

"You can learn it from Jack Tonn," she said. "Ask him who it was he robbed and left for dead a year ago along the lower Brazos. Lucky for him my father didn't die."

"Is your father still alive, along the Brazos?"

"He is."

"And your mother?"

"She passed some years back. Enough questions."

"Maybe I'll take a little trip that way, just to visit him."

"Suit yourself. Now, help me onto the horse and forget you ever met me."

"Should you be on the trail alone?"

"I have my own way of doing it, Mr. Windham, if you hadn't noticed."

"Suit yourself," I told her.

I watched her ride into the brush, never looking back, losing herself in the shadows of a south Texas night. I felt a strange mixture of relief and anxiety. I was glad, of course, to have my horse back. Real good ones are hard to come by. At the same time, I was a little apprehensive about how things would be with her loose on the trail. It would be hard for men everywhere to get used to her, and I worried for them.

AFTERMATH

By the light of a bedside lamp, Chad Simmons ran his hands over the gleaming barrel of a TEC-9 semi-automatic handgun. On the bed beside him rested a sawed-off 12-gauge shotgun and an AK-47 assault rifle, complete with ten fully loaded clips.

Near six feet, well-built and solidly muscled, Chad sat with a towel wrapped around him, his red-brown hair still wet from the shower. Outside, the day had begun but the sun's light had been slow to materialize. The summer had been long and hot and today, September 11, dawned with the Colorado skies cloudy and the air cool.

Chad admired the weapons, hard-pressed to pick his favorite. It was the handgun, though, that made him feel totally in control—like he could go anywhere and have it where no one could see it.

He had acquired it the night before from his regular supplier, who said there was plenty of ammo for it. Just come for it whenever he was ready.

It would work nicely into the Plan, these weapons, so lethal and so cool.

Yes, the Plan, well into its planning stages, soon to come into its latter stages, the most important and anticipated event of his young life—something he and Donny were calling the Christmastime Massacre.

Donny Riggs, his friend and co-general of the operation, had decided at the beginning of the summer that together they would make history and be known forever at Longs Peak High School, or what was left of it when they had finished. Donny had attended a "boot camp" in the dense forest of the central Rocky Mountains, far from the Interstate that ran through the heart of Colorado. Many boys from many different western states had attended, to learn and earn their place in a new regime that was to come, a promised regime that followed the teachings of Adolf Hitler.

Chad had wanted to go, but Donny had insisted he wait until the following summer. "You're not quite ready, but you will still be able to learn from me, and be a part of what we've been putting together for so long now."

Chad thought of himself as ready, always ready for what he now saw as his fate.

Soon it would be time to head for class. Yet there were a lot more important things to do. What was school good for, anyway? If you didn't fit the profile the teacher expected of you—or your classmates, allowing yourself to be typecast—then you were an outcast. First of all, it wasn't part of Chad Simmons's makeup to be typecast, and he certainly didn't want to be an outcast.

He was actually neither one, adrift in a form of limbo where the other students didn't necessarily see him as totally odd, but certainly not one of them, nonetheless.

Most of the kids did their own thing and left everyone to theirs—live and let live. But then there were the jocks, the school rulers. They had no idea about anything that you might be able to do for yourself, or want for yourself, aside from the cheers of the crowd. And those who weren't on the field, or the court, or the mat, who fit into a rich kid's kind of sect, stayed to themselves, also, and a lot of them had their own ways of making fun of anyone they didn't see as meeting their criteria of cool. Most of them had SUVs, or BMWs, or something like that. But even if you drove the right automobile, and they didn't want you, you still didn't count.

Chad had watched it all, over the first two years of high school. There were other kids like him, who didn't fit a particular profile. That made him and those like him fair prey for the jocks especially. He could take the snide, uppity looks and whispered comments of the rich kids, but it was the jocks who always insisted on getting physical. He had taken a few of them down, but they had a way of exacting revenge in groups. The jocks had never learned to watch their step, so they would have to learn the hard way.

Chad had petitioned the administration many times. The highest he could ever get was to the office of the assistant principal, a large man with a disheveled suit, and a face to match, named Dirk Arnold.

He had asked Dirk Arnold numerous times to speak to the school bullies. "They go over the line with their pranks and hard-assing," he had told Arnold.

"Don't you think you're overreacting?" Arnold had asked him on one occasion. On another, Arnold had said, "Just tell them to knock it off. Handle it, Chad. You can do it."

So, that was where the administration stood on it all. And what good was his dad in helping out?

"Chad, if you'd go out for football and wrestling,

like you did in middle school, you wouldn't have this problem."

Over and over Chad had heard the same things: ignore it, which was impossible, or conform and be like everyone else. He wanted to just vomit.

So, what was left? Time to take some drastic steps. Time to make it all stop. There was no sense in going on with this kind of life. It couldn't change, no matter what, so it made sense to rid the world of the blight called Longs Peak High School.

Chad had taken the five hundred or so his parents had given him as spending money each month and had purchased guns. Nothing difficult about it. Some good planning and a lot of time spent learning how to go about it and it would all fall into place.

Chad dressed for school. Above his bed a crucifix hung slightly askew. His mother made it her mission to keep it straight, but it always tilted back again, soon after she was out of the room. That was the only reason she ever came into his room, to check on the crucifix. She had them planted all over the house. He didn't go to mass that often anymore, either. It made his mother alternately mad and sad, but he had told her repeatedly that if she made him go anymore, he would stand up and make a scene.

So they had compromised. Christmas and Easter duty—that was about it.

It hadn't stopped her from ragging on him, though. Carol Simmons had tried repeatedly to get Chad to understand that their good standing in the Church was the reason God had blessed them with their wealth. His dad had gotten a lot of plumb contracting jobs because he was in the Knights of Columbus.

He had made the mistake, a few years back, of asking his mother why they had never said anything to anybody when he had told them he didn't want to be an altar boy anymore. He didn't want what he saw happening to Artie Sullivan to happen to him, because old Father Fitzpatrick had already touched him there once.

But Father Fitz was in charge of getting the contracts out for the work. Don't mess with Father Fitz.

But enough of all that. He had work to do. He wrapped the weapons in the heavy blanket he'd been keeping them in and laid them carefully behind a section of loose paneling in the back of his closet. He set the paneling back into place, carefully, leaving no signs of what was behind it.

He sat down at his desk, peered into the computer screen, and unlocked encrypted E-mail from Donny. He found a message about the Plan—an update on what they would do at various entrances to the school, to maximize the damage and casualties, and how they would block the exits. Bombs with timers would be in place. No students were allowed to escape unless he and Donny Riggs dictated it.

There would be two soldiers under them, but no more. These were also students willing to give their lives for the cause of the New Reich. They no doubt could have recruited a few more, but too many would increase the chances of a botched raid. They didn't want to spoil what they had taken so long to put together.

Chad read the E-mail. It began, of course, with the pledge. "I do hereby solemnly swear to live for and uphold the virtues of the New Reich, and to give my life's blood for the just cause of the regime's tradition. . . ."

It took a few minutes to get through, even though he and Donny had pared it down from the longer version on the Web site. They had learned it together, by heart, on line, to the sounds of boots marching in the background. Black boots, Nazi boots, heavy and clear.

Tromp! Tromp! Tromp! Tromp!

Marching to destiny! Marching for the New Reich!

He put on his headset. He had recorded those

sounds. Boots slamming against the ground, stomping the information into his mind. Sealing the resolve in his heart.

He just couldn't keep from listening to it. His brain called for it, wanted it in the worst way, intoxicating him with adrenaline.

But he had to be careful. His father had threatened to take his headset away again if he didn't leave it alone in the mornings, before school.

Besides the E-mail, Donny had also sent him a URL for a new site he'd discovered on staging successful raids and dealing with prisoners. There were some he might care to take prisoner, just to watch them squirm. Others weren't worth the bother. They would need plenty of ammunition.

His mother called from the bottom of the stairs.

"Chad, I have your new coat ready for you to wear today."

At first Chad didn't hear her. But a sense of someone wanting his attention brought him out of his trance.

"Chad, did you hear me?"

"What, Mom?"

"Your new coat," she shouted from the bottom of the stairs. "It's ready for you to wear today."

"Thanks, Mom."

"It's sheepskin. Very soft and wool-lined."

"I know, Mom."

"You'll be late for school."

"In a minute, Mom."

"Really, Chad, it's getting late."

"Okay, Mom."

Chad put his headset aside and closed out the files. He could hear the television downstairs in the kitchen. It was a regular routine: the television in the kitchen and his mother, humming a religious tune.

At the bottom of the stairs, he picked up his backpack and slung it over his shoulder. He always had his books ready to go and everything set for the day, right by the door.

His mother sat at the kitchen table with her coffee, watching a morning talk show. She glanced toward him.

"Are you skipping breakfast again, Chad?"

"I'll grab a Pop Tart. Okay?"

Chad didn't care if it was toasted or not.

"Bet you're excited," she said.

"About what, Mom?"

"About Cindy enrolling in school here."

"What are you talking about, Mom?"

"Oh, Chad, I told you the other day. Your Uncle Matt is moving back from Iowa, to work with your father. I told you that. Remember?" She sipped coffee and stared at the television screen.

"No, Mom. You didn't tell me."

"Well, I believe I did. In fact, your cousin Cindy and her mom are already here, in their new house."

"I would have remembered that, Mom. That means she'll be starting school here pretty soon."

"I think her mother told me she would be starting today, in fact."

"I would have remembered that, Mom." He started for the door.

"Chad, don't forget your new coat."

"Sure, Mom. A sheep coat. Got to be one of the flock, you know." He set his backpack down and examined the garment.

"Oh, Chad, you're a silly kid. Don't you like your new coat, dear?"

"Sure I do, Mom."

"Really, Chad. What kind of coat would you like?" She pointed to the screen and laughed at something someone had said. "Another leather one? What?"

"Hell, it doesn't matter, Mom."

His father's voice rose from the easy chair in the living room. He had already put his paper down in his lap. He had been listening to the conversation for some time. Chad had come to learn that gesture always meant he would be getting a dressing-down.

"Chad, come over here."

Tromp! Tromp! Tromp! Tromp! The boots in his head.

At the chair, Chad stood in front of his father.

"Yes."

"What's going on with you, son? You don't care about anybody or anything. You're rude. You're crude. You've got everything a kid could ever want. What the hell's the matter with you?"

Chad shrugged. "I don't know."

Tromp! Tromp! Tromp! Tromp! The boots in his head.

"Is that all you can say?"

"What else is there?"

"I don't appreciate you getting smart with me, okay?"

The tromping boots grew louder.

"Things have been kind of stressful, that's all," Chad said.

"Yeah, well, you're not the lone ranger there."

"I understand that, Dad. But you don't understand my position most of the time."

"I don't understand your position any of the time, anymore. I don't like it."

"Maybe you should take the time to listen to my side of it. But then again, maybe not. You're always right."

"Wrong thing to say, Chad. Now I want you

home right after school. Understood? No going over to Donny's, or anyplace else, for that matter. Make that for the rest of the week. Got it?" He went back to his paper.

The boots were like a loud, continuous pounding.

"No," Chad said, "I'll get back here when I'm damned good and ready."

His father looked up. "What did you say?"

"You don't get it, Frank. You don't *own* me."

Frank bolted from the chair, his paper knotted in his right hand.

"You listen to me, young man. I'm your father and 'Frank' is not acceptable. You got that?" His breath was ragged. "I said, you *got* that?"

Chad stood defiantly, his eyes ablaze, his head echoing with the march of the New Reich.

"And as long as you're under this roof, I own your ass. Don't you ever forget it."

"You don't even own your own ass, Frank."

Frank brought the paper downward and Chad blocked the blow. His father raised his arm again and Chad tackled him to the floor, knocking over the coffee table, spreading figurines across the room.

Frank tried to lunge up but Chad locked his father's arms behind him and turned him over with a wrestling hold, rolling him over onto his back, stacking him up on his head and neck, and then rolling him over onto his stomach, crushing him downward.

Frank grunted loudly as the air whooshed from his lungs.

Carol Simmons rushed from the kitchen.

"Chad, please, don't do this."

"He wants me to be a jock, Mom. So, I'm being one."

Frank Simmons growled a muffled curse. Chad held him down, both arms locked solidly. The harder Frank struggled, the more facial burns he sustained as Chad allowed him to partially rise, then drove him forward again, over and over, ramming him headfirst into the carpet.

Finally, exhausted, Frank went limp. Chad got off him and stood to one side. Frank climbed to his feet and breathed heavily. He brushed a trickle of blood from his nose with his fist.

Chad looked into his father's eyes. "You'd like to kill me, wouldn't you?"

"I want you out of this house. Now!"

"Sure thing."

"Frank, no!" Carol's eyes had already filled with tears. Now they plunged down her cheeks.

"I won't have this, Carol. Not in my house. Never."

Chad had already started for the stairs. His mother grabbed his arm.

"Chad, he doesn't mean it."

"Yes, I do, by damn!" Frank's voice boomed from behind them. "And there's no more damned allowance, either. Never, by damn!"

Carol stared at her husband, eyes wide. "Frank, what kind of language is that to use in a Christian home?"

Upstairs, Chad stared at his computer, well aware it might not be there for very long. He wished he'd uploaded his files to a server somewhere that he could access another time, if needed. Too late for that right now.

He grabbed some clothes from a dresser drawer and stuffed them into a duffel bag. He could get back into the house for whatever else he needed when it was dark.

His mother met him at the bottom of the stairs. He noticed that his father had seated himself back in his chair and that his head was buried in the paper.

"Where are you going to go, Chad?" Carol asked.

"Who knows. But I'm outta here."

Frank raised his head. "You aren't taking that car I gave you, either. It's registered under my name, remember?"

"Yeah," Chad said, "I know that."

"I don't want you taking it. Understood?"

"I don't want anything to do with it anymore."

"Good, because if you take it, I'll report it stolen. Got that?"

"I said, don't worry about it," Chad repeated. "Don't you understand English?"

Frank glared from his chair, starting to rise, but didn't.

"Go ahead and get up, Frank, so I can kick your ass again."

"Chad, please," Carol said. She suddenly stopped crying and turned to look at the television in the kitchen.

"Get out or I'll call the cops," Frank said.

"Call the cops, I dare you," Chad challenged. "Just think of it, the cops laughing among themselves, seeing how a guy's kid kicked his ass so badly."

In the kitchen, Carol's favorite television program had been interrupted by reporters who were discussing breaking news. One of the trade towers in New York City was aflame, near the top. His mother stared at the screen, chewing her nails. His father continued to glare at him.

"What are you waiting for?" Frank asked.

Time to leave, Chad decided.

"Chad," Carol Simmons said as her son opened the door. "Don't forget your new coat, son."

Donny Riggs paced the hallway at Longs Peak High. Slightly built, he fairly swam in his clothes, loose pants and shirt and a crusty bomber jacket he had discovered in a Dumpster two years previously. He cut his own hair, unevenly, and had dyed it a light blond, with a white blotch in front.

First period had just ended and there was still no sign of Chad Simmons. The school wasn't going as usual, though. Someone had flown planes, somehow, into the trade towers in New York City. He didn't know what it was about, but it wasn't any big deal at this time. He had other things to think about.

He toyed carefully with a large swastika pin, being careful not to attract attention. He kept it pinned on the inside of the bomber jacket lapel, so he could flip it back and look at it whenever he wished.

It bothered him considerably that school officials had declared there be no visible effects of any "negative" kind on anyone's person. No skulls, no devils, nothing of the sort. And why not? Mr. Strasser, one of the history teachers, kept a large Nazi flag pinned to the wall of his classroom, and a long bench lined with German war paraphernalia of all kinds—helmets, boots, an SS uniform, a pilot's goggles, a rifle, and a copy of Adolf Hitler's *Mein Kampf*.

But Mr. Strasser was a teacher, and it was all in the name of education. Certainly.

Mr. Strasser had been there a long time and was a pillar of the community. Right.

So, that made Mr. Strasser able to do any damned thing he wanted. Most certainly right.

And that day, late the spring before, when Donny had secretly flashed the swastika for Mr. Strasser to see, the older teacher had merely smiled.

Donny had asked him then if he knew anything about a secret society that kept a Web page active for students who were interested in the Third Reich. Again, the teacher had smiled, and had remarked, "It's good to know the history of the world. Don't you think?"

Good old Mr. Strasser.

While he paced, he noticed another student leaning against a nearby locker. Donny motioned him over.

Milton Cross wore dark pants with a sweater—nothing unusual or sinister about him outwardly. When he approached Donny, he said, "I'm ready to kill."

"That's good."

"Those terrorists got it done in New York, didn't they?" Milton Cross smiled. "We could only hope to cause that kind of problem here. But we'll make our point."

"And you'll die to do it."

"I have sworn to that," Milton said. "I uphold my word."

Donny studied Milton. "Are you up to speed on how this will go down, when the time comes?"

"I've read everything, learned everything, and know what's expected. I want to attend the meetings and also take Chad Simmons's place."

"I'll get back to you on that, Milt," Donny said. "Just be patient about that part of it. Okay?"

"Ah, but patience is my trademark," Milton Cross said with a wink.

He eased away from Donny just as Chad Simmons entered the building, but not quickly enough for Chad not to have noticed.

Donny approached Chad.

"Where you been, damn it? We had a meeting, remember?"

"What's going on with Milton Cross?" Chad asked. "Secret meetings behind my back again?"

"Oh, relax, would you?" Donny said. "There's big things going down in New York City. What, did you spend time at home watching it?"

"No, I walked to school."

"Ah, the exercise kid today, huh?"

"Back off, Donny. I'm in no mood." Chad's fight with his father had defused some of the anger, but he wasn't interested in listening to Donny Riggs's mundane chiding.

"Touchy, are we?" Donny asked.

"More than just touchy," Chad replied.

"Yeah, well, you need to keep that attitude, if you want to keep your position beside me."

"What are you talking about?"

"We'll talk later, Chad, my boy," Donny said. "For now, let's just savor what's going on in New York. It was a fricken triumph for tearing down what's here now, don't you think?"

"I don't know that much about it yet," Chad said. He looked around. Teachers and students were roaming the halls in a daze. A lot of kids were calling parents on cell phones. Others were headed out the door for home.

"Heavy," Donny said. "Wild."

"Yeah, this is really big, it looks like," Chad said. "Guess I'll find a TV."

"Well, whatever, Chad. I need to remind you again, though, that you can't skip out on our meetings or you'll spoil the Plan. We have to keep the schedule, remember? Visit those places in the school every day. No matter what else happens around us, we stick with what we need to do. Right? You know what we learned."

"Yeah, I know." Some of the girls were crying, looking for their friends in the hallways.

Donny nudged him. "Hey, I'm right here, guy. Pay attention."

"Listen, Donny, it's been a fricken weird morning in a lot of ways already. Know what I mean?"

"Every day's that way. Why complain?"

"Right, why should you complain? Your parents aren't on your ass all the time."

"No, because they're never around. They spend most of their time in Aspen. I guess they think I'm supposed to be okay with that. The housekeeper loves it." Donny laughed heavily. "Maybe you and I should invite our parents to school the day of the Plan."

Chad grunted. "I'll need to crash at your place, until I can find a permanent hangout somewhere. Okay?"

"Why? You running away from home?"

"Something like that."

"Good for you. Shoot the place up when you get the chance."

"Yeah, I'll do that."

"You think I'm joking?"

"Damn it, Donny, get off my ass!"

"I fricken mean it, Chad. You've got to get your head into the Plan. They tell us that we need to concentrate at every meeting."

"Well, Donny. I haven't been invited to any of the fricken midnight meetings yet. Remember?"

"You've got to show you really want this, Chad, in the worst way. That's what I'm saying. Then they'll invite you. That's how it works."

Chad noticed Donny reaching into his coat pocket and sneaking a quick trip to his mouth.

"Hey, give me some of those pills, will you?" Chad insisted.

"Take as many as you want. My mother gets them by the truckload."

Chad chuckled. "And she never misses them?"

"Never," Donny said. "That's the way I like it."

Chad had heard Donny discuss the meetings at the river, held once a week, and then three days in a row during each full moon. The meetings were always under cover of darkness and were held by people outside the schools, guys of various ages, with an allegiance to Adolf Hitler and the late Führer's teachings. The guys in charge were always dressed in Nazi uniforms, with black cloth over their faces. At each meeting there were always steins of German beer passed around among the attendees, the kids from the various suburbs who wanted to take their schools down and level them to nothing.

Donny Riggs had made it clear from the beginning that his intentions were serious. He would follow through. He seemed to get extra attention, and extra refreshments.

"Best beer you can find," Donny would say. "Best buzz you'll ever have, too. Get with the program and you'll see."

According to Donny, the Plan required meticulous attention to detail, and that meant adhering strictly to certain protocol, as set forward by the statutes of the New Reich. They were a demanding group, according to Donny, and demanded strict adherence to their authority, which would someday, they promised, bring them to the world that the Führer had envisioned.

"It is important to remember that all that exists now must be destroyed, so that what must be can rise from it," Donny was always saying. "That is foremost."

Chad had decided that he agreed with it, for the most part. There wasn't anyone else, any other organization, who cared a whit about making things better for kids who didn't fit a certain profile.

So, for Chad, the New Reich was it. Whatever it took to get the school to change somehow, to learn the hard way that the present system had created a raging storm within him.

Sergeant Tom Lopez had been assigned to Longs Peak High just the week before, when the previous officer, Max Lucino, had retired from the force. He had taken Lopez aside and had complained, "You'll find that you're going to be beating a dead horse, like I did. These kids are changing too fast and there's no point to it anymore."

Lopez had settled into his new position with uncertainty. A lot of what Lucino had said seemed true: the halls were filled with a number of students who could care less about where they were or what they were doing. There didn't seem to be any direction in their lives. It wasn't the majority of the population by any means, but certainly a large enough percentage to merit concern.

Today, though, there was no yardstick to measure anything by. The halls were filled with dazed and confused students, all wondering at the events of terror that were still unfolding on live television.

Among them was Chad Simmons. He knew Chad only because he had pitched a no-hitter against the Little League team he had coached some years back. Chad had been quiet, even among his teammates after the fabulous game. Lopez had made it a point to try and follow Chad's athletic career as he grew up, but learned that Chad had decided not to remain in athletics.

Today without question would change world history, and all the kids knew it. It seemed like a good opportunity to approach Chad Simmons.

"Remember me, Tom Lopez?" he said to Chad. "You did quite a number on my Little League team some years ago."

"Sure, I remember," Chad replied. "You're the new resident officer here these days?"

"What a time to start, huh?" Lopez said. "Were you thinking of going home, like some of the others?"

Chad started down the hall, Lopez beside him. He felt trapped.

"I don't think so."

"I guess this is a time to be with friends and family," Lopez said. "I called my wife and told her I loved her. If school lets out completely, I'll go home."

"Yeah," Chad said. "Friends and family."

"What have you been up to these days, Chad?" Lopez asked.

"Ah, well, not much," Chad replied.

"I'm surprised you didn't go out for football," Lopez said. "And that you're not wrestling, either."

"Not interested in that anymore," Chad said.

"You must have some hobbies, then. Something to occupy your spare time."

Chad studied the officer. "Did I do something wrong?"

"Oh, no, not at all," Lopez told him. "Why?"

"I feel like I'm being interrogated."

"Sorry, no, I just want to say hello is all."

Chad watched television in one of the classrooms where a number of students had gathered, thinking about Tom Lopez while he watched the chaos at the Twin Towers unfold on the screen. He wondered if it was possible that Lopez had somehow gotten wind of the Plan.

That didn't seem logical, so Chad finally dismissed the thought. All of it was changing, though, and he became troubled as he thought of it. He had spent a lot of time getting himself in tune for the Plan. Somehow what had just happened in New York, Washington, D.C., and in some field in Pennsylvania had reached deep inside him, disrupting the stomping of the boots and the messages that went with it.

Now there was a new, ironic source of anger.

Chad knew with classes suspended for the day

that Donny Riggs had taken the opportunity to meet again with Milton Cross and a couple of other students to discuss the Plan, leaving him out of it. He was beginning to feel like an outcast from the very concept that he had envisioned would elevate him to another status, before leaving this life to remain in that status in the next life.

As he watched the screen, he wondered how someone could assimilate enough hate in their system to run a plane filled with people into a tower of steel, glass, and concrete. Had to be pretty determined, pretty programmed, actually.

He was glad he didn't have a mirror to look into. He just might see the face of a fanatic there, since he had pledged himself to die for the New Reich when the Plan went into effect.

But that wasn't something he could discuss with anyone, the fact that he had come to believe that he could effect a better place for himself by killing jocks, and anyone else who didn't believe in the destiny of the New Reich. And now that he was beginning to question it, his mind divided itself into a voice that said, "The Plan is a bad idea," and the old drill master, who argued, "Nothing is any different! You can't abandon the Plan!"

Chad left the classroom and the building, sat in a park across the street, and gazed across to the school grounds. Straight up noon and, ordinarily, kids would be wheeling in and out of the parking lot, filling the area with automobile noise and laughter. Today, the few drivers left were cautious. The relative quiet was deeply unnerving.

Chad stood and walked around the park, searching for a place among the trees, out of sight, where he might throw a sleeping bag, once he went home and got one. Staying at Donny's place didn't seem like such a hot idea anymore. Everything within him was topsy-turvy. With everything going through his head at once, he felt completely exhausted.

He decided to head back home. No need to wait for darkness. His father would be at work, no matter what, and his mother, since it was Monday, would likely be at her altar society meeting. And she would no doubt be there longer than usual, possibly watching the terrorizing events, and praying about them with the other women. She would certainly be confused about how to act and what to prioritize in her life. She would go to church and light a row of candles and pray for the victims of the hijackers, and also pray as hard as she could that Frank would allow their son to come back home.

Chad had no sooner left the park than a car pulled

alongside the curb. Cindy Malone stepped out from the driver's side and ran around the car to him.

Cindy was petite and easy to look at, even for a cousin, and would no doubt become part of the popular crowd. She seemed to fit in with most everybody.

She hugged him tightly. "Chad, what are you doing walking the streets? I've been looking all over for you. I'm feeling really weird."

"Yeah, aren't we all?"

"Mom took off early to shop for furniture. Said she'd be gone all day."

"Not a furniture day anymore," Chad remarked.

"So, what are you doing without your car?" Cindy asked. "Did it break down?"

"No. It's a long story."

"Why don't you let me give you a ride?"

Chad got in and tossed his duffel bag in the backseat.

"Not a good day all around," he said.

"I can't hardly believe this is happening," Cindy said. "We're going to war now. No doubt."

"I guess I'll be in a war, one way or another," Chad said.

"You're too young, Chad."

"I'm at war at home. Big time."

"More trouble with your father?"

"Yeah. A lot more."

"A couple more years and you'll be out of the house," Cindy told him.

"I'm already out of the house," Chad said. "Got in a fight with him. Not just words this time. He kicked me out."

"Oh, geez, not really."

"Yeah, really. I'm homeless."

"That can't be for real."

"I'm considering it for real," Chad said.

"Give it some time," Cindy suggested.

"Nah, there's no time left." Chad took a deep breath.

"What do you mean there's no time left?"

"I don't want to go back there, is what I mean."

"What will you do?"

"We'll see."

Cindy drove without speaking for a time. "After what's happened, your parents will want you back right away."

"I'm not counting on it."

"It doesn't make sense," Cindy said. "Nothing makes sense. Can you imagine hating a country so much that you could spend time in that country, planning how to do something more terrible than anyone could imagine, and then kill yourself in the process? I mean, how crazy is that?"

Chad felt funny in the pit of his stomach as he stared out the window. Maybe he was having second thoughts about the Plan, but Donny Riggs and Milton Cross sure weren't. If anything, it had fueled their desire for blood even more.

"So, what made you want to go to Longs Peak?" he asked Cindy.

"I know it's kind of sudden," she said. "Dad wanted to make the move before the holidays. Get us settled in and all."

"Don't you think Lake Valley would be a better school for you? I mean, they have that International Baccalaureate program and all. Better education, you know."

"I wanted to be in school with you, Chad," she said. "Is that all right?"

"Sure it is, Cindy." He turned from the window. "But I'm not all that special."

"You were to me, when we were younger. Remember, in the fourth grade, when my best friend, Paula, got killed in that car accident? You really helped me through that."

"I'd forgotten," Chad said.

"You told me how important it was to keep her memory with me. That she wasn't really gone."

Chad turned and looked out the window again. The knot in his stomach grew tighter.

"I know that I'm going to be new at Longs Peak High," Cindy continued, "but I want to do something, like maybe organize the students to dedicate their Christmas to the victims. Don't you think? A special Christmas, to their memory, to help heal the country? Are you listening, Chad?"

"Yeah, I suppose you're right."

"You don't sound very enthusiastic. In fact, you sound confused."

"Maybe I am. Just drop me off at my house. Okay?"

"You sure?"

At the house, Chad grabbed his duffel bag. His mother's car was in the driveway. But there was no place left to go, for the time being.

He noticed Cindy looking at him.

"You want to come in for a while?" he asked.

"Is it all right? I just want to be with somebody right now. Do you understand?"

Chad entered the house, not knowing quite what to expect from his mother. Cindy would be a good buffer.

Inside, Chad discovered his mother in a chair in the kitchen. The television was on and she was crying.

She stood up and stared at Chad and Cindy.

"I thought you'd be at your altar society meeting," Chad said.

"Some of the women are still meeting, I guess. I hoped you'd come home." She walked over to Chad. "Let me hold you a minute. Okay?"

Chad felt his mother's arms around him. The knot in his stomach had turned into what he believed would become a permanent ball of something solid that held him down like iron.

Tears rolled down Carol's cheeks, and Cindy's as well.

"It's a terrible thing that's happened," Carol said. "All those poor people."

Cindy was staring at the television screen. "It seems like a movie," she said, "but it's real."

"Can you imagine being a terrorist's mother?" Carol wondered. "I mean, how could she sleep?"

"Their mothers are likely proud of them," Chad suggested.

"But how do you know that?" she responded. "I mean, deep down inside, each of them has to be ripped apart, no matter what their crazy notions of their religion are."

"Those women have to be human, too," Cindy agreed.

Carol Simmons looked at her son. "Did you tell Cindy what happened this morning here?"

Cindy answered for him. "He just touched on it, is all. He said everything would be all right."

"Yes," Carol said. "Everything will be all right." She turned to Cindy. "I just got a call from your mother. She's on her way over here now, and was hoping you might check in here. And Frank is coming home from work. He actually let his men go today, told them to be with their families."

"That's not like Dad, to miss a day of work, no matter what," Chad said.

"Things are different now, for everybody," Carol said.

Chad shuffled his feet. "I can't stay, Mom."

"Nonsense, Chad. You can too stay," she insisted. "It's going to be all right."

Ten minutes later Frank Simmons entered the house. He hugged Carol and then Cindy, telling her that her mother was pulling into the driveway.

He turned to Chad and hugged him for the first time since Chad could remember.

"I notice that you haven't cleaned your room in a while, son," he said. "How do you intend to live in that mess?"

By mid-October, Longs Peak and the other schools were settled into regular classes and other activities, but still leery of what could happen on the domestic front. By the arrival of Thanksgiving, everything was running even more smoothly. Though the cleanup in New York and Washington, D.C., was still in progress, and the horror of what lay beneath the rubble of the trade towers was continuously coming to light, there was a sense that no one had died in vain. Together with that, everyone watched updates on the news regarding the ongoing war against terrorism. As Chad saw it, a lot was going on that was seemingly hidden and covert, and he wondered how it could ever end.

His cousin Cindy had settled into classes and extracurricular activities with ease. As promised, she had started a drive to dedicate the holiday season to the memory of the fallen and their families. She kept Chad updated on the project's progress, urging him to become an active member of her planning committee. He had managed to beg off for the time being, citing too much homework. But that couldn't last. Cindy was just too persistent.

Officer Lopez had worked to become friendly with him, taking opportunities to discuss things other than sports events. Chad didn't care for plays or musical gatherings, so there was little to give Lopez to work with. Still, the officer persisted in striking up offhanded conversations at any given time.

It made Chad nervous, but not the way it had the first time they had met. Since the September terrorist attack, he had looked at his guns just twice, both times feeling strange in the pit of his stomach. One voice pleaded with him to get rid of them, while the other denounced him for betraying the New Reich, for not maintaining his anger and reciting the words he had learned by heart, and listening to the stomp of the boots.

Chad hadn't talked with Donny Riggs but for a few times when Donny had announced to him that they were putting off the Plan until further notice. But at school, he noticed Donny hanging around with Milt Cross a lot, talking in whispers, and at times hanging out with two other students. The Plan certainly wasn't off—they just didn't consider him a part of it anymore.

At least that's how it seemed until Donny approached him after school one afternoon in late October.

"Hey, listen, Chad," he began. "It's been a while since we talked."

"Yeah," Chad said. "You've been avoiding me. Why?"

"It's not that, it's the cop you've been hanging out with."

"I haven't been hanging out with him. He likes to talk, is all."

"What have you been telling him?"

"Nothing."

"That's good. Say, I've decided it's time you took in a meeting, down at the river."

Chad stood silent with shock.

"What's the matter? Don't you want to go? Aren't you a part of this anymore?"

"Yeah, sure," Chad said. "The full moon is at the end of the week."

"Friday night, Chad. Our Halloween meeting. I'll give you directions Friday morning. Okay?"

Chad entered the office of Dirk Arnold, the vice principal. It was time to give the man another chance to make some changes at the school. Time was running short.

Dirk Arnold closed the door and offered a chair. "Chad, have a seat."

Chad rested uncomfortably in the chair.

"You having problems with bullies again?"

"Mr. Arnold. I want to tell you that I believe this school is in danger."

"From terrorists?"

"Well, yes. Of a kind, certainly."

"Are you having nightmares about New York, Chad? Would you like for me to arrange for some counseling?"

"I just want you to arrange to listen to me for a moment," Chad said. "Is that possible?"

"We need to show some respect here, Chad."

"Yes, and the operative word is *we*," Chad agreed. "So far, you haven't given me any, and you really never have."

Arnold leaned across his desk. "Okay, Chad, what's this all about?"

"There is an attack planned against this school, a Columbine-style assault, for the week before Christmas break."

Arnold studied him. "And how do you know this, Chad?"

"Word gets around."

"That's all you can give me?"

"Just tell whomever you need to about it. Okay? Anyone you think should know."

"I'll need more than that, Chad."

"What if I gave you the names of the students?"

"It's not that simple, Chad. We would have to take some time and watch them for a while."

Chad shuffled in his chair. "Could you call in Officer Lopez, please?"

"That's a good idea, Chad. I'll be calling a lot of people in. I have some questions for you, and I'm sure the other school officials will too. Maybe you want to call your parents."

"Can we talk to just Officer Lopez first?"

"I'm afraid not, Chad. You've opened a can of worms here."

Chad stood up. "Let's just forget the whole thing. Okay?"

"We can't do that, Chad. Stick around."

Chad left the office with Dirk Arnold right behind him. In the hall, Arnold grabbed him by the arm.

"I told you to stick around."

"Let go of me," Chad demanded.

"He's right, you'd better let him go." Officer Lopez stood off to one side, having just walked in from the school grounds.

"He's made some serious accusations," Arnold said.

"And that allows you to manhandle him?" Lopez asked. "Mr. Arnold, let's you and I go into your office for a minute. Chad, wait out here."

After ten minutes, Tom Lopez came back out. "Let's go for a drive, Chad," he said.

Chad sat silent in the squad car.

"You hungry, or want soda of some kind?" Lopez asked.

"Sure, I guess."

They picked up sodas with some burgers and fries, and cruised the heights around Chad's neighborhood.

"Okay, so the meeting with Dirk Arnold never happened," Lopez said. "I told him that I would handle it and that if he so much as raised his ugly head about anything, I'd have you sue the school district, and that I would be a witness. So, he's out of it. Now, what's going on?"

Chad told him everything, from the very beginning. Lopez didn't appear shocked at anything that was said, anywhere along the way.

"Did you already know about this?" Chad asked.

"How could I have?" Lopez replied.

"Because I haven't seen any reaction yet."

"Believe me, I'm aware of a lot of things that aren't public knowledge," Lopez confessed. "What you've just told me is a problem that hasn't been faced yet in this country. There's a lot of hate being instilled in this country's youth by any means possible. There's a lot of things happen to them when they're small children that plant the seeds of hate. But it's all taboo. Nobody wants to face that. Now, maybe, with the events of September eleventh, that will be looked at more closely."

"What could make people hate that strongly, to fly into a building?" Chad asked.

"I think you can answer that, Chad. It starts when they're very small. Despicable things are done to them, to break them down. After a time, some of them don't even believe they're human any longer, so they are easy to train. Easily taught to carry out missions in the name of all things right and holy, when none of it is right or holy at all."

Chad thought a moment. "Are you talking about brainwashing?"

"That's one term for it," Lopez replied. "It can get complicated."

"Is that what happened to me?" Chad already knew the answer.

"Maybe it didn't take as well with you," Lopez stated. "Thank God."

"Even if I'm no longer involved in the hate, nothing's going to change."

"You have to believe that it will, Chad. That things will change. It's all in how you want to move forward. I can't predict your future, Chad. Only you can. Only you can decide how much value you give to yourself and the world."

"People don't care how I fit into the world," Chad said. "They don't care how anyone fits in, unless there's something in it for them. So they can use you."

"Do you think that's fair, Chad?

"It's all a game, all of it. You've got to be part of the flock. I'm not."

"So what if you don't quite fit in. You don't have to be like everybody else."

"You pay for it if you're not."

"The point is you are responsible to only yourself, to find your true self. Do what *you* want to do, in life, Chad. Be who you're supposed to be and it works out better."

"I don't have a lot of say at home. In fact, I don't have any say there."

"Not many kids do. But that's how it works. You have to understand, no matter what you feel inside, that you have a purpose here or you wouldn't have been born."

"I don't go for that religious stuff. Not anymore."

"Call it what you want. Any way you cut it, you owe yourself and nobody else."

"You must have had good parents," Chad said.

"I lost my parents when I was three."

"Oh, I'm sorry. Car accident?"

"My father shot my mother and then himself. He thought he'd killed me, too, but I survived. Sometime I'll show you the scars, if you'd like. I have only one kidney."

"Who raised you, then?"

"I found some people who cared, some people who didn't. The system isn't perfect. But there's always someone who comes along to validate you. I found him in the form of a drunken bum under a bridge, when I was living on the streets of Chicago."

Chad thought a moment. "So, you really think I can make a difference?"

"Without a doubt."

Chad looked into the officer's eyes. "I'm going to need your help."

The moon had risen full, and Chad took a seat on a fallen log near the river. Donny Riggs was certain to arrive soon, to take him where the meeting was to be held. He had promised he would, just that morning. It was, as Donny had said, the Halloween moon, a blood moon.

Chad sat for over an hour, toying with the bare branches and briars of a wild rosebush. Still no Donny Riggs. Something had to be wrong.

Chad was set to leave when he heard a noise behind him. Milton Cross emerged from the shadows.

"Sit back down, Chad," Cross said. "We need to talk."

"Where's Donny?" Chad asked.

"He's disappointed in you. He's asked me to take over for you as the co-general on all this."

Chad stepped toward Milton Cross. "Why didn't he come here himself?"

Milton Cross gave no ground. "Donny has other plans tonight. As do I, when we're through here."

Cross pulled a 9-mm pistol from the pocket of his jacket and placed it against Chad's stomach.

"Don't move at all. And don't say anything. Just listen."

"You would shoot me?"

"Shussh! Just listen, Chad."

Chad backed up and sat down on the log, close to the rosebush.

Milton Cross sat down. He laughed. "Are you afraid of me, Chad?"

"You've got a gun," Chad said. "What's to be worried about?"

Cross's voice was a hiss. "You haven't been part of the Plan for months. Why would you think Donny would want you now?"

"He told me that he wanted me to attend my first meeting tonight."

Milton Cross grunted. "Why? You never did believe in the New Reich. You were never a keeper, you know."

Chad wanted to make a break for it but Cross now had the gun in his face.

"You just aren't cut out for what must be done. We know who our true followers are."

"Did Donny send you here?"

"You are supposed to *listen*, Chad! Remember?"

Chad held his breath.

"Everyone knows you've been very disconsolate since all the happenings with the terrorism in New York and all."

"Disconsolate?"

"Unhappy and frightened and unsure, Chad. You want out of it all. This is the kind of place where people come to shoot themselves."

Chad grabbed Cross's wrist and aimed the gun skyward. It discharged into the night air. While he and Milton Cross struggled on the ground, Tom Lopez and two other officers converged on the two students.

"Break it up here and stand up, both of you."

"You took long enough." Chad's breath was coming in heavy gulps.

"We wanted him to talk more about Donny Riggs and the others," Lopez said, twisting Cross's arms behind him and applying handcuffs. "We didn't want to be detected."

"You believe you have me, but you don't," Milton Cross said. "Long live the New Reich!"

With those words he slumped forward, unconscious. Lopez caught him and laid him out on the ground where he began to convulse, a white froth appearing at his mouth.

"He's poisoned himself," Lopez said.

"He must have had a capsule in his mouth," one of the other officers said. "In case he was caught."

The other officer was carefully removing a small microphone that had been secured within the rosebush near the log.

"At least we have some evidence here," he said.

"Not enough to do any good," Lopez said with disgust. "Guys like this New Reich bunch, who prey on kids, hide behind the scenes and use the kids for their own purposes, but never get caught."

Chad Simmons looked down at the body of Milton Cross, now still in death. He looked into Officer Lopez's eyes.

"But they will be caught," Chad insisted. "There has to be a way to do it."

"It's a mission that has to be undertaken," Lopez agreed.

"I intend to work toward that purpose," Chad said. "And with your help, maybe we can carry on here."

"You'll have a lot of support now," Lopez promised. "Of that you can be sure."

TALL GRASS MONDAY

I remember how the sun rose that morning, filling the horizon with a streak of mixed red and purple, against a sky as soft as blue powder. It was to be a day where I would come to a firm understanding that things are never as they seem, and that working in the field of natural resource management can be a bit dangerous at times.

I was two years out of college and ready to reinvent the wheel. At the time, I was employed by the old USDA Soil Conservation Service, known as the SCS, now the Natural Resources Conservation Service. A better term for this day and age, I guess, and hopefully more effective in some ways than the older version of the agency. Who knows for sure about those things?

My title was Range Conservationist, and my job was to assess grazing pressure on grasslands. I would identify the vegetation species present and through various formulas, conclude what condition the native rangeland existed in, and how many cattle, horses, or sheep should be allowed to graze over a year's time.

I had come to know what grasses suit cattlemen best and which ones are a warning of overuse—too much grazing by too many livestock, on not enough range to support them. Some of the landowners showed concern about it, others never did.

It was supposedly my job to make the lives of these people easier to bear, should they be interested in improving their return on their investments. A lot of them didn't see anything that had to do with the government as a benefit to them, and didn't hold back about saying so.

There was, however, a group of cattlemen in the county where I worked who had made an effort to help educate the stock growers at large concerning proper grazing practices. These men, five or six in number, if I recall correctly, sponsored tours and workshops every summer as a means of educating young people and adults alike in the identification and understanding of grass and browse (that's what deer do, as opposed to grazing—they browse) species within the natural environment.

I still hold my hat off to those guys, breaking new ground in a culture of pioneer folk so tightly locked with tradition. Most went by the adage that what was good enough for Dad and Grandpa was good enough for them. But these men saw fit to make a change.

They got a lot of odd stares from those landowners bent on doing things the way they'd always been done, and ruining the resource in the process. Ownership of a resource, in their eyes, included grazing lands leased from the government.

On the other hand, some of those very same people, who wanted no one telling *them* what to do, eagerly stepped forward when it was announced that the government would pay a good percentage of their costs to improve their ranches, should they desire that. Well, certainly, if they could get a free buck here and there, why wouldn't they want it?

The only catch was they had to sign a document called a Great Plains Conservation Contract.

In exchange for going along with recommendations for agricultural improvements, the landowners were allowed a certain percentage of federal aid for their projects. Such things as land leveling for irrigation, fences, and springs, and stock water wells and pipelines, all received government payment on a percentage basis. This enabled the landowner to improve his farm or ranch to a great degree, with the help of federal funds, if he agreed to place his entire holdings under a plan to manage his natural resources.

The idea had presented itself as a result of the Depression years, and the savage loss of topsoil on farm and pastureland to drought and horrendous winds. For the most part the concept had done wonders for the millions of acres of open farmland in the West and Midwest, and also for grazing lands throughout the Rocky Mountain and Great Plains regions.

I had already written a half dozen of these contracts when I watched that sunrise on that bright June morning. I was scheduled to meet Dick Whitman, another range conservationist, who had asked me to accompany him on a job way up along the Missouri River.

I worked out of the Glendive field office at the time, writing conservation plans and Great Plains contracts over a three-county area. I was to venture over into a county I didn't usually work, and it didn't make a whole lot of sense to me.

There were a few things I needed to pick up at the office. I was packing a field bag when Ted Lane, the conservation technician in the office, arrived. He was responsible for doing a lot of the engineering work on dam and irrigation projects as laid out in the conservation plans.

"Jim," he said to me, "you're up way early." He laughed.

"Too early," I said.

"Hangover?"

"No, I stayed home last night."

"First time in a long time."

"Yeah, big day today, they tell me."

Ted laughed again. "Get those contracts done. Push, push, push. Waterfield is riding everyone's ass, all over the area."

Buddy Waterfield had the top job in the eastern part of the state. An area conservationist, he oversaw a number of field offices, the Glendive one included, and had made it his life's purpose to drive for as many Great Plains Conservation contracts as he could make happen.

He was in his first year at the job, a lateral transfer in from Texas. Rumor had it that he'd been caught with his secretary in someone's new-mown hay. He had to make good or find another career.

"I understand that this is a new contract up there along the Missouri," I said to Ted. "That right?"

"New and very interesting, I'd be willing to bet." He laughed again. He looked at me and added, "So you're really going to do it?"

"What?" I asked.

"Guess you really don't have a choice, huh?"

"What am I missing here?"

I had been out on vacation the previous week and had learned about the assignment from a message on my answering machine. Everyone else seemed to know a lot more about it than I did.

"What's the big secret?" I asked again.

Warren Lane, District Conservationist, and boss of the Glendive field office, stepped in the door just then. Ted hurried to his desk and began to look busy.

"Hey, Jim, you'd better get going," Warren told me. He was a tall man, middle-aged, with a raspy voice. "You've got a long day ahead."

"I don't know a lot about it," I told him. "Fill me in, would you?"

"And you've got to get back here and finish another two plans before the end of the month."

"You've reminded me about those other two plans four times, already, Warren. So why am I even going out on this one?"

Warren ignored the question. "Just reminding you about finishing your plans is all. Buddy Waterfield has called twice this week, wondering how we're doing."

"Why doesn't Buddy Waterfield write some of them himself? Get off his office ass."

Warren glared at me. He didn't like Waterfield any more than anyone else, but in his world, you kept your mouth shut.

Ted was shuffling stuff on his desk, smiling to himself.

"Ted, you need to get going, too," Warren barked.

"Yeah, just about ready," he said.

Warren turned to me. "Make a good show of yourself with Dick, and don't overstep your bounds."

"What's this guy's name up there?" I asked.

"Get on the road," Warren said. "Let Dick Whitman fill you in."

It always gave me great pleasure to find a stand of native grass that grew tall and thick, healthy and vital. In those days we gave those choice grasses a title: We called them Decreasers. Simply put, they were the first grasses that grazing animals went for when searching for food. If there were too many animals in one place grazing on these grasses, they decreased in number, giving way to smaller grasses, shrubs, and various forb, or flower species, which we labeled Increasers.

In time, if the grazing pressure was too severe as to clean out the Decreasers and the Increasers both, the range was left with Invaders. These were species like cactus and various sticky or hairy flowered plants, and a few very unpalatable grasses that nature uses to cover the soil but are too coarse and bristly to graze on. They grew to fill the void and keep something on the bare soil. When a pasture fell into poor condition, in a climate where rainfall is scarce, it usually meant the resource was ruined forever.

Few places still remain where the land is covered with tall grasses, mixed with some sagebrush, or other kinds of native brush, and flowers—a condition called Pristine. These locations are generally the top of buttes and inside of old cemeteries, or places far away from any existing water, where grazing animals can't get to or use rarely. Over the years I've seen most of those kinds of places in that wide-open piece of the world known as Eastern Montana, where the wind never lets you catch your breath.

It is a place that has never known time, lost in the wild reaches that once saw buffalo by the thousands, just south of untamed stretches of the Missouri River, and very far from any part of the world that's ever known a lick of change.

Call me crazy but when I would be working alone out there, I swore I could hear sounds on the wind—besides the distant calls of hawks or eagles or the rumbling of afternoon thunder. It's a reality that the land is still alive with the past.

The Sioux and the Crow fought over these hunting grounds, as well as the Blackfeet and Assiniboin. Later came the fur traders and then the cattlemen. A lot of secrets were laid to rest out there over the years.

To the north of these open fields and grasslands the Missouri River Breaks, as they're called, rise in a collection of deep and twisted canyons filled with rock and timber that stretch out on both sides from the Missouri River. It's a true place of isolation. Stretches of that country will likely never change.

Charles M. Russell, the famous cowhand-turned-artist of the late 1800s and early 1900s, once painted a scene of thousands of buffalo fleeing a massive prairie fire. It was after dark and the herd was swimming the Missouri, lurching up the banks to safety on the opposite shore of the flames. Their eyes were rolling and their tongues hanging out. *When the Land Was God's* was the title of the painting.

In the beginning, I didn't want to work that country, really, so isolated and windtorn and bleak throughout the year. I'd come from the intermountain valleys to the west, and the divides in this area were no more than a cliff between two streams, or a segment of rolling hills that stood out above the endless sea of prairie.

But there was a strange and unsettling beauty within the bleakness, a form of soul-wrenching attachment that made you pause and reflect.

And the meadowlarks and lark buntings couldn't have been happier. They loved the area, where no one bothered their nests. While the females rested their feathered little bodies in hidden tufts next to the ground, the males rose into the air above the endless stretches of plain and sang the shrillest notes you've ever heard. They were in love, and the broad sky above carried their tunes for all to hear.

If you'd ever care to visit, though, there's something to consider. This part of the country is so far from anywhere, so off on its own, that it presents a world unto itself—a place where outsiders dare not ask questions. It's too far from any main road where people travel, and it's too easy to get lost and never come out.

I arrived in the little town of Circle, a road-stop where grain and cows were the heart of conversation. Whitman had just arrived from the area office in Miles City, the domain of Buddy Waterfield, who lorded over a seven-county section of the state. Whitman was the area range conservationist and also spent a lot of his time writing Great Plains Conservation contracts.

We met at the Double D Café, and ate pancakes and sausage and drank coffee for an hour. I asked him why he needed me to go with him.

"It'll be good experience for you," he told me.

He didn't look me square in the eye, and I persisted.

"You've never asked me to assist you before."

"That's true, but I need assistance this time. You wouldn't go up there alone, either."

"Why not?"

He looked puzzled. "Didn't anyone tell you? We're going to see Marvin Cobb."

"I don't work this county, Dick. Who's Marvin Cobb?"

"Let's just say he's eccentric. It's better to have two together going up there."

"How so?"

"Just take my word for it."

Since he was the area range conservationist, he held seniority over me. I'd gotten to know him a few years before, when I was assigned to a different location, and saw him as a regular kind of guy, doing better-than-average work. Today, he seemed like a different person.

“I suppose Buddy Waterfield is putting pressure on you, like he is everyone in the area,” I said.

“Listen, I have to see that guy every morning, unless I leave really early, like I did today. He always wants to know how I’m doing with my list of potential Great Plains operators.”

“Pushing pretty hard, then,” I said.

“Nothing we can do about it but get the contracts,” Whitman said, “wherever we can find them.”

We stopped at the local SCS office and checked in. We gabbed with the people there for a short time, all of them studying us closely, as if they might never see us again.

“A BLM pickup came out of up there yesterday with a hole in it,” a technician told us.

The Bureau of Land Management was generally hated by the stockgrowers. They saw the agency as a bunch of bullies who threw their weight around and fined them for grazing offenses they hadn’t committed, or weren’t worth being fined over.

“Was anyone hurt?” I asked.

“Just an accident that they weren’t,” the technician replied. “He leaned over to pull his lunch bag off the floorboards. Bullet just missed his back.”

“Did he report it?” I asked.

“Oh, yeah. For what, though?”

"Possibly attempted murder."

"Well, the law sees it as certain murder, of them, if they go poking around up there."

"Good to know we're safe," I commented.

Whitman had a number of aerial photos he laid out on a large table. We always used aerial photos to draw project numbers and descriptions on, and also as a means of designating rangeland condition and fence lines. Everything was drawn in with an ink pen. You could tell a range survey had been completed when you saw a bunch of symbols on the map: EC meant that the grass was in excellent condition: GC was good condition. There was also FC and PC, for fair and poor, respectively.

Close to water, the range usually ran from fair to poor. You saw a respectable amount of good-condition grassland scattered around, but excellent was, for the most part, nonexistent.

"I think we can survey most all of it today," Whitman was telling me. He was pointing to a particular pasture area. "He doesn't have a whole lot of grazing land. This chunk of range will be handy to look at on the way out."

"He wants his bottomland along the river turned into an irrigation heaven," the technician remarked. "That's what he wants."

The technician gave us instructions on how to get out there, and added, "You boys going to write a letter home before you go?"

I left my rig parked in front of the office and we left for the lost spaces in Whitman's truck. The sun was already climbing steadily and an air of silence fell over us as we traveled.

An hour into the drive we stopped to look at a stand of grass inside an old cemetery. I don't even remember now exactly where it was, except that I thought to myself at the time that this had to be a lonely place to die.

The highway we were traveling on paralleled and crossed an old stage and freight route that connected the Missouri River country to the north with the Miles City area to the south. Whitman said the site had been home to an old saloon, now just a few old decomposed logs on a broken rock foundation.

The cemetery was filled with kids and young women, mothers who had died of "childbirth fever" back in a time when doctors were scarce even where the population was stable. HE LIVED TO A RIPE OLD AGE said one tombstone. He had passed on at age fifty-one.

It was one of the few tombstones in the cemetery.

The rest were wooden markers whose faces were grayed and streaked by wind and freezing water.

I looked across the stretches of open grasslands that emptied out into horizons in every direction. Overhead, a small kestrel glided smoothly through the morning, its mate calling shrilly from a lone cottonwood along a distant bottom.

As we traveled on, I couldn't help but notice that the rolling hills just before the river were covered with little bluestem. I'd never seen so much of it in one place before. Dick Whitman grunted and said that it was interesting. He said that the year before, they had discovered the bodies of two fugitives in the grass along a hillside.

"The 'official' report in the papers said they'd shot themselves," Whitman said. "But there was a lot of talk that they'd come up here to hide out and overstayed their welcome."

"What did the autopsy say?" I asked.

He laughed. "Autopsy? They don't do those up here. You heard what was said in the office. The sheriff won't even come out here anymore."

"I don't understand."

"Too many private feuds going on. If he takes sides, he'll end up like the fugitives."

"What do I need to know about Marvin Cobb?" I asked.

"The less the better."

I was beginning to get the picture.

"So, I'm along on this thing for strength in numbers. Is that it?"

"Something like that."

We reached the Marvin Cobb place about eleven. The heat was building and the skies had turned hazy. The road had turned from gravel to plain dirt, two deep groves along a fence line that wandered along the bottom to a rickety farmhouse that hadn't been white for decades. Its sides were grayish, peeling from top to bottom on all sides, and the picket fence lay completely in ruins.

But flying proudly from a long pole nailed to the front of the house was a Confederate flag, frayed and bleached from wind and weather.

Three bluetick hounds chained to a tree bayed like sirens as we drove into the yard. Two men lay in the shade of an old truck with a back tire removed. They raised their heads to stare.

"You really want to go through with this, do you?" I asked Whitman as he came to a stop.

He took a deep breath and drummed his fingers against the steering wheel.

"Buddy says we need this contract, that we need

a lot of contracts this year to get the funding for next year."

"You told me that," I pointed out. "But if all I've heard is true, you know Marvin Cobb will have no intention of complying with the arrangements to do all the work."

"Not our problem," Whitman said. "Those jokers in the local field office will have to administer it."

We stepped out of the truck and a small woman in a faded orange dress appeared from inside the house.

"We been expecting you." She held a rickety screen door open. "Come on in."

She studied me with quick eyes. Her hair hadn't been fixed in some time and was in place with old-time pins that could have come from a cow-town dance hall.

The kitchen was dark, not because there were no windows but because they were encrusted with dirt. Two chickens stood on the breakfast table, picking at chunks of old egg and toast.

"I'm Ellie," she said, shooing them out the door. They turned around and rushed past her, back inside, and she threw up her hands.

We introduced ourselves and Whitman asked, "Is Marvin around?"

"Well, I figure he is," she replied. "All he can do

is talk about this Great Plans thing you came for."

"Great Plains contract," Whitman corrected her. "Not plans, plains. It's a contract that requires full compliance with everything in it."

She smiled. "But you got to plan it first, don't you?"

The screen door opened and a bear of a man entered wearing a battered straw hat. He held a .30-30 Winchester rifle in the crook of his left arm, an arm that was much smaller than his right, and badly deformed. His fingers appeared like a chicken's foot, clawed up in a tight, scrawny fist, likely never opened in many years, if ever.

He wore a battered, greasy hat and his face appeared to have several sessions with crisp bacon encrusted in his week-old beard.

"You boys are late," he told us. "Ellie, fetch us all some coffee."

"It might be better if we got started right away," Whitman said. His face had become pasty.

"We are getting started," Cobb said with a grunt. "I want to see those maps you said you would bring."

"That's a good place to start," Whitman agreed. "Let me get them from the truck."

Whitman made his way out and Cobb turned to me. "He eat something bad for breakfast, or something?"

"He just might have," I said. "He'll be fine."

Cobb grunted again. He took off his hat and laid the rifle against the doorjamb.

"You're a young feller, come along to learn all this. That it?"

"Yeah," I said.

"That's good. You take anything in your coffee?"

I'd gotten used to cream, but saw that the small pitcher, half full, had two flies swimming in it.

"Black," I replied. "As black as night."

He laughed. "She builds a mean batch of that stuff. I'll have her give you a knife along with it."

"Now, Marvin, that's such an old joke," she said. "My coffee ain't so strong that you got to cut it."

"It is if I say it is." He glared at her and she stopped laughing.

"It's good," I said, slurping as small a taste as possible, but making it appear large. I don't know how I kept from gagging.

"Did you two have breakfast?" Cobb asked.

"Yeah, remember?"

"Oh, sure. Your friend got sick on it. Where'd you eat at?"

"I don't even remember."

"None of them greasy spoons up there ain't nothing to brag on a'tall."

Whitman came in and removed the aerial photos

from a long case. Ellie grabbed dishes off the table and stacked them in her arms.

"Don't you drop none of them, Ellie," Cobb warned her.

Ellie called into a back bedroom.

"Carla! Come out here and help. You hear me?"

A girl of nine or ten appeared, her head bowed, stringy hair covering her face. She wore ragged shorts and a thin top, and she walked barefoot, with a slight limp.

"Get the rest of them dishes off the table so the men folk can do their maps," Ellie told her. "And don't drop none of them."

I stood off to one side while Whitman and Cobb fumbled to unroll the photos. Cobb was impatient and Whitman's fingers were shaking. I stepped away and looked at some old pictures on the wall, battered C. M. Russell prints of cowhands throwing lassos over longhorns and grizzly bears in the days when the old gravesites were being dug regularly.

In one corner of the living room, a darkened area, a small boy sat on a ragged couch, tearing the stuffing out of a teddy bear. I watched him while he ripped at the arms and middle of the bear, and slammed it repeatedly against the arm of the couch.

I got an odd feeling watching that small child. He

made certain I saw what he was doing, then ran into a nearby bedroom and slammed the door.

Whitman and Cobb pointed at the maps and nodded and jabbered about things planned and the great results to come of it. The engineer had been right. Cobb was mostly interested in land-leveling developments along the bottom, so that irrigation water could be brought from the river to grow huge crops of barley and alfalfa. He wanted to know explicitly what the government's share of the cost would amount to.

It would be an understatement to say that Marvin Cobb was a jumpy man. A vehicle door slammed outside and he lurched for his rifle.

"Ain't nothing but the hired hands," Ellie said quickly.

Cobb peered through the screen door.

"Just the hands, Marvin," she repeated.

Cobb looked to Whitman and me and set the rifle down.

"Some of our neighbors are less than friendly," he said.

"We can get started now, looking the place over," Whitman said.

"Tell you what," Cobb spoke up. "I'm going to have Ellie show you the horse pasture, just south, while I check on a few things. When you get back, we'll go down to the bottom and look at where the alfalfa fields will go in. Suit you boys?"

"Fine with us," Whitman replied.

Cobb led the way out of the house, his rifle at the ready. He paused in front of his pickup and cursed at the two men sitting in the shade of it, playing cards on the ground.

Ellie got into the cab between Whitman and me and sat rigid as stone.

"Drive thataway," she said, pointing, and settled into silence while the pickup bounced along the road.

"You grow up here on the river?" I asked.

She looked at me. "Marvin says to just talk business."

"Sure," I said.

The horse pasture lay a mile straight south. Ellie instructed Whitman to go two miles out of our way, around a field of barley, and then through a gate into the horse pasture.

We drove around the pasture and got out a few times to look at the grass, what little there was of it. We could see ten head of gaunt horses scattered in twos and threes, their noses in dried wisps of grass and sagebrush.

"How many horses does Marvin generally run in here?" Whitman asked.

"I don't rightly know," she replied. " 'Spect he'll tell you when we get back, though."

I didn't even want to look at the horses or the pasture any longer. As far as I was concerned, anyone who abused their animals and their range land that badly should be jailed, and the key thrown into a lake.

"I've got one question," I said to her. "We took the long way around to get here. Why didn't we just drive down that road over there that goes along the fence line?"

"Well, that barley field there belongs to Jed Hawkins. He and us ain't too friendly."

She went on to explain that earlier that spring, five of their cattle had crawled the fence into the barley field, grazing the young plants off to nothing and tearing the field up pretty badly.

"I can see how he was angry," she said. "And it would have been fine if he'd just shot them. But, no, he went and chased them all over that field with his truck until they were dead tired. Then he got out and broke their legs with a two-by-four and just left them lay. No excuse for that."

We got back into the pickup, and Whitman drove the long way around and back into the yard. Cobb stood waiting beside his old pickup, the flat tire having finally been changed.

I got out, with Ellie behind me. She hurried toward the house.

He grabbed her by the arm and said, "Did you show them the pasture, Ellie?"

"I did, Marvin, just like you said."

He released her and turned to us. "Ready to head down to the bottom?"

Whitman followed Cobb down a narrow dirt road toward the river. We arrived at some fifty acres of bottomland, open except for scattered stands of silver sagebrush. The ground had been plowed a number of years before and the effects of the old moldboard were still evident.

"Some old-timer tried to grow a crop or two down here, back in the Depression," Cobb laughed. "We'll do it up right this time."

"Who had this place during the Depression?" I asked.

"I 'spect it was Ellie's grandfather," Cobb answered. "Don't matter now, does it?"

"No," I said. I noticed Whitman staring at me.

"I own this country around here now," Cobb bragged. He swept his good arm in a half-circle, holding tight to the rifle with his crippled forearm. "All of it."

I began to walk toward a grove of trees in the near distance.

"Is that area where the diversion ditch for the irrigation will come out?" I asked.

Cobb was hobbling toward me, shouting, "Hey! Don't you go over there!"

I expected to see the muzzle of the .30-30 pointed at me when I turned around. I believe he had thought about it, but wanted the government money bad enough to restrain himself.

"What's wrong?" I asked.

"Nothing. Just don't go over there, is all."

I looked at Whitman. He shrugged.

"Where do you want to bring the water out of the river for this project?" I asked Cobb. "The engineers in town will want a place to look at."

"What engineers?"

"The ones that will have to survey in your land-leveling project."

"Yeah," Cobb said. "You just make sure I know ahead of time before they show up. You need to tell me."

"Nobody's coming out here without your knowledge, believe me," Whitman said.

"Good," he said. He seemed to settle down some.

"What else do we have to look at?" I asked.

"Nothing today," Cobb said. "You boys can come back tomorrow."

Cobb stood and watched to make certain we got into the pickup. He climbed into his, led the way out of the bottom, and held up at the county road. Whitman said to me, "Wait here," then got out and walked over to talk to him.

I watched them closely, realizing that they were discussing me, for the most part. There was a serious reason Cobb didn't want me in that grove of trees. Whitman seemed to have an idea what that might be.

When Whitman returned, he churned through the gravel and settled the pickup into an even pace toward town.

"What's the big secret?" I asked.

"It's only rumor."

"What's the rumor?"

"Maybe I shouldn't say."

"Maybe you should, since he went ballistic on me."

"Okay, but you didn't hear this from me."

Whitman began by explaining that Ellie had been Marvin Cobb's wife for less than a year. She had been married to a man named Harlen Baker, who had owned the adjoining ranch to the east.

"Harlen came up missing, for some reason," Whitman told me. "Ellie told the authorities he ran off on her. Maybe he did, who knows."

"But there's a better chance that he didn't," I said.

"It's all just rumor," Whitman continued. "There's never been a body found anywhere. Nothing like that."

"I wonder what's in that grove of trees?" I said.

"Do you want to go back and see?" Whitman asked.

"Let's skip it," I said. "I don't plan to be here tomorrow, either."

"Let's get that other pasture looked at and we'll head on out of here," Whitman suggested.

We drove into the pasture and did the surveying needed to determine the range condition. Parts of it were badly grazed and other parts not so badly. We determined that in order to take the pressure off the range in the other part of his pasture, he should have a stock-water dam built or a well drilled, to bring the cattle into the area where little of it was being grazed.

We selected a draw that seemed well suited for a stock-water dam. It was important to check the soil type closely to determine how well the soil would hold water. Heavier soils, with more clay, tended to make better sites for dam development.

After digging down with a sharpshooter spade, it became evident that the dam location would work nicely. A ways up the draw, it became obvious from the kinds of grasses that were present that the soil was turning from clay to a much sandier type. It wouldn't affect the runoff for the dam, but we were interested in just looking at the area.

Whitman stopped the pickup and we began to walk through a stand of tall grass that would normally be grazed out of the area. With the lack of any nearby water, there existed some two hundred acres of a large native needlegrass called porcupine grass—a species rarely seen in abundance anywhere in the northern grasslands anymore.

We had discovered what appeared to be a true pristine site.

It was amazing to behold, the stalks rising some three to four feet high, flowing like waves atop a vast green sea in the afternoon breeze.

We both strolled through it with our hands outstretched to touch the unusual seed heads, with their long awns that resemble a medium length of stiff, coarse hair.

We found some large depressions, also filled with grass. Buffalo wallows from *When the Land Was God's*, at least a hundred years before. Dozens and dozens of them, scattered closely together. I stepped into one of them and my foot touched a pile of bones. I parted the grass eagerly, expecting to find a buffalo skull. What I discovered was a human skull.

"Dick," I said. "Maybe you'd better look at this."

We both parted the grass and found segments of a human skeleton, the clothing mostly rotted away. Many of the bones had been scattered around, likely by coyotes or the few Canadian wolves that had ventured down from the north.

I looked closely and noted that one side of the skull was bashed in badly.

"What do we do now?" I asked.

We looked in every direction, expecting to discover Marvin Cobb's truck parked on a nearby hill, and him watching us through binoculars.

Whitman picked through the grass and discovered an old revolver, a Colt Navy, that appeared to be .36 caliber.

"This guy's been dead a long time," I said. "It wasn't Marvin Cobb who did it."

We took the sharpshooter spade, collected the bones, and buried the remains on the hillside, while a thunderstorm developed to the west. Whitman asked me if I wanted the revolver and I said sure, that I needed something to remember the trip by.

"Oh, I don't think you'll ever forget this day's work," he said.

I laughed. "Not likely."

———

I left the area the following spring to take a consulting position elsewhere. But not before the esteemed Buddy Waterfield received a cash prize at the annual SCS Appreciation Banquet for producing the most Great Plains contracts in the entire state. I wasn't there to witness it but I was told he stood up at the podium and talked about the many wonderful ways that the conservation programs were improving the natural resources. He took the check, they said, all fifteen hundred dollars, and waved to the crowd. He never thanked or mentioned any of us who did all the work.

Over the years, I passed through Glendive on rare occasions, on my way someplace else. During one stop I called Ted Lane, the technician. He had left the SCS to start his own surveying and construction business with his son. Ted told me that Marvin Cobb and Jed Hawkins had again ignited their feud, and were set to settle things in the fashion of the Old West. Then Ellie had showed up with a .357 Magnum, holding the pistol with both hands to steady it, and had forced Jed Hawkins away and eventually out of the county.

It seems that Marvin Cobb had rewarded her by running her off a few years later. He then took the daughter's hand in marriage. He and Carla, as far as

I know, are living happily ever after beside his irrigated hay and alfalfa fields.

As for the small boy who was so angry, so enraged—I still see his face now and again, and hear him gritting his teeth, tearing that little teddy bear to shreds.

GULLS IN THE SNOW

In the art of storing goods on a vertical plane, Charlie Hopkins had no peers. In contrast to those individuals who tend to keep order, Charlie was prone to pile things up until there was no room to pile any more. Various newsletters and books and magazines and reports and field notes and pieces of mail all found a home one atop another until the stack finally appeared too burdensome to add to. Piling things up this way wasn't something Charlie wanted to do; he just couldn't help himself.

He seldom found time to look at anything long enough to feel he had finished with it, so he would stack it somewhere until he could get back to it. He never dealt with anything right away; it was always just look at it and set it aside for later. He never read a story to its conclusion. He would read part of it and then set it aside for another time.

It was amazing that he ever finished a report or a contract bid or a story or article. He had lots going at one time and often forgot he had started one until he happened to find it while poking through one of his stacks for some reason. But to his credit, when he thought of something he needed to complete or refer to, he usually managed to find what he wanted.

His profession was archeology, so he worked in the outdoors most of the time. He was good at his profession and viewed his cabin as an extension of his work. He saw no reason why he should be concerned about crickets or creatures of various kinds. Most of them were just passing through anyway. He was aware that little animals needed spaces to crawl into and that his collection of stacked materials afforded an assorted number of hiding places. It made him feel good to be able to contribute to their needs.

These creatures traveled from far and near to see this incredible array of habitat. Besides the volumes of stacked magazines and mail, Charlie's bookcase—tucked neatly into the back wall—also served as haven for small jumping spiders. He welcomed them and looked forward to their antics among his many volumes.

Charlie had other things to look forward to as

well. The State of Colorado was anxious to give him a contract to study a particular rock wall in the San Juan Mountains, in the southern part of the state. Charlie had discovered the wall while hiking and had taken a number of pictures. The symbols were more than very interesting. They were something of an anomaly.

In all his work he'd never seen anything like them. Perhaps a connection to an ancient culture that predated all known cultures in the area.

Perhaps all known cultures on the continent.

Only Charlie knew the exact location, and since the state was interested, he had decided to take some representatives out there in a few weeks. The contract to study the site would make his life a lot easier.

And it would add a lot more paper and other documentation to his already overflowing situation.

It was time for Charlie Hopkins to get organized.

His one-room log cabin had items stacked nearly to the ceiling in virtually every corner of the room, and the walls offered little hope of ever revealing themselves. Too many things crammed into too little space. An expensive painting hung desperately on one wall, so Charlie made a special effort to keep the stacks along that particular wall below the frame line.

The top of his file cabinet was home to receipts and bills and papers of various levels of importance, all to be gone through later. The top of his television was home to his answering machine, complete with stacks of notes and notepaper that swallowed the telephone book. Various paperback novels and camera equipment sat atop his stereo, which was placed on top of his dresser.

The textures of plastic and paper and fake grain lamination piled in a row were disconcerting, but the colors went well together. Charlie didn't like a dirty place, in fact he felt very uncomfortable when he saw balls of dust poking out from under the bed. Each time he took a broom to the tile floor he promised himself that he wouldn't let things go that far again.

A small Monkey Ward refrigerator kept beer cold, lettuce far crisper, and pears from turning black. Charlie needed something to preserve fruit and vegetables longer than the normal cooler could, for he ate good food in spurts. He would get on a health kick for a time and then seemingly abandon the roughage for pre-fab meat pies and burritos.

This little refrigerator, turned up to just below the freezing mark, kept natural foods in subfrost suspension until Charlie remembered they were there and set about fixing a meal for himself.

Charlie Hopkins was lucky to have the cabin, an heirloom from the gold-rush days, completely modernized, tucked in the aspens between Lyons and Estes Park. His great-great-grandfather had ridden a red mule named June from Illinois to Colorado and had settled in the Denver area, content to sell dry goods to miners rather than pick up a pan and compete elbow-to-elbow in the mountain streams. There was plenty of gold to go around, they had said, but not many ever found it.

After a successful career in dry goods, the old man had retired to the little cabin above the Little Thompson River. Charlie was ever so glad for his grandfather's good fortune, which had trickled down to his own good fortune. He was struggling to keep from taking a nine-to-five job, and just barely making ends meet. A mortgage or a rent payment would have settled it.

Charlie's good friend Adam Parker came down from Estes Park to visit from time to time. Upon his arrival he would invariably say, "Charlie, there's a new pile of stuff every time I come here. I don't know how you do it."

They liked to fish together and roam the mountains whenever possible, snapping 35mm pictures of wildlife and hillside scenery. Adam worked in a bookstore and made it a point to know everyone's tastes. He belonged to Friends of Wilderness, an environmental group with ties all around the West.

Adam used the bookstore mainly for contacts. He got to know people and lined up outings and sold his photography frequently to outdoors magazines and wherever else wildlife and nature scenes were wanted. He had the best of everything, by his estimation. And unlike Charlie, he had no worries about money. A trust fund in a Boston bank would never run dry.

The interest they shared lay in educating people about the environment—how it was being used and abused for profit, with no concerns about replacing what was being lost. They had both concluded that a lot of what the public knew had nothing to do with what was actually going on.

Adam and Charlie had discussed the symbols in the San Juan area and had researched the Internet to see what they could find. There were pictures of many sites around the country, the West in particular, but none that matched what Charlie had found.

"This is unique," Adam said, studying photos Charlie had taken. "I know there are other sites scattered around with ancient symbols that have never been categorized. When you find a place like that, there's no mining or development or anything that ever takes place."

"Not everyone is anxious to have these sites discovered," Charlie pointed out. But he knew he was preaching to one of the choirboys.

"Before you take anyone up there," Adam suggested, "why don't we take some of my friends and a videocamera? Just to document it."

Charlie thought it a good idea. He didn't have to tell the state his intentions to make a detailed survey before the "official" one began. They would just get it done and then when he got busy on his contract and the state was ready to release information, a regular news crew could do a story. It all seemed pretty cut and dried.

With his good fortune about to unfold, Charlie Hopkins began a campaign to win back his girlfriend in Denver. Liz Jones kept a town home so neat you wanted to cry for joy. Charlie had always appreciated it, though he could never become as motivated as she was.

Liz had worked diligently to get him to move to the Highlands Ranch area and share her town home. Nothing doing. And she refused to accept the appearance inside his cabin. So they had contented themselves with Charlie's frequent visits to Denver, up until the previous month, when it seemed that Liz was suddenly unavailable a good share of the time.

Charlie was certain it had to do with his living quarters and wanted to tell her he would renovate with the money that came from the contract. Liz immediately responded and told him she sought to make up for her falling back from him by inviting him to a special banquet in the Adams Mark Hotel.

The banquet was to be sponsored by a number of local outdoor sport shops to commend corporations for their environmental attitudes. Charlie had his opinions about politics and the sales of outdoor sports gear. He agreed to go only because he wanted Liz back.

He and Liz had been very close, he believed, and he had hopes of learning why she had grown so distant. It couldn't be just his housekeeping. There had to be something else to it.

The evening of the banquet, he arrived to pick her up and asked, "So why have you been so hard to catch?"

"Let's not discuss it now, Charlie. How about we have a good time?"

Following bacon and eggs and a half-dozen cups of coffee, Charlie began to regain his sobriety. Framed in his mind was the banquet room at the Adams Mark, swirling and twisting around him as he stood atop a table, yelling to the crowded room.

The evening had been unusual in many ways. He and Liz had been seated at a table with a number of executives and field personnel from a large environmental consulting firm called North American Resources. He had discovered early on in the evening that they wanted to recruit him for a high-level resource position within the company.

Some of the state people had been there as well, wondering why he wasn't sitting with them.

It had all turned out badly, in many different ways.

What bothered him the most was the fact that he couldn't remember any of it clearly. Tidbits traveled in and out of his consciousness, as if taunting him.

It felt so very strange because he had never been in that condition before. He drank off and on, never to a great extent, and certainly never to the seemingly excessive degree he had the night before.

So he continued to ponder the mystery, sitting awkwardly in one of Liz's kitchen chairs, staring at a blotch of coffee he had just managed to spill.

He grabbed the pot and slopped more coffee into

his cup. Liz stared hard at him from across the table.

"You're a real ass, Charlie," she told him.

Charlie burped. "I love you, too."

"See what I mean? I must be crazy to care about you."

"Do you care about me, Liz? Really?"

She huffed a bit and asked, "Why did you behave like that? If it hadn't been for Don Sloan, your ass would be in jail right now."

He laughed. "That big shot sure had a hard time with his own speech after that, didn't he?"

Liz pushed herself back from the table and jumped up. "I fail to see the humor, Charlie."

He got up and walked over to where she was looking out a window toward the Rockies to the west. He put his hands on her shoulders and she twisted away from him.

"Fine," he said. "Be that way if you want. I'm beginning to see you in a clearer light now, I think."

She turned. "What do you mean by that?"

"How do you know Don Sloan? How do you even know about North American Resources?"

"I'm a legal secretary, remember? Our firm does work for them."

"Well, I decided this morning that I'm going to turn down Sloan's job offer. What do you think about that?"

"You aren't serious?"

"You'd better believe it."

"You'd throw away a chance to work for one of the nation's largest natural resource consultants?"

"North American Resources doesn't impress me, Liz."

"Don't be crazy, Charlie. Why would you turn it down?"

"They need a bag boy in their archeology department, Liz." He began walking the floor with his arms crossed. "They want somebody with my credentials to go out and gather a lot of data so they can spin it and allow the big corporations to do what they've always done."

"To do what they've always done?"

"You know what I mean, Liz. I don't make a good puppet."

"So what does that make you, Charlie? Mr. Do-Gooder or something?"

"I know a phony deal when I see one, Liz."

"I was really wrong about you," Liz said. "I thought you wanted to get somewhere. But, really, you're content with your lowlife bars and crummy contract jobs running up and down mountains."

"What I do is not crummy."

"You'll never amount to a thing. I should have known that."

"Liz, what I do is necessary to preserve the past. To give us a picture of who was here and how they lived, and what they saw as important."

"How much do you make, Charlie? I'll bet I make more as a legal secretary."

"And money has exactly what to do with it?"

She was shaking her head in disgust. "You aren't the quality of employee they want anyway. I can't imagine why they even offered you that position—especially since everyone knows you're crazy. Drunk and crazy, both, for that matter."

"What do you mean, 'Everyone knows I'm crazy?' "

"Oh, come on, Charlie. Do you think what you had to say on that banquet table didn't make you look as loony as they come?"

"What was it I said?"

Liz sighed. "Never mind, Charlie. Suffice to say, though, that you won't be working for anybody after last night. Not even the state."

Charlie stepped toward her. "What was it I said?"

Liz backed up against the wall. There had never been physical violence between them, only the abusive verbal spats that went with intimate relationships. Now, for some reason, she seemed deathly afraid of him.

"Charlie, stay away from me."

"What's the matter with you? You act like I'm going to hit you or something."

"Maybe." She moved along the wall farther away from him.

"You really are acting strange. I've never even come close to striking you."

"There's always a first time."

"Don't flatter yourself, Liz. You can't make me that angry. Now, what did you hear?"

Charlie stood with his arms crossed, waiting.

"Maybe you'd better go, Charlie."

"You serious?"

"Charlie, please."

"So, you want to end it for good?"

"I think it would be best."

"I'm not rich enough for you? Is that it?"

"Charlie, don't be a hanger-on."

"I get the picture, Liz. I'll get my coat and be gone for good."

Charlie opened the closet door while Liz began unloading on him about how he was really just a small-town bum and that she should have realized it a long time ago.

"My friends don't own three-piece suits," Charlie told her. "Is that it?"

She continued on about how she had never liked walking the mountains with him, but that he had always insisted. And she hadn't cared at all about the sunsets away from the city, away from the clubs, that he had never evened out the time for her.

"It was always about what you wanted, Charlie. Always."

Time to go home and cut his losses. Just another wrong turn in life, Charlie thought, as he cruised along I-25 through the heart of Denver and then onto the Boulder Turnpike. It was time now to question what he had just heard from Liz, the woman whose goal was company limousines and Caribbean vacations, the woman who had just forced him from her life.

He cared for her more than he thought, but it didn't matter now.

He wasn't a bum and he had legitimate goals. They just didn't meet her approval. Some people want to see life through a satin veil and settle themselves into the nighttime soaps. Some are willing to stay on the edge of existence, where the world is a late mortgage and an older model car. Charlie saw himself as somewhere in between. So what was wrong with that?

There was nothing wrong with that, as long as your friends had similar arrangements. But cross the line one way or another, you'd better prepare to look for a new crowd, and more often than not, a new girlfriend.

But what if she was right about the state not being interested in him now? He had counted on them. No use getting excited before he knew for sure.

Charlie began to feel more relaxed as he gazed at the rising peaks through his windshield. There had been some good times with Liz, but not all that many. Perhaps she had believed she was doing him a favor by trying to get him a job with NAR. But she knew him better than that. Or at least she should have.

In Lyons, he contemplated stopping somewhere for a beer. He pulled up to the curb, lost interest, and started for home.

In the cabin, he noticed the flashing light on his answering machine. A voice from the state alerted him that their meeting for the following day wouldn't be taking place. They suggested he wait for a while with pursuing the contract to study the symbols in the San Juan Mountains, until they got back to him. They would follow up with a letter.

Charlie found his favorite chair and quickly grew bored. Even with the multitude of satellite channels to chose from, he could find nothing interesting. He discovered a movie where a man and a woman were facing one another in a tidy kitchen, and within a matter of seconds, there were a lot of broken dishes lying around.

He thought of Liz and aimed the remote control. He found a dog doing tricks, a car chase, a heated family discussion over birth-control methods, and a rerun of the Old-Timers Baseball Classic. The pitchers threw a lot of slow curves and a ball was rarely hit out of the infield, but it was the class of the television lineup.

He quickly found himself relaxing, almost hypnotized by the slow drone of the game and the announcers' voices. He closed his eyes. Suddenly his field of vision was filled with a scene from the night before. Everyone at the banquet was staring at him. Their forms were blurry and misshapen. Some laughed and some yelled at him.

He was pointing to the wall. Why couldn't they all see it? The perfect outline of those drawings and carvings he had discovered on the face of the cliff in the San Juan Mountains. Why couldn't anyone see those pictographs but him?

No one had ever seen anything like them before and no one was ready to accept them. No one wanted any changes in how the patterns and theories of archeology had been handled in the past. It was to remain the same.

Changes are not allowed! No changes, understand? Absolutely no changes!

Now they were chasing him, men in black suits, all around the banquet room, out a door into the main lobby. From there he headed through the main doors into the darkness outside. But he couldn't shake them; the men were everywhere and they wanted him.

He awakened with a start and paced the room. He couldn't remember ever feeling so strange and having such an unusual dream. He couldn't ever remember a time when alcohol had caused that effect.

Charlie picked up the phone. Had it actually been ringing? He was aware that his breathing was intense.

"Hello?" he said hoarsely.

"Hello, Charlie." A man's voice.

"Yes."

"You're a hard man to catch. You know who this is?"

Charlie worked hard to settle his breathing. "No, who?"

"Don Sloan, with NAR," the voice said.

"Oh, yeah. Hello, Don."

"You sound like you've been running."

"Yeah, I have." He realized he was telling the truth. He still felt like he was trying to escape someone.

"Charlie, the reason I called is I've heard a disappointing rumor." His voice was smooth as silk. "I heard you were going to turn down our job offer."

Charlie held the receiver tightly. Liz must have told somebody right away.

"Charlie, you there?"

"Yes, that's true," Charlie replied. "I don't think I can come to work for you."

"Can you tell me why not?"

"I'm just not sure your company is going the same direction as I am."

Sloan laughed a little. "Well, I can assure you we are, Charlie. Has someone told you different?"

"No one has to tell me, Don."

"Charlie, listen to me. We've had our eye on you for a long time. I just wish you'd give us a chance."

Charlie thought a moment. He hadn't expected any of this.

"We are growing by leaps and bounds, Charlie. We need you to be our main resource man. We want you to travel to the kinds of sites you've written up in your reports for the state and give talks to different groups. We want you to show everyone how NAR is behind the preservation of the past."

"What about last night?"

"What about it?"

Charlie took a deep breath. The old-timers had finished their game on television and were all shaking hands. His head still hadn't cleared from the unusual dream.

"Tell you what, Charlie," Sloan said. "I'm going to make reservations at the Stock Exchange for this Friday night. Bring Liz if you want. We'll have a good talk and then you can decide. How's that?"

Charlie gave it a moment's thought. He had become very curious. Besides, he no longer could count on the state contract.

"What could it hurt?" he said.

"Great!" Sloan was bubbling with enthusiasm. "Friday night, around six."

Charlie hung up with a whole lot of questions running through his mind. Sloan's attitude seemed unusual to say the least, especially after the previous night's activities. Besides that, there were a lot of qualified people around who would jump at the chance to work for a company like NAR. Most of them had a lot more experience than he had, and certainly most had a lot better attitude.

He picked up the phone again and called Liz.

"Is that you, Charlie?"

Charlie took a deep breath while he tried to collect his thoughts.

"Why are you calling?" Liz asked.

"Why did you have to go blabbing about my decision not to work for NAR?"

"They have a right to know, Charlie."

"Wouldn't it be better if *I* told them?"

There was an awkward silence at the other end of the line, followed by muffled whispering.

Liz was preoccupied with something. More likely, someone.

He felt a sudden surge of anger and hurt, knowing she likely had somebody with her, male of course, who was asking her who she was talking to.

He decided to try and turn her around.

"Liz, I'm thinking about taking the job with NAR after all."

"Good. We'll talk another time."

"I want you to go out to dinner with me, to meet Sloan."

Liz was preoccupied again. The guy must be getting upset with her. Charlie heard her trying to shut him up.

"Charlie, I've got to go."

"Liz, push the jerk away for a second and just listen to me."

There was a sharp click as Liz hung up, and Charlie made a small dent in the doorframe molding near the phone by whacking it with the receiver. He called again. A male voice answered.

"Give me Liz, please."

"She doesn't want to talk to you."

"Listen, clown, I'm on my way over and you'd better have a good insurance policy."

Another hangup and a bigger dent now took its place next to the smaller one in the woodwork. One thing about those older phones, they could take a lot of damage.

He took a long breath and set the receiver back into place, and all he could see was Liz on the couch and some guy where he used to be. He switched off the television and pulled his car keys from his pocket.

In the car, he fumbled to find the ignition. He blasted the steering wheel with the palm of his hand a few times to release the frustration. Finally the engine roared and he took off. It was oldies night, and the radio was playing "I Got You, Babe." Charlie surfed stations until he found some light jazz. He was learning how to let things go.

Ten miles down the road Charlie pulled off at a fishing access and turned off the engine. The crickets in the grass outside were all trying to outdo one another. Seven million of them in one short length of ditch, paying attention only to one another. They apparently had less complicated love lives.

Complicated or not, at least they had love lives.

Charlie drummed his fingers on the steering wheel. Liz wasn't worth all this. Punching the guy out wasn't going to help. Liz would find kissing him awkward for a time, but nothing would change. Why worry? The crickets didn't care about her.

The night seemed softer to him now, the sounds more refreshing and uplifting. He would just turn around and head back to the cabin. It was almost late enough now for a decent old movie.

Lawrence of Arabia was always interesting to watch. Charlie always picked something out of the film he hadn't caught before if he could stay awake during the camel scenes, where they were crossing the desert with the theme song in the background.

The phone rang. It was Adam.

"You want to go fishing, Charlie?"

"Why not."

The following morning they packed their poles into Charlie's SUV and started for Horsetooth Reservoir, a ways north of Denver just above Fort Collins. A spring cold snap had settled in and it was rumored the fish were biting on everything.

Charlie and Adam both adhered to the old saying: When the barometric pressure falls, the fish rise.

Twenty miles from Fort Collins heavy clouds rolled in and fluffy flakes of snow began drifting down.

"Perfect," Adam said. "We'll catch a mess of fish."

They spent the day tipping beers, pulling in big ones, and watching a flock of gulls squawk in the falling snow along the shoreline. The birds haggled one another for the entrails that Charlie and Adam cleaned from the fish.

Charlie enjoyed watching them, and breaking up their fights by tossing chunks of hamburger bun into their midst. Actually, all it did was create more fights.

He listened while Adam talked about some new pictures he'd taken while driving Rabbit Ears Pass outside of Steamboat Springs.

"My agent says he can sell them many times over, to outdoor magazines and for corporate walls around the country."

"Good for you," Charlie said. "Maybe you can cover NAR's walls with them."

Adam laughed. "I think you took care of everybody's walls the other night, at the banquet."

Charlie stared at him. "How did you know about that?"

"I was there, Charlie. Two of us crashed the gates. You know we do that sort of thing, to get an idea of what the big boys are really up to."

"And you didn't say hello?"

"You wouldn't have recognized me, especially in your condition."

They both laughed.

"Really, what happened?" Charlie asked. "What did I say up on that table?"

"You don't remember?

"Last night was the strangest night I can ever remember," Charlie said. "I can't handle my liquor anymore, I guess."

"I would have to say that you weren't yourself," Adam agreed.

He went on to inform Charlie that he had roasted big corporations in general and even the state for being lax on environmental issues, essentially playing politics to keep the immense amounts of money flowing between those in power.

He had pointed to the wall and challenged the room to tell him why no new archeological finds, any place in the country, had been recorded in a very long time.

"You told them all that something was going on. Something was being hidden," Adam said.

"I don't doubt you, Adam, but I sure don't remember it."

"Did you take a truth serum before you came?"

Adam asked with a laugh. "Along with a memory loss serum?"

"Some kind of serum, I guess," Charlie said.

"Yeah, serums and drugs," Adam said dryly. "A pill to make you larger, a pill to make you small."

"Some that don't do anything at all," Charlie added.

"All of them do something," Adam commented, "and we're never sure just what."

They fished for a while. Charlie threw the last of his stale hamburger bun to the gulls.

"Don't you think Sloan is giving you a better than real deal, if you go with them?" Adam asked.

"Yeah," Charlie replied. "Too good to be true, eh?"

"It would seem that way. An archeologist disappeared about four years ago or so. Went out on a survey and never came back. The news said it was likely suicide, but I doubt it."

"What was he surveying?"

"An ancient site never before recorded. A wall layered with mysterious symbols that someone didn't want him deciphering, or the public to know about. Strange. I understand the wall was destroyed later, by who knows who?"

Charlie watched the gulls as they gathered and

inched their way closer to him, jostling for position, begging for a handout. It would be good to fish all the time and just feed gulls while it snowed lightly, the air just cool enough to enjoy hot chocolate and not get chilled. No other cares at all. Just fishing and feeding gulls and drinking hot chocolate.

Charlie walked into the Stock Exchange and Sloan waved him over to his table. The place buzzed like a sawmill. Everyone in the region knew of the Stock Exchange, Buffalo Bill's old hangout, still decorated in a Western motif. One of Denver's earliest social clubs, it had been the place to be seen in the latter days of the 1800s.

Now the Stock Exchange was a mixed Old and New West atmosphere, from rodeo cowboys in rawhide boots off the real range to combinations of turquoise and fringed leather, dark designer jeans, and wide-brimmed hats. Most talked of investment properties and out-of-the-way dude ranches while viewing the old animal head mounts crowded together on the walls.

Charlie had arrived in jeans and a sweater, while Sloan's clothes were cross-matched between a preppy from the East and the modern bear hunter.

"Glad you could make it, Charlie."

Sloan ordered drinks. He cringed when Charlie told the waitress to mix whiskey and peach brandy, light on the brandy.

"Will I have to call an ambulance?" Sloan laughed.

"My insurance will cover it."

"Just don't pass out on me," Sloan said. "I couldn't carry you out through this mob in here."

"I've learned my lesson," Charlie said. "Believe me."

"The Front Range will always be on the move," Sloan began, like he was moonlighting for the Chamber of Commerce. "A perfect place to be. Lots of culture, lots of good food, and lots of ladies."

That was Liz's cue. She slid through the crowd, took a seat next to Charlie, and smiled uneasily at him.

"I decided to take you up on the offer," she said.

"Well," Charlie said. "What a surprise."

He didn't ask her how she knew where they were meeting, or when, or even from whom she had learned their meeting place, for that matter.

"You still drinking those strong drinks, Charlie?" Liz said.

"You know what?" Charlie replied. "I'm going to have what you order this time."

He finished his drink and when the waitress arrived, ordered a Tom Collins to go along with Liz's.

"So what do you think, Charlie?" Sloan said. "This is your opportunity to make a real contribution to your profession. Give talks at meetings and publish papers on successes and new information you've obtained."

"I don't know, Don," Charlie said.

"What's the matter? You worried about the money? How much do you want?"

"Not the money, Don. Just the free reign to describe what I see and document it."

"Not a problem," Sloan said quickly. "You can go out to that site you were discussing, in the San Juan Mountains, as soon as you start work. Would you like that?"

"Will you excuse me a minute?" Charlie said. "I believe I'll find the boy's room."

He stopped on the stairs leading to the second level and the restrooms, and peeked around just in time to see Liz pulling a tiny vial out of her purse. He climbed the stairs and listened to a couple of musicians dressed like cow camp carolers for a few minutes and headed back downstairs.

He took his seat next to Liz and Sloan said, "They have all kinds of wild game specials here. Order what you'd like."

Charlie pointed toward the front door. "Isn't that Tom Selleck?"

Liz and Sloan turned immediately and Charlie made his move. He switched drinks with Liz slick as a whistle and said, "See there? Behind that crowd at the door."

Finally, when neither Liz nor Sloan could verify that Tom Selleck was in the restaurant, Charlie shrugged.

"I was sure it was him, on his way out."

Liz acted disappointed. Charlie took a gulp of his drink while Sloan watched him.

By the time the waitress arrived to take their order, Liz had finished her drink and was actively seeking a waitress to order another one. Sloan would not meet Charlie's glare, and instead lifted himself from his chair and slid out through the crowd like an eel.

In a few minutes, whatever was in the drink settled Liz into a zombie-like state. She followed Charlie out of the restaurant without question and got into his SUV and allowed him to drive her home without asking anything. She stared through the windshield and sang a song about a red robin that bobbed along.

At her Highlands Ranch town home Charlie found her keys in her purse, and after letting them both in, took her to a couch.

"Time to sleep, Liz," he said.

She yawned and stretched and curled up and Charlie covered her with a blanket. He placed her keys back in her purse and closed the door and started back north, along I-25, where people drove back and forth in their own world, whatever world that might be.

THE RED SKULL ROOM

As the sun fell into twilight, a light Cessna aircraft melted with the shadows just above the tree line. Below, boats of all sizes and shapes dotted an emerald blue surface in the waning light.

Just south of Glacier National Park, Flathead Lake sprawled some twenty-five miles in length and fifteen in width between high mountain peaks and forest wilderness. Long a sacred area for Salish and Kutenai Indians, the huge waters and the surrounding forest had become, over the years, the playground of the entitled.

With the arrival of the new millennium, cabins and summer homes had for the most part swallowed all the readily accessible beaches and hillsides surrounding the lake. Little was left the way it had once been.

Nothing foreseeable could stop the growth.

No one onboard the Cessna was interested in populations or real estate, though. The agents, three of them, were more concerned about being detected.

Brad Kemp, a small man with a smooth complexion but ruffled nerves, cracked his knuckles as he went over the plan in his mind. Next to him, Marty Feldman surveyed the surface of the lake though infrared binoculars.

Tom Carlisle, the senior agent, felt more at ease than the other two. What was another plane in the sky? There were always any number of similar aircraft aloft above the most active recreation spot along the northern tier between the Great Lakes and Seattle.

They had more important things to concern them, including how they were going to make this operation work when already a few things had gone wrong.

Marvin Blake's island lay six miles offshore along the western side of the lake. He had purchased his island in the mid-eighties for an undisclosed sum. It was widely rumored that the highly guarded compound he had built there had cost him twenty million dollars. Very few had ever viewed the lavish interior.

As the sun fell on the last day of December,

Blake's megayacht, the *Mission Lady*, lay moored at his private dock on the east side of the island. Blake was hosting his third annual New Year's Eve celebration among distinguished friends. He had spent the two previous months arranging for food and festivities certain to impress all in attendance. Colorful lights shone brightly off the boat's sleek two-hundred-foot length. Laughter and the clinking of drink glasses mixed with the strains of salsa music drifting out into the moonlit night.

Blake, a stout, balding man of medium height, would celebrate his sixtieth birthday in less than a week. He liked to tell his friends jokingly that he would surely have been a New Year's baby, but he had decided to wait the extra four days until *he* was ready to enter the world.

He lounged in a black leather armchair in the main lobby of his boat, watching over the guests he had invited for the evening. Sitting in his lap was an escort named Marlene. Her hair was long and dark, and her eyes mysterious. She could be part Asian, he thought. Possibly other nationalities as well. Her smile spoke of secrets she would never tell, not even on the last day.

She wore a striking purple gown split up the side, complete with a plunging neckline that Blake kept staring into. He had requested an interesting evening companion from an escort service he knew and trusted. He couldn't be more pleased.

Each of the club members had brought their own sexual entourage, plus a number of guests. The other men had as many as three or four men and women around them, serving them food and drink. But Blake was content to concern himself exclusively with Marlene.

Though he had married a woman he once considered glamorous and desirable, Blake's extramarital affairs had convinced him that his wife needed an education in pleasing her man. He had learned the name of a "charm school" from a business associate, but when he attempted to send her for lessons, she had slapped him across the face. He hadn't seen her since that time, some twelve years before. His business people had taken care of the divorce details.

Blake had inherited his great-grandfather's wealth, a fortune made from gold and diamond mining in the Rocky Mountains. He had barely known his father, who had been killed by lightning during a sudden storm while mountain climbing on Longs Peak in Colorado. Blake was only four at the time, and just three years later his mother left him to live with his grandfather. She then hit the road with a rock-and-roll band and was never heard from since.

Blake's grandfather taught him the fine art of the

strong business deal well before his teenage years. As an adult, Blake had added considerably to his wealth with oil and real-estate deals around the globe. Thirty-five years of wheeling and dealing among the strongest and meanest players the international trade empires had to offer had gleaned him a net worth, on paper, of twelve billion dollars. Hidden assets more than doubled that. He was known as a hard driver who could make or break anyone—unyielding in his demands, a man who always got what he wanted.

Almost always.

The one thing that had eluded Marvin Blake was winning the coveted New Year's Eve Sweepstakes, twenty-five million in diamonds awarded to the winner of a secret contest the club members had initiated before the first meeting.

The contest was the sole reason for their gathering.

Blake and the other four other men would each ante up their diamonds, five million dollars worth, the entire pot to be taken in full by the contestant who produced the most interesting and hard-to-obtain collectable. Each year's contest was based on a different theme, and each contestant was required to vote for an entry other than his own.

Each of the previous contests had been won with

a black market antique. Sal Leone, a New York City businessman seated immediately to Blake's right, had won the first year with a gold-plated Etruscan shield. Other entries had been Athenian silver coins, a miniature Greek sculpture, and a rare design of gladiator's blade from early Rome.

The second year had brought antiques from South America, the winner being an ancient Chilean headdress of parrot feathers and gold. The others had told Blake that his entry was interesting, but far too easy to come by. He had presented an ancient shrunken head from the Amazon, carbon dated to be nearly four thousand years old. Blake had argued that he might have agreed with their rationale had the head not been covered with long blond hair.

Subsequent years' winners had bought ancient artifacts that had been stolen from sites under excavation or from museums in different parts of the world. The previous year Blake had presented a map from a Chinese voyage predating Columbus by six centuries, complete with newly discovered Atlantic islands, no longer above the ocean's surface, and notes of the seafarers' adventures scribbled in the margins. The piece had been taken from the archives of a museum in Beijing. However, the map was only a partial, and there was no evidence of where the expedition had finally landed, or even who the explorers were.

The winner had been a Chinese businessman named Liu Cheng, who had unveiled a four-foot stone head from the Ming dynasty. Totally priceless, the antique had won unanimously.

Blake held no doubt that this year he would be the unanimous winner. They had all agreed on a Native American theme, but could enter an artifact collected only within the United States borders. So confident was Blake of his victory that he had arranged a side bet with Liu Cheng, who said he would gladly forfeit an extra five million should Blake prove himself right.

Sal Leone declined to get in on the side bet, as did the other two men in the club, one a South African businessman named Grenmoore and the other a computer software dealer from Los Angeles named Kirkman. Every one of the members had already declared their entry unique enough to claim the diamonds. It promised to be the strongest competition yet.

The contest always began one hour prior to the stroke of midnight, so that the winner could receive a New Year's toast to his good fortune. Though a full forty-five minutes remained before the start of the competition, Blake was eager to claim his certain winnings and proposed they get underway. However, Grenmoore, the South African, was in no hurry to dismiss his lady guests.

"Why don't we stick to the regular schedule?" he said. "Tradition, you know."

The others agreed. Blake sloshed down the last of his drink and stood up. He began to pace back and forth.

"What's your rush?" Grenmoore asked him.

"I'm in a hurry to win," Blake said.

"We're all in a hurry to win." Grenmoore laughed and then everyone laughed.

Blake ignored them. Marlene stood up and encouraged him to relax.

"I'm certain everything will be just fine," she said.

Blake pointed his index finger at her. "You can count on it."

Tom Carlisle watched the activity on the *Mission Lady* from the timbered shadows on shore. Marty Feldman and Brad Kemp stood beside him, each with his own pair of small binoculars.

They had left the plane and had driven to the shoreline without incident. They now monitored the yacht while going over the plan, and once again synchronized small, computerized clocks hanging from chains around their necks. They were dressed in the same clothes as the security guards patrolling the boat, and that was not by accident.

Carlisle had gotten to know Marvin Blake well during the past fourteen months. Blake had made Seaside Security of Seattle his main protection system, and Carlisle had infiltrated the company. They had no idea he was a special agent working with the International Criminal Police Organization, otherwise known as INTERPOL, and was using their company to document Marvin Blake's illicit activities.

Carlisle had dazzled Seaside's top brass with his knowledge of security systems, especially for use with high-profile people. Soon he had worked himself into their connections to Marvin Blake, and after impressing Blake, had become the top man in Seaside's Intermountain Division. Carlisle had made it his priority to stay in touch with the billionaire, to the point of flying to any location he might be at the drop of a hat.

Carlisle had used his position to install minicameras at strategic locations throughout the boat, including two in the main cabin, a place of secrecy that Blake called the Red Skull Room. Carlisle had been told never to enter there unless invited, even though he was the top security man in Blake's operation.

Carlisle had risked everything to place the cameras. If something had gone wrong, his cover would have gone up in smoke.

It had worked, and now that the New Year's Eve contest was set, so was the bust. Carlisle had an open pass to the festivities. Even Seaside Security didn't know what he was all about.

Kemp checked his 9mm pistol and returned it to the holster hidden under his shirt. He swallowed a handful of aspirin and cracked his knuckles.

"I've asked you not to do that," Feldman said.

"You tend to your own hands," Kemp told him.

Carlisle watched the boat while the other two continued to bicker.

"Will you guys give it a rest?" he said.

Kemp cracked his knuckles. "I don't get paid enough for this kind of crap."

"You signed on," Carlisle pointed out. "And you know what they say about the heat in the kitchen."

"So, Carlisle," Feldman put in. "How many kitchens have you seen as hot as this one?"

"I'll admit, it's way up on the scale," Carlisle replied.

Carlisle had done the majority of the planning, with the other two adding their expertise as needed. They had never worked together, so none of them knew how the other two worked, how they reacted to pressure.

Kemp cracked his knuckles again. "Maybe we should just cut our losses and call it a day."

"Yeah, he's right," Feldman agreed. "We need more strength for this one."

"Enough," Carlisle said.

"Tom, we went into this believing we knew what was going down," Kemp argued. "Now it's obvious there's more to this thing than meets the eye."

"He's right," Feldman said. "I don't feel good about it, either."

"We've put way too much time in on this to throw it all away," Carlisle protested. "We'll never get another chance like this one to bag these bastards."

"Or get bagged," Kemp said.

Carlisle listened as a transmission began coming through his earphone. A group of agents on a surveillance yacht a half mile away were helping with the plan. They were connected with the Cessna people who had brought Carlisle and the other two in.

"You're right, there's more guests than we counted on," an agent named Ted Brown was telling Carlisle. "We don't know them all."

"How hard will it be to check them out?"

"We're doing what we can, Tom."

"Okay, let me know what you find out."

Carlisle signed off and Feldman stared at him.

"Not good, Tom," he said.

"It will work."

"Everyone else thinks this is crazy, too. Don't they?" Kemp asked.

"You'd think neither of you had ever done anything like this before," Carlisle told them.

"Let's talk about some major concerns I have," Kemp said. He pointed to four men who suddenly appeared. "Who are they?"

Carlisle studied them. American Indians of mixed blood, all four of them. These men were the guests Ted Brown had alluded to.

Security officers quickly surrounded them and escorted them to the edge of the yacht, where they were forced to climb down into a smaller boat.

"I'll see if the surveillance guys can run a make on them," Carlisle said.

He radioed Brown and learned the four were members of AIM, the American Indian Movement. They had something other than a New Year's Eve toast in mind.

Kemp cracked his knuckles again, so hard that Carlisle asked him if he was trying to break his fingers off.

"Debilitating injuries. That will get you out of this," Carlisle said. "Is that what you want?"

Feldman had his binoculars trained on the four men as they brought their boat to the dock. He observed that the four were meeting with more men and pointing toward the island.

"They're not going home," Feldman commented.

"Maybe they liked the party," Carlisle suggested. "Don't you tell people about a party you liked?"

Feldman grunted. "That's gotta be it."

"Back to the plan," Kemp said. "You sure Blake and the other club members will go into their secret room when you think they will?"

"No doubt about it," Carlisle said. "I know exactly how they do things."

"What if they made some changes?" Kemp asked.

"Why would they?" Carlisle said.

Kemp cracked his knuckles one last time and looked at his watch. "It's time," he said.

"Are we going to do this thing?" Feldman asked.

"That's why we're here," Carlisle replied.

The three proceeded out of the shadows with caution and boarded a small boat manned by another agent. Carlisle had stationed three Seaside Security men who knew him well to greet guests. They were to check each I.D. thoroughly, comparing each name and picture with those on the guest list. Each individual invitee had been given a secret password that he or she was to present with their identification. If everything matched, they got on board. If not, it was good-bye.

For as long as Carlisle had worked for Seaside Security, no one had ever tried to crash one of Marvin Blake's parties. The guest list was very exclusive and many had brought their own personal security as well. That's why it would be simple to get Feldman and Kemp on board. Marvin Blake had great confidence in Carlisle and had entrusted the entire evening to him.

Carlisle led Feldman and Kemp past the security guards without incident. They made a circle around the upper deck, checking the positioning of various devices they had planted. Smoke bombs and noisemakers, hidden in small duffel bags under chairs and in cracks and crevices. Nothing lethal, just something to get everyone excited and confused. Create panic and make it much simpler to complete their work.

Everything had been set on remote control. Feldman and Kemp would get things going on the two upper decks and Carlisle would follow immediately thereafter on the main level. Carlisle had a small remote screen to view what the hidden camera was seeing inside the Red Skull Room, where the competition would take place.

They would remain in contact via small radios in

their ears, and also stay connected to Ted Brown on the surveillance yacht. Everyone would think they were just doing their jobs as security people. It would all go well. They had rehearsed it time and again. What could go wrong?

Carlisle ordered a club soda from one of the many bars and checked his watch. One half hour until the competition was to commence. Yes, soon it would all begin, and then a lot of things would change for a lot of people in just a few short minutes.

Blake was still seething about the other club members holding back on starting the competition. He wasn't used to being overruled by anyone. They obviously didn't understand. It was his yacht and he was providing a lot of entertainment for a lot of people. If he wanted to begin the competition early, he should be able to have that privilege.

Maybe they somehow realized that his entry had all of theirs beaten and didn't want to face it. None of them would back out, though. He was certain of that, for they had already had the meeting earlier in the week, where they all had their diamonds checked by a number of jewelers brought by the club members.

After pacing for a short while longer, Blake sat back down in his chair. Marlene assumed her place on his lap.

"You feeling better?" she asked.

"Hell no," he said, pushing her away.

He got up again. Marlene took her margarita from the coffee table and followed him to the bar.

"I'll get that for you," she said.

Blake pushed her aside, causing her to spill her drink. "Did I ask you to follow me over here?"

"I thought I could be of help."

"I'll tell you when you can be of help. Go back over and sit down."

Marlene turned to leave and Blake grabbed her by the arm. He pulled her close.

"I changed my mind," he said, rubbing his hand along her thigh. "Fix my drink for me. Strong on the scotch, light on the soda."

Marlene did her work with an expert touch. Blake was pleased with the result.

"What is this contest all about?" she asked.

"Just a friendly competition among gentlemen." He filled his mouth with scotch and ice. Each member of the club had agreed never to discuss their secret arrangements. The matter of the illegal antiques was enough. Knowledge of the diamonds would certainly bring professional thieves sniffing around.

"Why don't we go sit down and relax?" Marlene suggested. "Your competition will begin before long anyway."

Blake took another swallow of scotch. "Wait," he said to her. "We've gotten pretty close these past few days, haven't we?"

"Yes," Marlene replied, "we have."

"And you know how to keep a secret, right?"

"Certainly. What are you saying?"

Blake then made a big decision. He decided to let Marlene in on the club's business. He was dying to show somebody his winning prize. He needed a second opinion, a consenting opinion. He wanted to hear someone say that his antique was marvelous and beyond anything anyone had ever discovered, anywhere.

"Let me show you something." Blake took her by the hand and began to lead her through the revelers toward the stern of the boat.

"Where are we going?" she asked.

"You said you were interested in our contest, didn't you? Let's see what you think of my winning entry."

Marlene followed Marvin Blake toward the Red Skull Room. She stopped twice with him while he talked to guests. She began to develop a strange feeling in the pit of her stomach, some kind of fear that she couldn't put her finger on. She had known from the beginning that he would eventually confide in her. He had told her often that nobody appreciated him or the things he did, and she had consoled him. She had wanted him to include her in his secret world. That's what she had wanted all along. But now she was beginning to think that the world she had wanted to enter was far more dangerous than she had ever imagined.

Blake had his arm wrapped tightly around her waist. They pushed their way through the crowd toward the back of the boat, where Blake nodded to three security guards. The guards looked at each other and Blake told them to do as they were told. They moved a distance away while he fumbled drunkenly for a set of keys. Once he found them, he jammed one into the lock.

Blake was breaking all the cardinal rules. Never speak of the club or its activities. And certainly don't invite outsiders into the inner sanctum.

He took Marlene by the hand and led her into the Red Skull Room. It was luxuriously accommodated with a wet bar and a large circular table surrounded by leather-covered chairs. In the center of the table was an empty green bowl made of emeralds.

Beside the bowl rested a human skull, painted red in a pattern Marlene had never seen before, its mouth fashioned in an odd, nearly toothless grin.

The skull seemed active with an energy she didn't care to be around. But she couldn't tell that to Blake.

There were a number of items of various sizes located along one wall. Some large, some smaller, all covered with cloth. An unmistakable odor permeated the room.

Death, old and musty death. Three of the items had a peculiar ambience to them, like they had once been alive. They rested silently under their coverings. She wondered if they might be watching her through the cloth, and decided that they were.

She felt like she was invading an unsettled tomb, a temporary burial ground for ancient beings whose history was being compromised for the sake of pleasure. She knew, in fact, that an invasion had taken place, in some tomb or tombs, and that these desecrated artifacts had become nothing more than pawns in a rich man's game.

"What do you think?" Blake asked her.

"Very interesting," she replied.

Blake strode proudly to a small table where an object lay covered with a green velvet cloth. "Soon there will be an unveiling of sorts," he said. "The contest will begin and each of the club members will, in turn, disclose their cherished entrees. They will certainly be interesting, you can bet on that. But I have to say that this year, none will come close to what I have brought."

Carlisle eased down the hallway and into a rest room. He removed a small, flat monitor from his shirt pocket and flipped the switch.

He had noticed earlier that Marvin Blake and his lady escort were not with the other club members. Now, looking at the monitor, he discovered them inside the Red Skull Room.

At first he thought Blake had taken his escort's purse, but it seemed too old and worn for such an article. Instead he discovered the tycoon toying with an American Indian medicine bundle.

Carlisle stared at the monitor, trying to get a fix on the object. He wanted to see if he could recognize the beadwork. He knew beadwork and he knew the tribes the beadwork belonged to. But Blake wasn't cooperating. He kept moving the bundle around, making it impossible to get a fix on the bead pattern.

It didn't matter. He would see the medicine bundle up close soon enough.

Carlisle continued to watch the activity in the room on his monitor. He saw what appeared to be an empty emerald bowl on the table. What the bowl was for was anyone's guess.

And the skull. Yes, the skull. Their symbol of offering to something far less than holy.

He watched while Blake discussed the medicine bundle with his lady friend. She appeared uneasy and unsure of herself, and Carlisle worried about how she would be able to handle what was about to happen.

As if he were a magician of sorts, Blake pulled the cloth off the object. Marlene studied an ancient-looking deerskin bag. It was about a foot wide by eighteen inches long, like a long and slender skin purse, beaded from one end to the other in red and black and yellow designs.

"This is an American Indian medicine bundle," he said. "Very old."

"And you believe you'll win with that?" Marlene asked.

"No, no," Blake replied. "It's what I have inside the bundle that counts." He studied her. "You seem a little jumpy."

"I am a little nervous," she admitted. "After all, this is very secret information, isn't it?"

Blake chuckled as he untied a leather thong that kept the bundle closed. He eased the bundle open and allowed Marlene to peer inside.

"Do you know what it is?" he asked.

"Is it a baby?"

"No, it's not a baby. It's fully grown."

"How is that possible?"

"I'm telling you, it's a mummified little man, no more than twenty inches high," he said. "He's sitting cross-legged."

"Where did you get him?" Marlene asked.

"That's a secret," Blake said. "But there are more where he came from. Should make me a ton of money with collectors. Do you want to touch it?"

Marlene shrank away. "Oh, no. Don't take it out, please."

Blake laughed. "Why not?"

"Wouldn't it be bad luck if you took it out now? I mean, you should wait for the others, don't you think?"

Blake stared at her. "You think so?"

"Well, sure," she said. "You don't want it to lose its magic."

Blake laughed again. "It's not some kind of genie in a bottle."

"How do you know that?" she asked.

Blake laughed nervously. "You seem to know about these things."

"I just know when something feels strange to me, that's all."

"Maybe you're right," Blake said. He tied the

bundle's leather strings into a knot and covered his prize once again. He decided that luck, good or bad, had nothing to do with it. Still, he had inspected his cherished possession enough and would wait until the competition to take it out of the deerskin pouch.

"I've had considerable testing done," Blake said, "including DNA and carbon dating. The others won't believe the data that I'll present to them."

"What will happen to it after the contest?" Marlene asked.

"I'll take it home. Or maybe auction it off. We'll see."

Marlene turned to the doorway. Blake hadn't noticed the man standing there.

"As you can see, there will be no one who can top what I have here," he continued, tying the bundle's leather strings into a knot. "I'm looking forward to those rare diamonds, yes I am."

Liu Cheng moved into the room. "Mr. Blake," he asked, "just what do you think you're doing?"

"We're just talking," Blake stuttered. "Nothing wrong with that."

"But there *is* something wrong with that," Liu said. "The rules are specific. No one enters the contest room without everyone else. And you are expressly forbidden from bringing someone from outside the club in here."

"It's *my* yacht!" Blake shouted.

"But it's not your *club*!" Liu responded. "You should forfeit your right to participate."

"Now, let's not get carried away," Blake said. "There was no harm in it."

Liu stared at Marlene. "I'll just leave now," she said.

"No, you will not leave," Liu said. "You will stay right here. I will confer with the others about what to do with you."

The others began to enter the room. They all stared. Grenmoore asked why Marlene had been allowed inside.

"It's my boat and she's my guest," Blake said. "She's trustworthy."

The men looked at each other. Marlene knew without question what was on their minds. There was no way they would let her off the boat alive. She suggested again that she just leave quietly and allow them to go ahead with their contest.

Liu Cheng said sternly, "I said that you will not leave. You should not talk anymore."

"Don't be so hard on her," Sal Leone said. "Maybe she can do penance . . . with all of us."

Blake bristled.

"Just a joke," Sal said, laughing. "But you got to admit, we've got a problem now."

"Let's begin the competition," Kirkman suggested. "We'll take care of other matters later."

Each man went to his collection of items and produced a leather pouch, then poured his ante into the large emerald bowl in the middle of the table. Marlene's eyes widened at the sight. So many diamonds. So many sparkles. After each had contributed their ante, they placed their right hands on the table, their fingers touching the skull.

Marlene wondered at their strange ritual. None of them seemed at all concerned about her now. She thought of bolting for the door, but realized the three men outside would stop her immediately. She was trapped.

Carlisle radioed the surveillance unit that the plan should now begin. Then he told Kemp and Feldman to begin their respective roles.

Kemp radioed back that he would take one last look around the upper deck. Feldman said that he was ready and would begin the countdown.

Carlisle headed for the Red Skull Room, working his way through the crowd. He decided to slow down. He was too anxious. He couldn't reach the room too soon, for fear of throwing the whole plan off. Blake and the others had to be in the middle of their competition, the artifacts all in plain view and each club member well documented on film.

He radioed the surveillance agents again. They assured him that the audio and video on Marvin Blake's yacht were both coming in strong and clear.

"We'll be able to document everything they do," Brown said.

Carlisle slid the monitor back in his pocket. As he drew closer to the Red Skull Room, he rehearsed his moves in his mind. Just as the noise devices went off, he would enter the room and announce to Blake and the others that they should leave the room with him immediately, for security reasons. Blake and the others would no doubt be shocked, but he would emphasize the point and command them to follow him—right to where Kemp and Marty and two other agents would be waiting to arrest them.

Carlisle's thoughts were interrupted by a large man who approached him, dressed in a Seaside Security uniform, and asked if he had any identification.

Carlisle didn't panic. "I'm security," he said, pointing to the radio in his ear. He noticed that the man had a radio of his own, and that he appeared to be a mixed-blood American Indian.

"Really," the man said. "I'm security, too. Who do you work for?"

Carlisle looked around. Something was going on.

This man was no one from Seaside, and he was obviously stalling for time.

"I'm the one who should be asking the questions," Carlisle said. At the same time his radio came on. Kemp sounded breathless. Something about finding bags filled with explosives.

Carlisle stepped away from the large man. "Say again."

Kemp's voice was near panic. "I said I'm finding a lot of large bags, filled with plastic explosives. We've got to move right now!"

"Hold on," Carlisle said. "I'll get right back to you."

Another call was coming, this time from Ted Brown on the surveillance yacht.

"Get off the boat, Tom. There's an AIM raid planned."

Brown's voice choked off as muffled shots echoed in Carlisle's ear. More shots. Yelling. The surveillance yacht was under attack.

Carlisle quickly turned his radio off. He was supposed to have received backup from the surveillance members.

The big man stepped up to him. "Anything wrong?"

Before Carlisle could move, he was staring at a 9mm pistol.

"You're in the way of things here," the man said. "What say you and I go for a walk to the edge of the boat?"

"I don't feel like going anywhere," Carlisle said.

"I think you do. Or maybe you'd like some slugs in the gut."

Carlisle turned and started down the hallway, the big man crowding him from behind.

"There are a lot of agents and security people on this boat," Carlisle warned. "All I need to do is yell."

"Yell all you want," the big man taunted. "It will be the last yelling you ever do."

Marlene sat as still as stone on the arm of Marvin Blake's chair while the club members began their competition, fortified with drinks and cigars from the table. Marvin Blake's entry would be the last one viewed.

She eased off the chair and stood behind Blake, seemingly without his noticing. Or anyone else paying her any mind, for that matter.

She looked toward the door, wondering.

Grenmoore unveiled his artifact, a Tlingit Indian mask from the Pacific Northwest. Marlene eased herself toward the line of artifacts, one slow step at a time. Blake didn't notice. Nor did any of the others.

They were drinking and cursing, huffing and puffing on their cigars, arguing over the authenticity of the artifact.

Blake said it was too large to be a real mask and had to be a replica. Grenmoore argued it was authentic and had belonged to an unusually large chief. Each of the club members insisted on seeing documentation. Grenmoore had anticipated their demands in advance and dug into a briefcase. Each, in turn, would read the documentation and each would need to inspect it carefully and give it a score.

Marlene began to ease toward the line of entries, her eyes going from the medicine bundle back to the group of arguing men. She had hold of it when Blake happened to glance over.

He stood up. "What are you doing?"

Suddenly a huge explosion on the lower level rocked the yacht, knocking her off balance. She heard gunfire and immediately dove for cover behind Blake's chair, and then under the table filled with drinks.

Blake and the others sat momentarily stunned, then each pulled a weapon from under his jacket. The door flew open and three men dressed in black burst through.

The room was suddenly filled with smoke and arms fire. Men screamed and cursed and fell forward and backward and sideways, shooting in every direction. Marlene covered her ears and screamed as well. Liu Cheng's pistol fell behind his chair and bounced under the drink table where Marlene had taken refuge. She clasped her hands around it tightly and waited.

The blast took Carlisle and the big man by surprise. They both lost their balance and caught themselves against the outside wall of the vessel. Carlisle recovered and clamped his hand around the big man's wrist, turning the pistol downward. The gun discharged into the floorboards. Carlisle hoisted the big man over the side and left him hanging by his fingers.

Another explosion sounded and Carlisle steadied himself against the wall. The big man lost his grip and fell into the water, now mixed with high-octane fuel.

The boat came alive with screams and yelling. Carlisle hurried down the hall toward the Red Skull Room, pushing through a tangle of terrified guests.

Another explosion on the top level further added to the chaos. He clicked on his radio and called Feldman and Kemp repeatedly, but there was no response. In the background, he could hear automatic weapons fire.

He struggled through the terrified crowd toward the Red Skull Room. People were crowding each other to get off the boat. Many had jumped into the water and were swimming away from the burning vessel.

Carlisle reached the room and found the security guards sprawled in the hallway in widening pools of blood. He lurched into the room, gun ready, and discovered dead and dying men everywhere. It appeared that the three men dressed in black were all mortally wounded.

The club members were lying scattered around the room. Some were moaning while others lay still. They had all been hit at least once. Grenmoore was on his knees in one corner, crying, calling for his mother. Marvin Blake looked to be sleeping in his chair.

The green bowl on the table rested quietly, filled with gleaming diamonds.

The red skull, also untouched, smiled its grisly smile.

Carlisle realized that Blake's escort was missing. She rose from the floor with a pistol leveled at him.

"I want you to do exactly what I say," she told him.

"Who are you, actually?" Smoke from the fires onboard began to fill the room.

"No questions, just action, Mr. Carlisle. Pour the diamonds into that cloth bag on the table."

How did she know his name? She was obviously here for a reason other than to entertain Marvin Blake.

"You don't want to do this," Carlisle said.

"Don't make me ask you again," she said.

Carlisle obliged her. She grabbed the bag of diamonds out of his hands and then took the medicine bundle under one arm as she backed toward the door, holding the pistol on him.

"You'll never get away with it," Carlisle told her.

"Just don't follow me," she said. "Fair warning."

Carlisle waited a few moments, then eased out the door, his gun ready. He ducked as her fire took chunks from the doorframe. Then she was lost in the smoke and flame that was quickly engulfing the boat.

Behind him, Marvin Blake was leaning forward in his chair.

"What happened here?" he asked.

Carlisle threw one of Blake's arms around his neck and hauled him to the deck. Chaos continued to reign. The sounds of gunshots had faded but the screaming and yelling continued. Overhead, a law-enforcement helicopter circled, with spotlights searching the yacht. Other choppers arrived, marked with medical insignias.

Sirens from law-enforcement boats just arriving added to the noise.

Feldman was standing near the edge of the sinking yacht, waiting to be loaded into a law-enforcement vessel.

"Kemp's dead," he murmured. "At least I think that was him."

Carlisle would continue with Seaside and Marvin Blake. All the evidence had been destroyed, except for the medicine bundle and whatever was inside it. His cover was still intact, and the operation would continue.

It would be some time before it was learned whether it was truly an American Indian Movement raid or if someone had set it up to look that way. Whoever the young woman was, she had vanished. And so had the diamonds.

There was no way to know if Marvin Blake would ever organize another club. Time would tell. It seemed doubtful, what with the red skull at the bottom of Flathead Lake, Montana.

HANGTOWN

This has always been known as a place of perpetual sun, a paradise of warm days followed by soft nights blessed with southern winds off the sea. As I speak, the sun rises in the same glory it always has, but in those days the land was blighted by a fever—a sickness known to control even the strongest of men.

Gold was the force that drove men's lives. It perpetually consumed all thought and action, all meaning of life and desire. Along the foothills of the Sierra Nevada, emigrants and immigrants alike arrived by every means possible, and their lives changed forever.

For a time, I was one of those entrapped by the fever. I spent considerably long hours in the streams panning for gold. While the others played cards or drank or attended fandangos in the tent and clapboard towns, I washed gravel from pans with the aid of lantern light. It might rain or even snow at times, or the wind might blow, but I would always be wading in the streams.

My success was measured in a few ounces per week, if I was lucky, and more often that same amount measured over a month's time. I never saw enough to get more than a change of clothes and a stash of beans and bacon, or a bottle, or perhaps a good horse once in a while, for riding to other diggings that had just opened up, promising something more—always something more.

There were others who did well, of course. Some made their fortunes and went on to fast lives in fine houses in San Francisco, or in the quickly growing and very violent city of Los Angeles. Others had everything stolen from them, oftentimes their lives as well.

I kept to myself a great deal of the time. Being of mixed lineage, I had acquired few friends. My father was white and my mother was half white, the other half Spanish and Yaqui Indian. I was conceived in Santa Fe and born in a wagon on the road to Kansas City, and given the name John Carlos, John Carlos Lansing.

My father felt I should be John instead of Juan,

and let the Carlos part of it speak for my other half. As I learned life's lessons, I agreed with him, but my mother didn't. I believe now that she always resented her white blood, as it represented to her Spanish-Indian relatives the mark of something bad.

I had no way of knowing anything but what I felt from my family, and others around me. My father seemed to treat everyone the same, and I wanted to be like him in every way possible. My mother came close to disowning me many times. She would often spit at me, screaming, "You are no different from your father, but not full blood, as he is! You behave as if you have only white blood in you. Why would you betray your Mexican side?"

I disagreed with her on that point. Before the age of seven, I spoke English and Spanish fluently, and the Yaqui dialect as well. And I knew more about the lineage of my Spanish-Indian side than I did my father's relatives. He never talked about them. And my mother never knew her father, so that likely embittered her more.

I spent a part of my childhood on the outskirts of Kansas City, on a small farm my father bought with the profits from three seasons' catch of beaver fur. He was never one for settlements. My mother insisted that I turn to my Indian roots completely when he went back to Taos again to trap beaver and trade with the mountain tribes. She never forgave him for that.

Not long after my father left, she died. So much changed then, so very much. Times became extremely hard. A lot of it I've wanted to forget, but never have been able to. It has driven me during my adult years.

That was the legacy I carried with me to the gold fields. I had intended to better myself to an immense degree and pushed myself toward that end. It took a terrible toll on me until I realized the futility of it all and donned the robes of a Franciscan monk.

On the night this story begins, I had been wearing the Franciscan robes for six months. I will say that the life served me well, for that period of time that I lived it, and for the reasons I chose to do so. A man often makes decisions he doesn't expect to make, until he makes them. I was driven to the calling for more than one reason.

People had come to know me simply as John Jose, the Padre on Horseback. Since the mission era had all but vanished, I stayed to the trails with my sermons. I had learned some of the local Indian dialects, including Miwok and Yokut, and some Chumash. Well before the Gold Rush all of these people had been servants and basically slaves at the missions, tending orchards and cattle, and doing all kinds of work. But that had all passed, easily ten years before, and there were no reminders of what had once been, save some orchards and grain and bean fields tended by old Indians who had never learned to do anything else.

I was traveling with two young Miwok Indian men—Cholok and Ramon—whom I had freed from bondage at a huge ranch called the Seven Rocks, a day's ride south of Los Angeles. The Miwok people lived strong and happy in their days before the white man's coming. A lot had happened over the years and they had become a scattered people.

Cholok and Ramon had been born at one of the missions but had left to join a group of traditional Miwoks living in the foothills and mountains. As well as their own tongue, they spoke Spanish and fragments of broken English.

These two, along with three others, had retrieved their horses back from a group of *vaqueros*, who had taken them at the order of the ranch owner, a large and powerful Californio known as Bestez. Cholok and Ramon, along with the other three, had been captured by men working for Bestez and forced into bondage.

I had learned of the injustice, and since I needed

guides to lead me on a special journey, I traveled to the Seven Rocks ranchero. I wished to be guided along the gold field trails out of Los Angeles, to go among the outlaws that were raiding the southern diggings, the placer mines that lined the streams that spilled from the Sierras into the San Joaquin Valley. What is a priest for if not to help those who have chosen the wrong pathway?

That day, at the Bestez ranchero, Cholok spoke up on behalf of himself and Ramon, insisting that they were both excellent guides. The other three remained silent, preferring to stay in bondage rather than risk their lives looking for bandits.

Even the powerful Californio thought my own personal mission to be quite unusual.

"Why are you after these cutthroats?" Bestez asked me, rolling his tongue over a cigar.

"I have souls to save," I replied.

Bestez laughed. "Ah! Their souls are already gone!"

"Maybe one among them isn't," I responded. "That is enough."

I then bid Cholok and Ramon to come with me. Bestez complained that losing the two workers was a great injustice to him and demanded restitution in the form of a dispensation.

"I'll grant you no dispensations," I told him.

"Consider it your duty—a gift to God."

Needless to say, I wasn't the kind of clergyman Bestez found useful. He snarled at me, raising his fist, until we were nearly out of sight. God likely forgave him right away, but I didn't care one way or the other.

As I traveled with Cholok and Ramon, I discovered that I had certainly been given good information. The two proved to be invaluable as guides. They were young, barely twenty, and sharp-eyed at all times. They knew the country in and around the Sierra Nevada very well and could follow any trail left by man or beast.

Cholok definitely was more than ordinary. He was slim and solid, and taller than the average male of his tribe. He told me that he had grown up running constantly, so that his stamina was well developed. He told me that he had been named for a special place in Yosemite, where he had been born. His mother had birthed him at the foot of a waterfall and the name, Cholok, literally meant the Place Where the Water Falls Down.

The waters there were sacred, he told me. In addition, his birth had been viewed by one of the large, powerful bears that the area had been named for. My father used to tell me stories about them, before he left for the mountains. He called them silvertips, the mountain term for grizzly bears. Cholok considered them his protectors. To have an animal like that present at birth had to mean something special.

On the other hand, Ramon shunned me completely. Never once could I start any kind of dialogue with him. He was small and sickly and, according to Cholok, felt his life had been cursed from the beginning. He had a persistent cough I believed to be consumptive, but he wanted nothing to do with a white doctor, preferring to wait until he could find a traditional medicine man among his people. He kept making the sign for death, saying that it knew his name, so I decided not to press it and left him to his fatalistic tendencies.

If Ramon wanted to convey something to me, Cholok spoke in his behalf. I believe now that Ramon considered me to be bad medicine, a category most of the padres had been placed in over the years. At first I believed Cholok wanted to be friends and form a close bond; but after the first week, it became apparent that he was beginning to share in Ramon's bitterness toward me.

As we rode that night, I came to realize that both of them believed that I had intentionally tricked him into riding to their deaths—that I had personally set up their demise at the hands of the most notorious outlaw in all the gold fields.

I came to realize it that evening, when we stopped to water the horses and the pack mule in the twilight. Ramon dismounted and slipped off by himself to sing a traditional song that Cholok informed me was a death song.

"I don't understand," I said. "I never misled either of you, not at any time."

"But you didn't tell us everything."

"I told you about going to find *bandidos*," I said. "You knew that."

"Ah, but not just *any bandido*," Cholok pointed out. "You say you are looking to save the lives of those outlaws, but we are headed toward the hideout of the worst of them all." He stared hard at me. "Why Joaquin Murrieta?"

"It is my mission to find him," I replied.

"You must find *him* more than any other?"

"Him, and those who ride with him."

"Maybe if you'd have said this, back at the ranchero, we wouldn't have come."

"You said you would come with me for *any* reason, go *any*where. Have you forgotten already?"

Cholok bowed his head. "You remember my exact words."

"Yes, I do. We should be going."

The horses were nervous and flared their nostrils

repeatedly. The mule seemed to take everything in stride.

Cholok worked to settle his horse and turned to me.

"Maybe we should camp here and go on when the light returns."

"We'll lose Joaquin's trail. He'll be gone."

"He already knows we're following him."

"All the more reason to hurry, then."

"Just because you're a priest, do you think he will spare you?" Cholok asked.

"Even an outlaw doesn't want to die with a priest's blood on his conscience," I replied.

"You don't know all outlaws," Cholok argued. We finished watering the horses and he added, "I believe you are searching for something that you're not willing to discuss with me."

"I have personal reasons for why I do things in life, as you do," I admitted. "Does that make me wrong?"

He took a handful of my robe in his fist and shook it at me. "You wear these. You're not supposed to ever be wrong?"

We mounted and as the light faded completely, a strange wind began to blow. The darkness became filled with small, whirling twisters called dust devils. From my mother I always knew them to be wandering spirits, the dead having returned, lost and searching for vengeance.

When you see them in the daytime, it is a reason for caution; when they come at night, it's certainly a very bad sign.

The darkness held us fast as we rode. The wind cried, I swear, like a woman who had lost her child. I thought about the outlaw I looked for, Joaquin Murrieta, who carried a price of a thousand dollars on his head, dead or alive. He was said to be ruthless and without a hint of conscience. And there were those who said he was just retaliating against Yankee aggressors who had driven him from his gold claim, injuring and killing members of his family in the process. For this, they said, he had every right to take vengeance.

By this time it had gone far beyond that. Terror thrived like a feeding demon in the gold camps and along the trails. Vigilantes combed the hills and valleys, searching every camp and every wagon. No one knew what to expect or when it would come—death in a land supposed to be promised.

I had a plan in meeting with this outlaw. As a priest, I would approach him from the standpoint of his vengeance—something that God alone should have authority over. I could see some merit in the concept that Murrieta might be angry over injustice; but, I would tell him, nothing can change what happened.

He would hear what he wanted to, of course. I knew that beforehand. But he wouldn't soon forget my visit.

There were other important reasons for the unrest in the gold fields. A Foreign Miners Tax had been imposed the previous year, and many Mexican and Chinese miners in the Southern Mines had been forced off their claims. That's when the bandit problem really began. A lot of cattle and horses were leaving the region, stores and saloons were robbed and destroyed, and traveling the trails, unless you were in a large group, was suicidal.

As I understood it then, there were as many as five separate outlaw bands working the area, all of mixed white and Chicano and Latino races. There were plenty of Yankees, also, who would rather take their gold already bagged than wade in the streams for it. A Mexican *bandido* was never opposed to having a white man with him, as long as he carried knives and guns, and did his share for the band.

These gangs had spread themselves from San Francisco to Los Angeles, and all stops in between, each of them led by someone named Joaquin. To add to the confusion, all of the Joaquins were related. No one could be certain which Joaquin was the one sought after.

In addition to the bounty on the outlaw's head, the state legislature had passed an act, in May of 1853, the year I tell about, providing for the formation of a company of California Rangers, commanded by a man I had met named Harry Love. Big and hard-eyed, I might have thought him a *bandido* himself had he not been wearing a badge.

I had talked to this man more than once and I became certain right away that he had no use for me. I was only interfering in his own mission. He and his men were well armed and carried a couple of cans of wood alcohol to preserve Joaquin's head in.

None of that mattered now. I knew we were close to finding the Joaquin I wished to talk to, and both Cholok and Ramon became ever more nervous.

Just ahead was Hangtown. As the camps grew, more and more of these stops popped up in the gulches along the main trails. One was as ripe for the plucking as the next, and I was certain Joaquin and his men were camped nearby, poised to raid the little town.

It was late but we could see a few scattered lanterns flickering in the distance among the tents and log-and-clapboard buildings. I was ready to tell

Cholok to lead the way when a group of riders surrounded us. We hadn't heard them coming at all, not even a slight sound.

We could hear the clicks as rifles and pistols were cocked. Cholok and Ramon asked me what we should do.

"Is there anyone who would shoot a priest?" I asked.

"We'll see," Cholok replied.

I heard someone telling us in Spanish to sit easy on our horses, and asked if I was wearing a padre's robes. I responded that I was a Franciscan and that he and his men had nothing to fear from us.

A large man then rode forward. His wore a beaten sombrero lowered over his eyes. Bandoleers crisscrossed his chest.

The moon suddenly appeared from behind the fleeting clouds, and he laughed.

"Yes, you are a padre? Are you lost?"

"No. I am where I want to be," I replied. "Who among you is Joaquin Murrieta?"

He sat up in the saddle, surprised, and turned slightly, looking toward a slim man sitting his horse among the others.

The big man turned back to me. "Did you come all this way to hear his confession?"

The *bandidos* all laughed, all except the slim man, who watched me carefully.

"I want to see each of those men here in front of me, one by one," I said. "They can ride by me. I will light a lantern."

The big man balked. "You give orders in your own place, padre. This is our place."

"God owns all places," I told him. "Would you dispute that?"

He grunted and rode back to the slim man, who sat calmly. The big man rode forward to me again. He studied me a moment, his left hand holding the reins across the saddle horn. I noticed that the thumb and first finger were missing.

I had heard of this man also. His name was Manuel Duarte, but was better known in the gold camps as Three-fingered Jack, a dangerous man in his own right. He was a cousin to Joaquin Murrieta, and I felt certain we had found the famous outlaw at last.

"I can see that you are Joaquin's cousin, Mr. Duarte," I said. "So Joaquin is here, too."

"How do you know so much about me?" he asked.

"It is my job, as a priest, to learn many things," I replied. "When can I have your men pass in front of me?"

"Why would you study everyone here?" he asked.

"I want to see if their souls cry out for salvation."

"As a priest, you should be able to tell that from a distance."

"It's the darkness," I told him, "and the wind. You understand."

"Light your lantern," he said.

I dismounted and went to the pack mule. I had one bag that I'd filled with hard candy, as an offering whenever I needed it, and also as a treat to the children I often came upon. In another bag was a pistol and a lantern.

After lighting the lantern, I stood at the edge of the trail and waited. The slim man rode up and leaned over.

"I will show my face to you," he said. "And I heard that you already know who I am. But my men wish to decline your offer, whether or not it comes from God."

I was astounded at his English. Not mastered but certainly very accomplished, especially for someone I had assumed was uneducated. So much for assumptions.

I held the lantern high but still couldn't see him all that well. Still, I did notice that his features were rugged and strong, and that the flickering light pulled blond highlights from his hair. It was evident to me that his blood was a Spanish-Indian mix, like most of his men, except a few Anglo Yankees who rode with them.

"Are you Joaquin Murrieta?" I asked him, wanting him to admit it.

"It doesn't matter who I am, Father. I'm sorry for having done wrong and if you would forgive my sins, I would be grateful."

I studied him for a moment and he winked at me, then turned his horse to leave. Looking back, he said, "It is a dangerous night. If you and the Miwoks wish to remain safe, you will follow me."

I kept the lantern lit and mounted my horse. Joaquin took the lead and spoke to his men by hand signals, ordering them into a structured formation.

After a short distance, he selected four of his men and had us dismount.

"This will take but a few minutes," he told me. "My apologies, but it is necessary."

I studied the four men closely, all young but very sure of themselves. They proved very adept at handling horses, calming our animals and fitting them quickly with a form of rawhide boot that slid neatly over the hooves. The boots were tied on securely with thongs and the men returned to their saddles.

"Now we can all be quiet," Joaquin said.

I understood why they had ridden up on us so

easily. The soft leather muffled the hoofbeats.

"You do know your business," I told him.

They led us to a grove of oak trees a short distance above the outskirts of town, off the trail and very secluded. There were signs it had been recently used as a campsite.

"I want you to stay up here, no matter what you hear from down below," Joaquin warned. "Is that understood?"

"I'm not used to taking orders," I told him.

Joaquin spoke evenly "You need to get used to it for now, Padre. This is Hangtown."

In but a few moments, he and his men had vanished into the darkness.

I told Cholok and Ramon that they had paid their debt to me and were free to go, if they wished.

"Listen," Ramon said, "we are safer with you than anyone else. Don't you think?"

"Most of the time," I agreed. I wondered why he had suddenly decided to converse with me.

"I thought you would bring harm to Cholok and myself," Ramon told me. "Instead, you have brought honor. We found Joaquin and he didn't kill us. Your medicine is much stronger than I thought."

"You are a protected man, it would seem," Cholok added. "Why would we want to leave you?"

We hobbled our horses and the mule, and sat together at the brow of a hill. The wind that had howled all night suddenly ceased, as if a dark hand had smothered it. The town below seemed quiet enough, but Cholok and Ramon were both extremely uneasy. They obviously knew something I didn't.

Soon the shooting started. It was a few pops at first, here and there. Then suddenly Hangtown erupted into a chorus of gunfire.

My guides continued to sit stoically. Each passing minute seemed like an hour. But in less than five minutes, the fighting lessened. Men yelled and cursed and occasionally a woman screamed. It was all I could do not to mount my horse and go down, but I realized Joaquin had been right: it would be foolish; I wouldn't be able to change what was going on.

Finally, it appeared to be over. I noticed a half-dozen riders leaving town as fast as their horses could carry them. They were too far away to recognize at all. When they were gone, the three of us mounted.

We rode to the edge of town cautiously, passing three men who had been hanged from a cottonwood along the creek. I lit the lantern and studied each of them. Cholok and Ramon said nothing, waiting for something from me.

"They must have been bandits," I said.

"How can you tell?" Cholok asked.

We rode into the center of town and discovered a group of people gathered in the street, holding torches and lanterns over two men who lay facedown.

I dismounted and the people parted.

"Two different bands opened up on one another," a miner told me. "These two fell right here. There are more scattered around."

The men were both Caucasian, likely not over twenty years old. Their faces still held the pain of their deaths. I was certain, as I knelt and made the sign of the cross over them both, that they hadn't been with Joaquin's group of *bandidos.* Another band had to have come into town at or near the same time as Joaquin's.

I whispered prayers for their salvation while everyone looked on, including a girl of fourteen or fifteen, and a striking woman whom I assumed was her mother, with wavy red-brown hair that held a glint in the light of the torches and lanterns. They both wore long dresses and what appeared to be either homemade or Indian-made leather footwear.

"It is a shame this has to happen so frequently," the woman said. "When will it end?"

"When the gold is gone," I replied. "Probably not before."

I looked down the street to see two men pulling

another victim toward me by the heels, dragging him behind them like some fallen game animal. The woman told me that one of them, the larger one, was a storeowner named Rusk who sold dry goods at a very high price, and that the other man worked for him.

I recognized the man they were dragging to be one of the young *bandidos* of Joaquin's gang.

"Why do that to him?" I asked them. "Just leave them all lying where they fell. I can go to each one in turn."

"Well, this one fell inside my store, and I didn't want him bleeding all over my feed bags," Rusk said. "I can't sell produce covered in Mexican blood."

The girl and her mother stepped forward. The girl said, "How much more is your precious produce worth drenched in Yankee blood?"

"You'd best curb that child's tongue," the storeowner said to the woman.

"I think it was a fair question," the woman responded.

Rusk looked to me and I couldn't help but smile. "They just want to know why you'd value feed bags over human life," I said. "I suppose if I were bleeding in your store, I'd be worth very little as well."

The owner held his lantern up and finally noticed that I was of mixed blood. Not very obvious, but certainly noticeable to anyone who wanted to look that hard.

Rusk and his helper turned and left. Some of the other men in the street also departed, and those who remained asked how they could help.

"It would be best if the dead were buried right away," I suggested. "And dig the Mexican graves just as deep as the Yankee ones."

Caroline Rutgers and her daughter, Frances, insisted that my Miwok guides and I spend the night in one of the tents they maintained at the edge of town. They were both wearing Miwok moccasins, given to them as presents by Miwok women who had come to know them.

While settled near a fire to keep off the mountain chill, the girl kept telling me that all her friends called her Franny, instead of Frances, and that I was welcome to do that. She was interested in how someone came to choose the life of a Franciscan padre, and why there were no women in robes. She kept the questions coming until her mother appeared and changed the subject.

She had with her a number of children, ranging in age from toddler to early teens. They were of many different nationalities, including Chinese, Mexican,

Latino, Chicano, and various mixtures in between.

They were all dressed better than most of the children I ran across in the gold camps, and all appeared to be in good spirits.

"Can you bless the children, Father?" Caroline asked.

The children smiled, and the smaller ones touched my robe. A toddler made his way to me and touched my face. I took his little hand in mine, feeling unworthy of the attention I was receiving.

"They see you as holy," Franny said.

"Small children are holy," I said. "Adults have to work hard just to tread water."

The children all took seats near me. I asked Cholok to get the special bag from the back of the pack mule. He returned, and the children giggled and waited patiently while I handed out the lumps of hard candy.

"These kids are up awfully late," I said. "Where are their parents?"

Franny looked at me with sad eyes. "Life here hasn't been fair to them."

"Orphaned?" I said.

"Most have lost their parents to disease or violence of some kind," Caroline replied. "A few, like the small one who touched your face, were left behind when the last announcement of a new strike reached here. His parents rode off and left him behind. They haven't been back for him."

"They appear well fed," I observed. "Your husband must have made a good strike. Where is he?"

"No, he's working a claim to the north," Caroline replied. "He chose not to help us here, but to chase the eternal hope of instant wealth, just like the rest. Who knows when he'll return."

"How can you afford to feed all of these children?"

Caroline and Franny glanced at one another. Franny gave her mother a hard look.

"There are those who contribute to their cause," Caroline said.

"That is very commendable," I told her. "It's not all that common, though."

"It isn't," Caroline agreed. "But it does happen. A lot of odd things happen here, like a padre showing up in the middle of the night."

I saw no reason to hide anything from her.

"I have been looking for the *bandido* Joaquin Murrieta for some time. I found him tonight but didn't get enough time with him. I believe he came down here and was involved in the shooting."

Again, Franny eyed Caroline, as if to say, "Be careful what you tell him, Mother."

"It was very dark," Caroline said, "and very hard to see."

"Would you know him if you saw him?" I asked.

Franny spoke up. "Why would you be out on the trails following outlaws?"

"Outlaws need prayers, too," I told her.

"And outlaws can be answers to prayers," Franny said suddenly.

Her mother laughed. "She's a romantic at heart."

"Well, the two of you seem to be enacting a miracle of some sort here," I said. "You should have your tents set up at Angel's Camp, not here in Hangtown."

Again, it was Franny who spoke. "If everyone was as anxious to take care of one another as they are to find gold, there would be no need for soup kitchens or orphan homes."

"I do agree," I told her. "Do you think the time will ever come when we as a society will see that?"

"It's doubtful," she said. "It's very sad."

Franny left to care for a baby that began crying in one of the tents. I turned to her mother.

"She's taken on a lot for a girl her age."

"She's more than just a girl," Caroline said. "She has the heart of a dozen good women. She is very remarkable."

"How do the two of you manage, with your husband gone?" I asked.

"We have angels of our own taking care of us," she replied.

"I know a group of rangers was supposed to come through here, looking for Joaquin," I said. "Did they make it?"

"You saw those poor men hanging when you rode in here, didn't you?" she asked. "They didn't need to be hanged. The men who did it said they were rangers."

"I doubt it," I told her. "That's not how they operate."

"There are a lot of people looking for Joaquin Murrieta," she said. "Most of them are vigilantes. They think like Rusk, the store owner. They feel justified in killing Mexicans. Chasing them off, all under the guise that they're looking for Joaquin." She held up a paper from the town of Stockton, with blaring headlines about another attack by Joaquin Murrieta on a gold camp. "If people were to believe all this, he'd have to be in five places at once."

"There's no clear solution," I said. "But it seems you are safe here."

"Wherever there are children, there is no fear of Joaquin Murrieta," she said. "Let me show you something."

She took my lantern from me and led me into a log cabin. In the middle of the room sat a crude wooden table where she said all the kids ate. They bathed, she added, in a large tub in one corner of the room. She moved to the back, along the wall, and shoved a small trunk aside.

"Move closer and hold the lantern, please," she said, kneeling down. "And watch the door for me."

After brushing some dirt aside on the ground, she opened a buried wooden box. Inside was a large bag filled with gold nuggets.

"You have contributors who give to your church, for your own cause," she said. "We have contributors, also." She told me that once a week she paid a mule skinner in gold to drop off freight for them. "The kids get good, solid food and dry, warm bedding to sleep on. That's all they ask for."

I didn't have to ask where she got the gold to keep the supplies coming. She had worked as hard as anyone I had ever run across to defend the honor of Joaquin Murrieta.

"You know," I said, "an outlaw can kill one day and do something for penance the next. It's a cycle."

"I can say only that the man who is hunted, the man Franny and I know, does not harm women and children," she told me. "He protects them whenever he can. That's more than I can say for those who chase him."

She told me that the little toddler who had

touched my face had lost his mother to illness, and that Joaquin and his gang of *bandidos* had brought him to her.

"He risked his life and those of his men to do that," she said. "The little boy would have likely died without care."

"Likely he would have," I agreed. "I hope you don't think I am judging him, or anybody. I am a priest doing his duty before God."

"Perhaps God is glad for your work," Caroline said. "How are you rewarded?"

"My reward is yet to come," I replied.

She looked at me in the lantern light and said, "I've been meaning to tell you this, but it seems so strange."

"What's that?" I asked.

"One of Joaquin's men could easily be your brother, you look so much alike."

I stared at her. "My brother?"

"I told you it was odd. You seem a lot like him, in a way. Hard to explain. I'm sorry."

"Don't be sorry," I said. "Do you know this man's name?"

"I've seen him just one time, and spoke to him that same day," she replied. "He brought the baby in that Franny's attending to now. He told me that the mother, his wife, died in childbirth."

"Very difficult," I said.

Caroline continued. "Then he said that he wished he and his brother had had someone like me to live with after their mother died, near Kansas City. I don't know the place. Do you?"

"Yes," I told her, "I do know Kansas City. And I do have a brother, and our mother died when we were young. We were placed in an orphanage. After a year, a young couple took him to be part of their family. I never saw him again."

"So that's why you've been looking so hard at every face you see," she said. "Even the dead. You've been searching for your brother, haven't you?"

"It's true," I conceded. "I've spent a lot of time looking for my father as well. I believe Indians killed him, but have no certain proof yet."

Caroline had brought out a lot of the past I had been trying to keep buried. Much pain and anguish had found its way to my brother and me during that period, and many times since. It was something I needed to look at and work on within myself. That I knew.

We walked out of the cabin and toward the fire, where Cholok and Ramon were telling stories to Franny and the children.

"So, you think God will aid you in your search if you wear the Franciscan robes?" Caroline asked me.

"Perhaps," I replied. "Life is surely complicated."

"There is no surer truth," she agreed. "But it could be made much simpler if there weren't the quest for so much power. What good does it do in the end?"

"That is best answered by those who have had it and lost it," I replied.

"Where will you go tomorrow?" she asked.

"To find Joaquin again."

"And your brother," she said. "More so than Joaquin."

"I have to find one to find the other."

"Will you ever return here?" she asked.

"Perhaps," I replied. "Life is surely complicated."

Not long after meeting Caroline and Franny, I found my brother under very unusual circumstances. It was just a week before Harry Love and his rangers ran into a group of *bandidos* at a place called Arroyo Cantúa. The papers ran an extensive story about the gun battle there, and the taking of Joaquin Murrieta's head, and the hand of Three-fingered Jack.

The head and hand went on display for all to see, but there were more than a few people who believed that Harry Love had collected a bounty for the wrong man. He also collected some five thousand additional dollars from the state coffers, besides the initial thousand, a mystery no one seems to have solved to this day. Surely his expenses couldn't have run that high.

I did make it back to Hangtown, and my visit with Caroline and Franny, with my brother along, was a pleasant one. They didn't seem as upset as I might have thought about the publication of Joaquin's death.

"The angels are still at work," Caroline told me.

I wanted to learn the truth for myself and decided to search it out. The gold region was alive with interest in what had taken place in Arroyo Cantúa and the report the rangers had given on their finding and killing the worst bandit ever to terrorize the gold fields.

My brother wasn't anxious to travel in the open and I left him in another gold camp, panning for nuggets in a little stream, while I traveled to Stockton to take my turn viewing the display that was so prominently advertised on a broadside:

THE HEAD

OF THE RENOWNED BANDIT

JOAQUIN!

AND THE

HAND OF THREE FINGERED JACK!

THE NOTORIOUS ROBBER AND MURDERER.

To this day I think about what I saw when I entered that saloon and, after the people parted, peered into a large jar. It was late evening and I asked that all the light be put out. Franciscan padres are obeyed most everywhere, and when the establishment was dark, I lit my lantern and held it up to that jar.

The face was distorted and the alcohol that preserved it a little cloudy, but try as I might, I couldn't get any blond highlights in the matted hair to register that night. Perhaps the hair was too damp, or the light wrong. I will never know for sure.

I am fairly certain, however, that the head in that jar was likely not that of Joaquin Murrieta. For in all the time I stood there, studying that face, there was never even a hint of a wink.

ON TREACHEROUS GROUND

I

The big house against the hills outside of Great Falls, Montana, shone brightly with holiday lighting. Sam Grant drove his prized '67 Ford Mustang up the winding road and into the yard and parked. The cold weather had finally broken and a slight wind blew, settling what was left of the snow into rivulets of muddy water.

"We have arrived," Grant told his date.

Jane Connors swung her long legs out of the car. "Quite the digs. You do run with some high rollers. Not what you told me earlier."

"I'm a little surprised myself." Grant closed his door. "But I'm sure you'll see this party is pretty backwoods. I thought you might get a kick out of it."

Grant had chosen a spot down the hill, a short distance away from the other vehicles parked everywhere, at every angle.

"Who did you say was throwing this?" Jane asked, looking at the odd mix of mud-covered pickup trucks and expensive cars.

"An accountant. The invitation said it was a stockholder's meeting. I didn't know he had a big-time corporation."

Jane smiled. "It seems he may have more than one. Most of them hidden, no doubt."

"You uncomfortable?" Grant asked.

"Nah," Jane replied. "Just curious."

Grant had met Jane two weeks before at a Christmas play in Lincoln, a little mountain town nestled beneath the Continental Divide. Grant had been watching a small nephew haul incense and myrrh onto the stage, drop one of the canisters, pick it up, and declare, "Jesus will still like it," to the audience.

Jane had come to the area from Los Angeles to do winter sports articles for outdoor magazines, and had taken in the play for kicks. She had dropped her bag of goodies from Santa, and Grant had kindly come to her assistance.

The week before had been dinner and dancing. Just a friendly evening. It had ended with Jane helping Grant fix his car along the side of the road. Something in the electrical system had malfunctioned, and she had discovered the problem handily.

After laughing together over her mechanical genius, they had decided to go out again. It appeared their date this evening might prove very interesting.

As they neared the mansion, Jane asked, "So, how did you get to know this guy?"

Grant explained that he had met Jinx Morales, who had moved from Seattle to Great Falls the previous summer, at a fund-raiser for a local charity called the Sunrise Foundation. Grant had contributed generously to the Sunrise Ranch, a part of the foundation built as a safe haven for teens at risk. Morales had been doing the foundation's books for free.

Grant's past had left him sympathetic to troubled teens. When Grant was five years old, a hit-and-run driver, who had thrown an empty whiskey bottle out at the scene, had taken the lives of his mother and father, instantly. Grant and his half-brother, Tom Carlisle, seven years old at the time, had been sitting in the backseat. Both had somehow escaped serious injury.

The two boys had bounced from one foster home to another, with no luck in finding a family who wanted to keep them. Finally they had been separated to live in different homes, and hadn't found one another again until adulthood, while both were serving in a covert operation in South America.

Tom Carlisle was now in law enforcement, and Grant rarely saw him. After their separation as children, Grant had found himself at odds with the law as a teen and young adult, and had learned to distrust authority.

Since meeting Jinx Morales, Grant had become interested in helping the Sunrise Foundation in any way he could. Jinx had recently talked to Grant about contributing to the foundation for a new venture that would help even more kids. All he would say was that they would discuss it further at the Christmas party.

Now that he was there, though, he wasn't certain that everyone in attendance was thinking about the Sunrise Foundation.

Jane stopped a moment to admire an ornamental display that covered the entire front yard. The lawn glowed with a dazzling ribbon of white Christmas lights that ran downhill off the side of the property like a mystical stream, where a wandering Rudolph had stopped to drink. Atop the roof was old Saint Nick himself, unloading his sled while the rest of the reindeer stood patiently.

Jane studied the area. "This guy would be a highroller even by LA standards."

Grand agreed. "I've never been up here before."

Jane turned to Grant. "Why don't most of these pickups have license plates?"

"They belong to people who don't believe in local, state, or federal government," Grant explained. "They don't believe they have to live by any law but their own."

"Their own law?"

"The law as they see it, not as the federal government sees it."

Jane paused. "Are you talking about those militia types? Did you know they were going to be here?"

"I didn't know who all was going to be here. We don't have to go in."

"Yeah, we do," she said. "I've never been to a militia party before."

Jinx Morales greeted Grant at the door and slapped him on the back. "Good to see you, my friend. And the young lady as well."

Grant introduced Jane, and they followed Jinx into the living room. It was a catered event, complete with servers in black tuxes. Tables covered with hot and cold food, as well as seemingly every kind of alcoholic beverage known to man, filled the center of the room, with space at the far end for dancing.

A deejay spun recordings from the past through large speakers, filling the room with everything from the Bee Gees to Country Joe and the Fish.

Jinx flashed Jane a broad smile. "What does the lady want?"

She pointed, and he grabbed a bottle of lemon tonic water.

"What with it?" he asked.

"Just plain, thank you."

"Oh, c'mon, pretty lady. Loosen up a little. Sam has plans later for you, I'll bet."

"You worry about your own plans, Mr. Morales. Okay?"

Jinx handed her a glass of tonic water, with ice. He growled low in his throat, still smiling.

"A she-cat with sharp claws," he said. "Please, you can purr at my house."

He dropped ice into another glass, filled it with Yukon Jack, and handed it to Grant with a laugh.

"I already know what you drink."

Grant frowned. "How would you know? I've never drank with you before."

Morales smiled and shrugged. "I keep track of you. You're a friend."

The house was alive with revelers dressed in everything from expensive suits and dresses to boots and jeans. Jinx's wife, Chi-Chi, hurried from the kitchen, her large breasts spilling out of her low-cut gown.

"Oh, Sam Grant!" she shrieked. "Why didn't someone tell me you were here?"

She grabbed Grant around the neck and planted a huge kiss on his lips. Everyone cheered.

"Hello, Chi-Chi," Grant said. "I see you're having a good time."

"How have you been, you lady killer, you?" she asked. "And who's your friend?"

"Jane, this is Chi-Chi Morales."

Chi-Chi looked Jane over. "You're not from around here." She looked back at Grant. "At least not yet." She laughed quickly and pinched Grant's cheek, then turned to Jane. "You take good care of my loverboy here. And always remember, he's mine first and yours second." She laughed and hurried off to refill her drink, her tight-fitting dress clinging to her large hips.

Morales hurried over and sidled up to Jane. "By rights, it should be my turn to kiss you. Ah, but maybe in a minute, when I know you better."

Jane smiled. "Yeah, maybe later."

"Jinx, tell me," Grant said, "who are all these people?"

One of the guests hung over the railing on the second level. He waved and spilled his beer onto the carpet below.

"Sam Grant, where the hell you been all these years?"

"Don't you recognize your own neighbor from long ago?" Jinx laughed and joined some other guests.

Willie Jens, in his mid-twenties, looked more like a bodybuilder than a farmer. He wore a cutoff shirt with soiled denims, and a cap encrusted with field dust.

"Perfect holiday attire," Jane said to Grant.

Willie had been a younger childhood neighbor from just down the road. It had indeed been a long time.

"Hello, Willie?" Grant said.

Willie made it down the stairs and stuck out his hand. "Really good to see you, Sam," he said. "So you're going to join us, I see."

"Join you?"

"This is a pledge party. For the Mountain Patriots."

"I thought it was Jinx's Christmas party."

"It is. But it's *our* party, too. We can use you with us."

"That's not why I came, Willie."

"But you belong on the team."

"Not really."

"Tell him, Miss. Ah, Miss?"

"My name is Jane."

"Tell him, Jane, that we need him."

"Willie, I've got a lot going these days," Grant said.

"Whatever, Sam. Let me take you upstairs to meet some people."

"We were just about to leave." He finished his drink and set the glass down on a coffee table.

"No, it's okay," Jane said. "We just got here."

Grant stared at her. "I'm not joining any groups of any kind."

"Go with him," Jane insisted. "I'll help Jinx and Chi-Chi serve drinks."

"You sure?"

Jane laughed. "Relax, the night is young."

Grant climbed the stairs to the upper level, where a group of men were passing around bottles of beer and hard liquor. He looked down to see Jane enjoying herself below, fitting in with Jinx and Chi-Chi like she'd known them forever.

On the second level, the guests were far more subdued. They weren't laughing or joking at all, but spoke in low tones. Grant realized he didn't know any of them.

Willie arrived with a new beer and a bottle of tequila.

"There's someone here who wants to see you," he told Grant.

Willie ushered him over to the group and they stopped their conversation. A large man dressed in faded blue jeans and a faded flannel shirt walked out of a nearby bedroom and stared at Grant with steel-blue eyes. He had a puffy, unshaven face and graying blond hair. He worked a toothpick from one side of his mouth to the other and adjusted his cap, the front of which bore a U.S. flag with a black lightning bolt through the middle.

"Sam Grant, it's been a while."

Grant extended his hand. He hadn't seen Charlie Steadman since the end of Desert Storm. They had fought side by side through a lot of the war. He had pulled a wounded Steadman from a foxhole just before a barrage of missiles had hit their position. Grant had been given a commendation for bravery.

"I'd heard you were hiding out in Arizona," Grant said to him.

"Arizona. Idaho. I'm all over these days." He laughed.

"What brings you here?"

"You, Sam."

Charlie Steadman had been the main leader of a militia group in Michigan. He had moved to Montana to begin the Mountain Patriots movement five years earlier, and had succeed in uniting a group of militants angry enough at the U.S. government to secede from the Union.

After an altercation on the streets of Billings, Montana, the previous spring, he had been arrested and indicted on twenty-three federal counts, including syndication, malicious damage to property, and intimidation and interference with federal officers.

While awaiting trial, he had been under transfer to a holding facility in the central part of the state when two pickup trucks had suddenly arrived at a county road crossing. A barrage of gunfire had killed the federal escorts, breaking Steadman and three other Mountain Patriots free. Now accessory to murder had been added to his rap sheet.

Grant had followed his friend's escalating crime career in the press, wondering how he could have become so hateful.

"You're sticking your neck out by being here," Grant told him.

Steadman shrugged. "I'm among friends, aren't I?"

Willie Jens was listening in. He handed the bottle of tequila to Steadman.

"He knows what he's doing, Sam. Listen to him."

"Willie, why don't you go visit with the others?" Steadman suggested.

"Sure, Charlie. Good idea."

Grant watched Willie leave and noticed two men staring at him from one corner of the room.

"Is the shorter of those two Bert Pearson?" Grant asked.

"Yes, it is. He's with me now."

"Really? You two have never gotten along."

"He's decided I know what I'm doing. He wants to be my right-hand man."

Grant smiled thinly. "You sure of that, Charlie?"

Steadman shrugged. "That's what he told me. So far he's been cooperative. I mean, he's been more than that."

"He hated you at one time, Charlie, for drawing away most of his men from his own group to the Mountain Patriots. Have you forgotten that?"

"How do you know about that? Especially after not seeing me for so long?"

"I play poker in the back of the Stockman Bar, out in Stanford."

Steadman grunted. "Well, that answers a lot of questions. But I'm certain that Pearson really believes in me now."

"That's good, Charlie. Just watch your back. Who's the other one?"

"An Air Force officer named Rossler. He shares our views."

"Really? A man on the inside?"

"There are more of his kind than you think, Sam. An awful lot has changed, you know, since the attacks in New York and Washington in September. We're all being squeezed tight, even the boys with the uniforms on."

"I don't see any of us as worse off, not really."

"You're blind, Sam. Can't see it, or don't want to."

"Do Pearson and Rossler have a clear vision of things?"

"Very, it seems to me."

"So, let me talk to him then," Grant insisted.

"Rossler's not ready to meet you yet. Not until you're established with us and trustworthy. Those are his words."

Grant studied the two men, staying to themselves in the shadows of the room.

"Interesting," Grant said. "Trustworthy, you say?"

Steadman led Grant into a corner bedroom. Grant felt the stares of both Pearson and Rossler boring into his back.

Steadman took a drink of tequila and offered the bottle to Grant, who declined.

"There was a time you'd drink with me, Sam."

"I'm the designated driver tonight."

"You know, we really need to be together now, since a lot's going to happen very soon."

"Charlie, things are never what they seem."

"And that goes double for you, Sam. You know they're going to use that terrorist war as an excuse to take away our freedom and enslave us. It's already happening."

"I don't see it the same way as you do," Grant said. "And tonight's a bad time to bring all that up, okay?"

"I don't understand you, Sam. You should be mad as hell, especially since Camille was killed the way she was."

"Listen, Charlie, she was my wife and your sister, but bringing it up all the time won't bring her back."

"But they killed her, and your son inside her!"

Grant stared hard at him. "What's the matter with you? It's Christmas, and all you can do is talk about stuff that tears me up inside."

"It tears me up, too, damn it!" Steadman hung his head. "Sorry, Sam. But just hear me out, would you?"

"No more about Camille, Charlie. Got that?"

"No more. I promise."

They moved to a large window, where they looked out over the city and across the broad flow of the Missouri River. The moon shone a milky glow over the rising hills and the spreading lights of the city.

"That's a damned pretty sight, Sam," he said. "Do you want to see it all change? When the dark army shows up, nothing will be the same."

"How do you think a 'dark army' is going to be able to take over a whole entire nation, Charlie?"

"They have it all planned out. Maybe that terrorist thing was a part of it. Do you think you can enjoy life in a One World army detention camp?"

"I told you, I don't see that happening," Grant said.

"You're damned right it won't," Steadman insisted. "There's a bunch of us around this country who'll see to that."

He showed Grant a series of maps laid out across the bed, each one covered with scribbles and notations. It appeared that a strategic plan lay waiting to unfold.

"Things are going to happen before long," Steadman huffed. "Our people are going to move to stop this thing from ever taking shape."

"What are you talking about?" Grant asked.

"If we have our own country within the borders of the U.S., we'll make our own laws, and stand by them."

"Why not just go to congress and seek a hearing on the laws we already have, if you want to make a scene about them?" Grant suggested.

"It's too late for talk, Sam. There's a new bill being introduced to allow federal takeover of foreclosed-on private lands."

"I hadn't heard about that."

"Of course not. Very few have. It's in the planning stages as we speak. But we're going to stop it before it happens."

Steadman took a folder from a dresser top and handed Grant what appeared to be a legal document, but legal only within the bounds of Steadman's new nation concept.

The document read:

In Justice Court
The Sovereign Mountain Patriots' Nation

BOUNTY

Know All New Nation Parties by These Presents:

One Million Dollars of Legal Money

The sum of One Million ($1,000,000) Dollars of Legal Money in the form of partial assignment of perfected securities will be tendered over to any just man who successfully causes the arrest and subsequent conviction of the following named suspect, but not limited to:

U.S. Senator Shelby H. Barnes

For his willful and knowing participation in the crime of treason against the just citizens of the Sovereign Mountain Patriots' Nation (SMPN). Public record of said crime and the facts leading to this warrant is contained within File Q 1896 S 107th Congress, to establish a Federal Loan and Acquisitions Act, foreclosure and acquisition of such private lands that would fall under the jurisdiction and boundaries of such Act. Said Act is against the foundations set forth by the SMPN, and such attempts are herewith declared to be punishable by death, if such attempts are found to be attributed to the accused.

This bounty is subject to change until final judgment and final decree, with appropriate remedy when it occurs, in and for the Sovereign Mountain Patriots' Nation.

Signed: *Charles H. Steadman*
Leading Enforcement Officer,
Commanding General,
Sovereign Mountain Patriots' Nation

Steadman had left his fingerprint to show that his signature had not been forged.

"Barnes will be tried by a jury of his peers and hanged accordingly," Steadman said.

"That's more than I care to know, Charlie," Grant told him. "I'm out of here. Have a good new year."

Steadman stopped him. "You haven't heard it all yet, Sam."

"You're way off the deep end here, Charlie. There are lots of ways of voicing your opinion. Hanging a U.S. senator isn't one of them."

"Whether you believe it or not, Sam, there's going to be a revolution."

"Don't you think you're pushing a self-fulfilling prophecy here, Charlie?"

Steadman wasn't listening. He had turned his attention to downstairs, where someone was announcing that the cops were coming.

Grant and Steadman both peered out a window

to see a sheriff's vehicle pulling into the yard. Two officers got out.

"Settle down, Charlie," Grant said.

"Do you expect me to just give myself up to them?"

"Maybe they just want Jinx to turn the music down," Grant suggested. "Just wait."

Steadman went to the corner of the bedroom and picked up an AK-47. He left the room and ordered the rest of the men upstairs to arm themselves also. They opened closet doors in three different rooms and took out a number of pistols and rifles, many of them automatic.

Grant noticed one of the closets was stuffed full of wooden boxes, the kind that held explosives.

Below, the music played on and people continued to dance.

Jinx Morales hurried up the stairs.

"Everyone remain calm," he said. "Okay? Calm."

Grant peered over the railing and saw two deputies standing just inside the doorway. Chi-Chi was doing her best to charm them. He didn't see Jane anywhere.

Jinx went into a bedroom and again emphasized that everyone remain calm. Steadman grabbed him by the arm.

"Why'd you let them inside?" he demanded.

Jinx pulled away. "Have some respect."

"I asked you a question."

"Someone's truck came out of gear and rolled into a house down below," Jinx replied. "An older red blazer."

Everyone turned to Willie Jens, whose face twisted into a frown.

"No, it couldn't have been my rig." But he knew that it was indeed his vehicle. Willie rubbed his sweaty palms on his pants. "We'll get it straightened out."

Jinx and Willie eased down the stairs toward the waiting deputies. As they talked, Grant realized that there was no doubt that Willie had no license or insurance, and that more problems would soon develop.

Steadman called Grant back to the window and pointed to another sheriff's vehicle that was parked a short distance down the road. The officer behind the wheel was on his radio while the other got out and began shining his flashlight on the parked vehicles.

"Just what do they think they're doing?" Steadman said. He rammed a clip into his rifle.

"Wait until the two downstairs leave and just go out the back," Grant suggested.

"It won't be that simple," Steadman said.

He stared out the window again. In the distance, a number of law enforcement vehicles were en route, lights flashing.

"See what I mean?"

"You don't even know that they're coming here."

"I'm not taking that chance."

"Let's think this thing out, Charlie," Grant told him.

"No time for that now!" Steadman shouldered past Grant and the others to the railing and shouted down, "Jinx! Get the hell out of the way!"

Morales dove to one side. The two officers looked up and Steadman opened fire on them, killing one instantly. The other staggered out the door, fumbling for his revolver.

The women began screaming, rushing for cover. Willie yelled up for a weapon and someone threw him a 9mm pistol. He laughed, eased open the door, and fired six rounds into the wounded officer.

Steadman and the others rushed past Grant and down the stairs. Steadman yelled instructions, dictating position as if on a battlefield.

Grant hurried down the stairs and began searching through the panicked guests for Jane. She was nowhere to be found. From outside came the wailing of sirens. Flashing lights lined the road below and officers poured from vehicles, guns drawn.

Grant slammed through a set of French doors and was met by two armed deputies. One of them screamed, "Down on your belly! Hands behind your head! Now!"

Grant knelt down as automatic weapon fire burst from behind him. Bullets sang over his head and back. The two deputies yelled and whirled in bloody circles, pitching into the mud and snow.

Steadman and the others rushed through the door past them. They shouted and cursed and began shooting toward anything that looked like a law-enforcement officer or vehicle. One of the officers fired something into the house that turned the interior into flames.

Grant circled along the side of the hill to where clumps of heavy brush choked a small draw. He held tight in a prone position as law-enforcement personnel streamed across the hillside above him, their guns ready.

A barrage of fire from Steadman's men raked through them. They stopped to return fire, screaming and yelling. One fell and rolled down into a clump of brush near Grant, mortally wounded.

Grant quickly slipped away through the shadows. At the bottom of the hill the moon shone down on a steady stream of flashing lights, curving up the hill toward the house like an escort at a state funeral. Overhead, a helicopter appeared and a dozen streaks of flame began spurting up toward it from various positions along the hillside.

The chopper veered away and Steadman's men cheered loudly.

Grant heard an explosion in the house. An upstairs window burst, raining a fireworks display of ashes and flaming debris out into the night.

He crossed over the hill to where another road led to another subdivision, separate from Jinx Morale's mansion. Along the road sat his Mustang, with Jane behind the wheel.

Out of breath, he approached the car. Jane stuck her head out of the driver's side window.

"Sam, what took you so long?"

National headlines:

SIX DEAD, TWELVE WOUNDED
IN NEW YEAR'S EVE FIREFIGHT!

FOUR LAW ENFORCEMENT,
FIVE MONTANA MILITIAMEN DIE
IN CONFRONTATION.
TWELVE WOUNDED.

The television stations and newspapers ran a lot of stories over the following couple of months. Some took the slant that law enforcement had overstepped their bounds by raiding a private party, while others spotlighted Charles Steadman and his men as American terrorists on the loose, compounding the global problem.

The general populace took sides, and the press

never let up. Grant found it odd that he was never officially brought in for questioning by local authorities. They had left it to the feds. It was a certainty that his name had come up somewhere along the line.

Jane Connors was uncommonly cool about it all. For never having been to a militia gathering, she had managed to conduct herself in amazing fashion. He couldn't get a straight answer from her, though, as to why she had left the party and had hot-wired his Mustang just prior to the siege at Jinx Morales's mansion. "Just intuition," she had told him. Whoever she was and how it had all come about, she had saved him, he believed, from being an accessory to murder.

It hadn't saved him from a continuous barrage of questions regarding his affiliation with Charles Steadman, though. The FBI was the main agency on the case. They wanted to know everything. For the time being, they took his word for it when he insisted that he didn't share Charlie Steadman's views on life and never would. Still, they would certainly be tailing him for some time to come.

Grant was certain they knew where Steadman and his men were hiding out, but were reluctant to force anything and create another media feeding frenzy. Better to do it tactically.

II

The newly remodeled Stockman's Bar in Stanford was packed. Saturday night and Sunday's upcoming C. M. Russell Stampede and Rodeo had brought visitors from everywhere. The middle of town had vibrated since early evening with a battle of the bands. Onstage, as the last bits of dusk disappeared in the west, Marty and the Outlaws held session with a strong country-rock beat.

Sixty miles from Great Falls, this little community of five hundred remained solidly in the past, rooted in the history of its forefathers. After the Indian wars, cattle barons claimed the grassy slopes below the mountains, and wheat farmers laid their plows into the flatlands.

Settlement had come hard. Winters were tough, and summers dry. Early in the century, a white wolf had haunted the ranges, its fangs tearing holes in the sheep and cattle population. Finally brought to stockmen's justice, the wolf now stood fully mounted, behind glass, on the second floor of the courthouse, an inspiration to high school athletes through the years.

Grant walked through the bar's front door, making his way past staring patrons. He eased himself through a door and into a back room, where a tableful of poker players looked up in unison.

"Sam Grant!" the dealer said. "Good to see you."

"How you doing, Jake?"

"In the mood for some poker, Sam?" Jake asked. "Always room for you."

Jake Marker was a fifth-generation rancher in the area. He had known Grant's parents well and had been a pallbearer at their funeral.

Jake dealt a hand to Grant and to one of the other players, a small man they called Spence.

"The feds leaving you alone now?" he asked Grant.

"They've all gone fishing, Jake," Grant replied.

"Too damned warm for fishing," another player said. "Too damned dry."

Spence toyed with his cards. "Has your girlfriend from LA been around lately, Sam?"

Grant frowned. How did word spread so fast? Jane had been up for a week on another magazine assignment, and had left just the day before. They had been careful not to stay in the area, deciding instead to make their way into the northwest part of the state and enjoy some privacy.

Someone must have found out.

"Is it getting serious?" Spence persisted.

"Just friends," Grant replied.

Everyone chuckled.

"How you handling the drought, Sam?" one of the other players asked.

Grant studied his hand. "I'm going to have to bring some more hay in to feed, and likely sell off some cattle."

"It's that way all over," Spence said. "Hard times."

"You'll break even at least, Sam," Jake said. "You always do."

Grant smiled and studied his cards. "Jake, you know that I play too much poker to break even."

The door opened suddenly. A young farmer who looked like a bodybuilder entered, clutching a can of beer.

Willie Jens grunted and said, "Don't all of you stop talking on account of me."

"Willie, you're putting us all in danger," Jake pointed out.

"Nah, I'm just here for a beer or two, and gone." He took a chair next to Grant. "So, when you going to join us, Sam?"

"When are you going to stop asking, Willie?"

Jens bristled. "After the Christmas party, I heard a lot about you. A lot of folks believe in you. But you can't be everything they say you are."

"Nobody is all that, Willie," Grant pointed out. "So stop bothering me."

"I wouldn't care, but Charlie's a good friend. He wants you to survive this with us, not go down with the rest of them."

"Charlie should be talking to me then."

"No, I'm talking to you, Grant, and you'd better damned well listen."

"Willie," Jake said, "lay back, now."

"I ain't afraid of him, no, I ain't." Willie drank from his beer.

"You'd better get back with your group, Willie," Grant advised. "If time is so short, they'll be missing you."

"Okay, Mr. Special Forces Man," Willie said. "Don't say I didn't give you a last chance." Willie finished his beer and crushed the can. "The time's long come. Those that ain't with us are against us." He got up and threw the crushed can against the wall and left.

The players relaxed a bit. "He and his brothers are set to lose their place," one of them said. "That's part of it."

"That's no part of it," Spence argued. "If he was good as gold solvent, he'd still have a gun in his hand."

"Word is Steadman and all of them are coming down out of their hideout. They've got something planned."

"What do you suppose they're up to?" Spence asked.

"I heard a rumor that they plan to go after the Arab terrorists themselves," Jake replied. "Because they don't see it being done right by the government."

"There's nothing to that," Grant said. "An impossible task. Steadman is fanatic, but he's not that stupid."

The back door opened again and everyone turned to see a woman enter the room.

"Sam, you need to come with me, please."

Jane Connors, dressed like a country girl in jeans and halter top, appeared in a big hurry.

Grant rebounded from his surprise. "I thought you'd left."

"I'm back. We need to go."

Jake and Spence and the other players were smiling. Grant cashed in his chips and hurried out the door behind Jane.

When they left, the room erupted in laughter.

"I guess it is serious after all," Jake commented.

Jane ushered Grant into a dark sedan with an out-of-state license plate. She zipped through the shadows along the back streets of town like an Indy 500 racer.

"Tell me something," Grant said. "Is this car untraceable?"

"Something like that," Jane admitted.

"And you're an FBI agent?"

"Let's just say an agent."

"I'll admit, I have been wondering. But why didn't you tell me from the beginning?"

"Sam, you know that's not how it works. I was assigned to you, to learn who you are and what your thinking is. You're not one of them, so mission accomplished, as far as I'm concerned."

"So, they think I'm part of Steadman's group? And that you can learn what he's up to through me?"

"I've told them there's no way you're implicated in this."

"But they don't believe you?"

"Some of them do. It's complicated, Sam. Right now I'm getting you to where you need to be just as quickly as possible."

"I just need to be back at my ranch, with my Mustang, safe and sound."

"Your Mustang will be fine."

"Is there someone else around who can hot-wire as well as you?"

"Believe me, at least one or two, Sam. Don't worry about it."

"I need to know what this is all about."

"Something's about to go down, Sam. You need to be where you're not in the line of fire. Just sit back and enjoy the ride, please."

Grant sat in the darkness of his living room, looking out his picture window onto the moonlit pastures below the mountains. The room was quiet, except for the clinking of Jane Connors's drink glass as she set it down.

"You okay, Sam?" she asked.

"I'm in the middle of all this," he said, "and I never asked for it."

"You're tied to Charlie Steadman," Jane told him. "That's what your problem is, if you can call it yours."

"It's a good thing I have you," Grant said. "They'd be on me a lot worse if it wasn't for that."

"They think I'm compromised already," Jane admitted. "But they're wrong."

"What happens when they jerk you from the case?"

"I'll quit and stay with you," she replied. "They know that."

Grant took a deep breath. "So, what's going to happen?"

"It isn't clear. Only that Steadman wants to kidnap Senator Shelby Barnes and try him for treason, in his militia court. He's obsessed with that notion."

"So Barnes has a lot of extra security, I suppose."

"Lots of extra security. But Steadman and his men are good. Real good. The feeling is they'll make a play for Barnes, sooner or later, at a place and time least expected."

"Why hasn't Steadman been arrested yet?"

"You know the answer to that, Sam," Jane replied. "When it happens, it's going to be a bloodbath, no matter how they do it. Steadman and his men are not going to give themselves up. That's it. There's enough going on without compounding it all."

"Surely a Special Forces unit can capture him without everyone knowing it."

"They've already tried," Jane said. "Ten of the best. Not a one of them came back, or has been heard from. No one knows if they're alive or dead."

"No news about that, not a story anywhere?"

"It was a closely guarded mission," Jane explained. "I didn't know about it until someone asked me to check into some names and see if I could stumble across something."

Grant thought a moment. "Steadman and his men have killed lawmen outright. This time the public understands that he has to be brought to justice, don't they?"

"The public doesn't know what to think. They've got way too much on their plates already. No use trying to second-guess what's going to happen with Steadman. You need to be patient and just sit tight here until it's over."

"That's impossible," Grant said. "I have work that needs to be done."

"You stay here at the ranch and I'll see to it that you get what you need."

Grant studied her. "I need to ask you about a rumor that Charlie wants to take on the terrorists in his own way."

"Doesn't that sound absurd to you?"

"Even if he knew where they were in this country, he couldn't just go after them."

"Right. So don't give it another thought." After a moment, she said, "You've never shown me a picture of your wife."

Easing himself from the chair, Grant sat down on the floor near a lamp stand. He switched the light on and pulled a large photo album from a cabinet in the stand.

Jane eased herself down next to him. “She’s a nice-looking woman. Vibrant. You made a good couple.”

“She was four months pregnant at the time of the accident,” Grant said.

“It must still make you a little nuts, how it happened.”

“At times.”

When Grant had first told Jane the story, her reaction had been predictable. “What a freak thing,” she had said. He had run it through his mind thousands of times over the past two years. They had been driving along a mountain road at dusk in their SUV when two men in a dark sedan had passed them at breakneck speed, spewing gravel everywhere, followed closely by a sheriff’s vehicle with its pursuit lights on and siren blaring. Grant had edged over to the side of the road, as close as safely possible, but the sheriff’s vehicle had rounded the corner and slid into them, knocking their SUV down an embankment, where they had smashed sideways into a large pine tree.

Grant had remembered regaining consciousness to the strong smell of gasoline and his wife lying twisted in the seat, impaled by a tree branch that had come through the windshield. He had struggled to break the branch loose and pull her from the vehicle through his door, and quickly away from the vehicle. But he had known already that she was gone.

A young sheriff's deputy had made his way down the slope to express his apologies for the accident. When paramedics arrived they found Grant holding his wife in his lap and the young officer sitting next to him, semiconscious, both of them watching the SUV burn. That night a hundred acres of forest had gone up in flames before firefighters and a thunderstorm had contained it.

"One thing I've always wondered," Grant said as they looked at more photos of happier times, "is who that young deputy was chasing. He didn't know, and he never got a license number."

Jane was shaking her head. "You never know how things are going to turn out, do you?"

"You never know," Grant replied.

III

Dressed in camouflage, his face blackened, Bert Pearson rode in the passenger's seat of an older model army Jeep, an AK-47 rifle propped against his thigh. Middle-aged, with thinning hair and a patchy gray beard, Pearson had seen combat action both in Vietnam and the Gulf. He had been decorated three times for bravery under fire.

No longer in the military, he now had little to do but dwell on his past glories and his increasing rage, including the reason no one had ever given him any answers about Agent Orange, which he maintained had taken his brother's life. And no answers for the threat to freedom as it was now being played out by world powers bent on destruction and control.

Pearson's young driver, Private Melvin Karst, stared straight ahead at the road. He drove with his lights off, confident that the 3 A.M. half-moon would provide enough light to negotiate the twisting road along the base of the mountains.

Karst stopped the Jeep at the crest of a timbered hill and turned off the engine.

Two large Suburbans filled with camouflaged men emerged from the deep shadows of the nearby pines, followed by a pickup truck covered with a camper top. The vehicles churned onto the road and came to a stop behind the Jeep.

Pearson disembarked the Jeep and took position as the men left the vehicles, fifteen in all, and fell into formation, staring straight ahead.

Pearson barked, "Command, at attention!"

"Yes, sir!" the ten men replied in perfect unison.

Pearson and Karst opened the back end of the

camper top on the pickup and lowered the end gate. Inside rested a stack of fifteen AK-47 rifles.

He and Karst began the process of preparing the men for their mission. Each received a rifle and a hundred rounds of ammunition, plenty enough to complete their assignments.

Pearson watched the men methodically take their weapons and enable them for firing. This bunch looked as poised as any he had ever seen.

Poised and didn't even know it. He laughed to himself as he studied them.

Had they the conscious awareness of what they were about to undertake, not a single one of them would be there.

They had each been programmed by an "instructor" for the duties of the day, to carry out a segment of the Plan that, in Pearson's mind, would prove to be the most important of all. If it worked as he believed it would, he would gain a large measure of satisfaction.

The men who had worked with the soldiers to get them ready were so secretive that Pearson had never met them in the daylight. Just their voices from the shadows of a darkened room. They insisted on being called "instructors," when they were actually programmers. Human-brain programmers. Their "instruction" techniques paralleled those of the most severe of their kind in all of recorded history, torturers obsessed with instilling undivided loyalty within the divided mind of a subject.

Though older, these were a particularly vicious group of men. They had studied in the late fifties and early sixties under Nazi doctors from the Third Reich, including Josef Mengele, at secret outposts in South America and also within the United States. The idea of creating the perfect soldier, as well as the perfect spy, was still under development and experimentation. And they were willing to work with anyone's subjects, if the price was right.

Pearson wondered how—and if—the Nazi techniques differed from those used by the renegade Islamic terrorist groups that were active everywhere in the world. Surely they had perfected their own brand of mind control to provide a subject that would pilot a plane into a steel building without faltering. Pearson had already witnessed some of what the Nazis had accomplished. Many of their subjects had done some amazing feats without ever having remembered a thing about it.

Pearson studied the soldiers. The previous evening at the compound, each had been branded with a swastika, the mark burned squarely into his forehead. The smell of seared flesh was still pungent, yet not a one of them showed any hint of pain, a tribute to the men who had programmed them.

The special training methods, hypnosis, drugs, and torture had turned them into what they were now. Each of these fifteen men would follow instructions to the tee and later never know they had. They would, indeed, believe they had been to Disneyland, if so instructed.

But Disneyland had not been mentioned. Something far less entertaining had been planned for them. They would partake in a scheduled assault, and never know they had taken part in anything but what they had been told.

Pearson inspected the soldiers and stopped in front of the last one to his left.

"Red Cat One," he said. "Are you ready to do your duty?"

"Sir, yes, sir!"

"Why are you here, soldier?"

"I am shooting with true aim for the just cause of the Sovereign Mountain Patriots' Nation, sir!"

"Who is your leader?"

"General Charles Steadman, sir. And Samuel Allen Grant. They have sent me on this mission."

"Very good. If you are ever caught, if you are ever questioned, who will you say sent you here?"

"General Charles Steadman, sir. And Sam Grant."

Pearson felt certain at this point that under any

and all circumstances, he and Rossler would not be implicated in what was about to take place at the Alpha 1 missile launch facility. Instead, it would be Steadman and Sam Grant.

"Private Karst, give him a rifle and ammunition."

Karst did as ordered. Red Cat One received his weapon and held it at the ready.

Pearson said, "Step back in line, soldier," and he did, remaining at attention.

Pearson moved methodically down the line, requiring each one in turn to repeat his oath, and if captured, who had sent him on this mission. Each man was known by Red Cat, followed by his number. When he reached Red Cat Fifteen, he had them all kneel down, place their weapons on the ground, and clasp their hands behind their backs.

This was critical now. Pearson reached in his pocket and pulled out a piece of paper. He couldn't remember all the commands by heart.

"Can you hear the whistle of the flare overhead?"

"Yes, sir!" they yelled in unison.

"Are you ready to march toward the Alpha 1 launch facility?"

"Yes, sir!"

Pearson walked the line of kneeling men, touching each one on the forehead, pressing his first and index finger into the swastika, saying, "For the cause, for one and all."

Each soldier breathed deeply at the statement and closed his eyes.

"Red Cats, all rise and assume formation!" Pearson barked.

Again, the soldiers responded in unison, rising to their feet, placing their rifles over their shoulders.

"Forward, to your duty."

The soldiers began to march in a long line, down off the hill and across a field, through the shadowed predawn, toward the Alpha 1 launch facility. Pearson took a camouflage net from the back of one of the Suburbans and handed it to Karst.

"Follow them and do your duty, Private Karst."

"Yes, sir."

Pearson watched while Karst marched out behind the soldiers. Using night binoculars he monitored their progress. Partway across the field, Karst let out a low grunt and the line of soldiers stopped. They came to their knees and laid their rifles down, then flattened themselves on their stomachs.

Karst spread the camouflage net across the row of soldiers and secured it at both ends with small stakes. He returned to Pearson and said, "Mission accomplished, sir."

"Soon there will be more to do, Private Karst," Pearson said.

"Yes, sir!"

"Let's take our position in the pines and get some rest."

Charles Steadman neared the city limits of Great Falls in a recently stolen late-model SUV with phony plates. The midmorning sun rose in a cloudless sky, promising another scorching afternoon.

Steadman toyed with a 9mm semi-automatic pistol, holding the weapon in his right hand, savoring the feel, while steering with his left. As he slowed for city traffic, he rubbed the smooth metal surface of the pistol with the tips of his fingers, as if the weapon was his own private invention.

He laid the pistol on the passenger seat and turned north, toward Malmstrom Air Force Base. Just before the base, he turned left into a residential zone. He drove through and turned into a park area where one of his followers, a younger man named Wetzel, waited next to an outdoor barbecue grill.

Steadman pulled the stolen SUV to a stop behind Wetzel's sedan and looked all around. He got out and eased up to where Wetzel was examining a hot dog.

"I told you to just wait here," Steadman said to him, "not to have a picnic."

Wetzel smiled. "It's not too early, is it?"

"You'll be attracting kids and dogs over here."

Wetzel turned off the grill. "Yeah, I never thought of that."

"Where's Willie Jens?" Steadman asked.

"He said you told him to go with Pearson today. A change of plans."

Steadman ground his teeth. "Really? That's a change I certainly didn't authorize."

"I didn't think so," Wetzel said.

"So," Steadman asked, "what's the status on Barnes?"

"Senator Barnes?"

"Who else?"

"You forgot, I have a cousin named Barnes."

"Yeah, do you want me to hang him, too?"

"I see your point." Wetzel checked an earpiece cleverly hidden under a baseball cap and beneath neck-length shaggy hair. "His plane just landed."

"Everyone in place?"

Wetzel nodded. "We're all set."

"Wait another half hour, then," Steadman instructed. "If I'm not back, go ahead as planned."

"Got you," Wetzel said.

"Another thing," said Steadman.

"Yeah?"

"Put the hot dogs away."

"Sure thing, General."

Steadman returned to his vehicle and drove out of the park, then crossed to another street, looking for the address of a three-story apartment complex with a three-foot-high wooden bear in front of the door.

As he drove, he listened to a national news broadcast. Authorities were starting a massive search for him. He had seen to it that "leads" as to his whereabouts would take their search to the wrong places.

He smiled. The Plan was going just right.

He found the street address and upon seeing the wooden bear by the door, pulled to the curb. He looked up to see a man's face in the window. Arlan Rossler was watching him closely.

Rossler had so far provided a lot of useful information, even though he had advocated sending a team to take out Sam Grant. "He knows too much," he had insisted. "You'll be sorry if you don't listen to me."

Steadman wondered if Rossler wasn't jealous of Grant in some way. Grant was special and would never betray a friend, any kind of friend, whether or not he agreed with him. Rossler just had to learn to understand that, and to learn that he wasn't even close to being in charge.

Steadman took the pistol off the seat and made sure it was ready to use. He jammed it under his belt, and with the street empty, left his pickup and entered the complex.

Rossler met him at the top of the stairs, nattily dressed in a heavily starched Air Force officer's uniform. Tall and slim, with a confident gait, he could appear in charge in anybody's unit.

"You're late," he told Steadman, lighting a cigarette.

Steadman followed him through the building. They passed an apartment where the door was slightly ajar. An old-time cop drama was unfolding on the television, and the voices of an arguing couple carried over the gunshots into the hall.

Steadman checked his watch. "Early, is what I am."

"Our watches don't agree."

"My watch is what counts, Major Rossler."

They stopped at the apartment door. The cop drama and the arguing couple echoed in the hall behind them. Rossler puffed on his cigarette and unlocked the door.

"What are you worried about?" Steadman asked.

"It's an edgy day," Rossler replied.

Steadman studied the apartment's interior. Plain walls and plain pictures of flowers in fields and fruit in baskets hung on plain frames. Threadbare furniture rested on threadbare rugs over a worn hardwood floor, and it appeared that the drapes hadn't been changed since the mid-seventies, when the complexes were built and furnished.

Only the toaster in the kitchen and a full-length mirror on a living room wall were new, and the oscillating fans that forced dead air through the room.

"This is Lieutenant Hill's place," Rossler told Steadman. "It's not much but it's got a good view of the base."

Lieutenant Shannon Hill sat on her couch, cleaning a pistol.

"If you don't like my place, Rossler, you can leave. We'd be better off without you."

"It's Major Rossler to you."

"Not anymore it isn't. You were transferred out of special projects. Remember? You're in maintenance now, where you belong."

Steadman had gathered information on both Rossler and Lieutenant Hill from sources he believed he could trust. He couldn't be too careful regarding his associates at a time like this.

Rossler had been on base for five years, rising to a senior officer position within launch control. Two weeks after Lieutenant Hill's arrival, he had been transferred to the maintenance team. He had never received answers as to why he was transferred, further fueling his anger toward the military and his career hopes in general.

Lieutenant Hill had been at Malmstrom six weeks, assigned to the Launch Control Team. An electrical engineer and a crack pilot, the word among outside militia forces was that she had recruited a number of malcontents while on assignments in North and South Dakota. She had assembled a number of men willing to join a revolutionary cause they saw as just. They believed that controls over civilian and military populations alike had become far too invasive, and that the situation would soon turn into permanent martial law. A move had to be made to ensure that the power complex was compromised.

After departing, Lieutenant Hill had kept in touch with her old bases, promising Steadman that once the major plan went into effect, all loyal followers would break and join.

She looked up from her work. "I've been meaning to ask you, General Steadman. What does today's plan of action have to do with the overall objective?"

"We have to send messages to those who believe they're in charge," Steadman replied. "This will be a clear message, I can assure you."

"I wish I was assured," Rossler said.

Steadman thought a moment about the seemingly sudden turn of attitude. He had always been arrogant, but today was off the charts.

"This is no time for a test, Major," he said. "Am I understood?"

Rossler blew a cloud of smoke into the room and turned away. The arguing couple in the other apartment intensified their volume, their voices rising.

"Let's get ready," Steadman said. "Get those rifles packed."

Rossler balanced the ashes on his cigarette. "What's the rush?" he asked. "We've got some waiting to do."

"Everything needs to be in place," Steadman insisted.

"Yes, in place." Rossler blew more smoke into the room.

Lieutenant Hill got up from the couch. She walked to the window and opened it.

"What's the matter?" Rosser asked. "You don't like my smoke?"

"You, the smoke, it's all the same." She trained a pair of binoculars on the base.

Rossler flicked the ashes onto the couch and turned to Steadman. "Is Pearson ready with his end of it?"

"He's got things under control," Steadman replied.

At the window, Lieutenant Hill said, "They've arrived."

Steadman followed Rossler to the window. At the base, a military helicopter landed. Montana's senior senator, Shelby Barnes, disembarked with four security men. On the ground to greet him were Malmstrom's wing commander, Brigadier General Arthur Dolan, newly appointed, and a number of junior officers.

"Right on time," Steadman said. "They must want to do some serious drinking."

Lieutenant Hill continued to peer through the binoculars. "Looks like it. They're headed straight for the Officer's Club."

Steadman moved away from the window and dialed his cellular phone. When he heard Bert Pearson answer, he said, "The countdown begins. Zero minus forty minutes."

At first there was no answer. Then, "Arlan, is that you?"

Steadman hesitated. "This is General Steadman."

"Oh, sorry," Pearson said. "Yes, General?"

"Is everything on schedule?" Steadman asked.

"On schedule," Pearson said. "Ten-four that."

Steadman heard the phone click.

"Did you reach him?" Rossler asked.

"Yes, I did," Steadman replied. He studied Rossler. "When's the last time you talked to him?"

Rossler dragged deeply from his cigarette. "What do you mean?"

"Simple question. When did you last speak to Bert Pearson?"

Before Rossler could answer, Steadman had drawn his 9mm pistol.

"And the meaning of this?" Rossler asked.

"Things aren't adding up here," Steadman replied. He turned to Lieutenant Hill. "Take his cell phone and give it to me, along with yours."

She did as ordered, her face a pasty white.

Rossler crunched his cigarette into the carpet, creating a black and sooty spot.

"Foolish, you are," he said. "Again I ask, what are you doing?"

The voices of the arguing tenants grew even louder. They had taken their fight into the hall.

"What is your answer to my question, General?" Rossler insisted.

Steadman moved quickly and with precision. He took a pillow from the couch, jammed it into Rossler's midsection, and stuck the muzzle of his pistol against it. He pulled the trigger and a dull *whoomp* sounded as Rossler doubled over.

Rossler lay moaning on the floor as Steadman approached Lieutenant Hill.

"What's going on here, Lieutenant?" he asked.

"You tell me, General," she replied coolly.

"You don't seem a bit alarmed."

"If you intend to kill me, too, then do it."

"You and he had something planned, didn't you? Something against me."

"You just ruined it all, General," she said. "We could have gotten it done."

"That's not an answer to my question."

"You have all the answers, General Steadman. Or you think you do."

Steadman backed Lieutenant Hill into the kitchen and forced her into a chair. "Stay here for at least an hour, if you know what's good for you. It's your choice."

He left her sitting, staring at him, and backed up slowly toward the door. In the hall, he hid the pistol under his coat and started past the arguing couple. The man had begun to slap his wife. Steadman pulled the pistol and brought it down solidly against the man's nose, sending him to the floor.

Steadman left the wife doubled over her husband, screaming oaths at him.

Should have left well enough alone, I guess. Steadman thought it all the way down the street. *No one sees when they're being helped.*

Steadman pulled into the park. Wetzel saw him and rushed to the sedan. Steadman parked the stolen SUV and jumped in with Wetzel.

"Drive this thing out of here."

"Things really went south, huh?" Wetzel drove with restraint, careful not to attract attention.

"I had to shoot Rossler. Didn't bother me a bit. I told Hill to stay put for an hour."

"For an hour?"

"Are Jack and Reggie still watching to see that she's staying put?" Steadman asked, referring to another pair of his men whom he had stationed down the street in a second floor apartment to watch his back.

"Not anymore, General. She came out not a minute behind you and Jack got her with one shot."

"No one saw them?"

"They got away clean," Wetzel said. "Lots of cops around there now, though."

"Damn it!" Steadman said. "Now we have to start all over. With everything."

"Better than falling into a trap," Wetzel pointed out.

"I still intend to make Barnes pay for his crimes."

"He will, in time," Wetzel assured him. "What tipped you off that it was a trap?"

"I called Pearson and he was expecting Rossler to call."

"Yeah, see, Sam Grant was right." Wetzel negotiated his way out of town along the back streets, careful to stay with the flow of traffic.

"He has a habit of being that way." Steadman wrung his hands. "I wish to hell he'd join us."

"Doubt if he ever will," Wetzel remarked. "But if I were you, I'd sure as hell keep in touch with him."

Pearson sat in the Jeep with Karst again behind the wheel. The soldiers still lay out in the field, covered with the net, awaiting the signal to advance. Just so none of them broke their programming.

He had other worries now. He fretted about having mistaken Steadman for Rossler on his cell phone. Not a smart move. He didn't want to try and call Rossler now. Better to wait until Rossler called.

For now, he had a lot of work to do before the operation could begin.

He ordered Karst to turn the Jeep down a private roadway, off the county road. After a half mile, there appeared a secluded set of buildings along a small stream.

There a soldier named Densen greeted him. He stood in front of a large water truck, awaiting his orders. Willie Jens was supposed to be with him.

"Private Densen, where is Private Jens?"

"He said he was going hunting, sir."

"Hunting?"

A boom sounded and Willie appeared at the brow of a nearby hill, pointing out into the distance.

"What does he think he's doing?"

"I don't think the shot will be of consequence, sir."

"You don't, do you?"

"No, sir. Somebody's taking target practice out here all the time."

"Get him the hell down here," Pearson demanded.

Densen started up the hill at a trot. Pearson paced, checking his watch. Karst sat in the Jeep, staring out into the countryside.

Pearson had always wondered if Willie was going to work out as part of the Plan. He had attended classes with the others, but the instructors had mentioned more than once that Willie had a difficult time assimilating the information presented to him and keeping everything in order in his mind.

"Even with the new computer-generated programs," one instructor had observed, "he's a very difficult file."

Pearson was always amused at the various instructors' choice of words. All their subjects were referred to as "files" and "processing units," never as soldiers or men. Perhaps these "instructors" didn't know anymore what the word *human* actually meant.

Or perhaps they never had known the meaning of the term.

No matter, Willie Jens had somehow misfired under the curriculum. He had fractured too badly under the techniques used on him. He wasn't able to disassociate and then return to core consciousness well enough to create the multiple layers of personalities needed for the program. Every successful "candidate" had become a number of different people, internally and mentally, within a single individual, and was then able to complete missions without failing, and without even knowing they had been involved.

Densen had become well programmed and was ready for the operation. They had said no such thing about Willie Jens.

By Pearson's calculations, Willie would be better off back in the main encampment at the edge of the Missouri badlands, where he would be harmless and out of the way. If he was a difficult "file," he had no business being a part of this operation, especially one of this magnitude.

But it had been at Arlan Rossler's insistence that Willie definitely play a major role. All Rossler would say is, "You'll understand my reasoning when this is over."

Willie and Densen came to a halt in front of Pearson. Willie, disregarding Pearson's questions about his absence from rank, held up a Sharps buffalo rifle, 52 caliber, and smiled. "I got me an antelope."

"We're not hunting antelope today, Willie," Pearson reminded him.

"A damned fine shot I made. I should be a sniper."

"Willie, we've got a job to do and we're running late."

"Can I gut my antelope out before it spoils?" He laughed.

"Where's your weapon, Willie?"

"My sugar baby?"

"Where is it, Willie? Get it and join me and

Private Densen at the water truck. Is that understood, Willie?"

Willie saluted. "Oh, yes, sir."

Pearson and Densen left for the water truck.

"Please, sir," Densen said. "I'm sorry about Willie. I really had no idea."

"It's all right, Private. I didn't expect you to have to baby-sit him."

At the water truck, Pearson lifted the tarp off the back. Jammed in next to the water tank was a wire cage. A large jackrabbit bounced back and forth off the sides, its eyes wide, its nostrils flaring.

"Well done, Private," Pearson said. "He's a nice one."

"He'll do the trick, sir."

"That he will."

Willie Jens arrived with his sugar baby, an M-60 assault rifle, the stock filled with notches. Few men were strong enough to handle such a weapon, but Willie was among them. Around his shoulders he wore two large belts, which held a number of clips for the rifle. Without a word he jumped into the passenger side of the water truck.

Densen saluted. "I'm ready, sir."

"You will wait for my radio dispatch. Is that understood, soldier?"

"Yes, sir!"

In the passenger seat, Willie Jens filled his mouth with gum and stared out the windshield.

"Wish I could have gutted that antelope," he said.

Karst sat staring from the driver's seat of the Jeep. Pearson got in and instructed him to drive.

"Yes, sir. Ready, sir."

Pearson thought about the upcoming events as Karst drove the Jeep further along the base of the mountains. The day promised heat, likely approaching one hundred degrees.

No matter the weather, no matter anything, Pearson had decided by now that getting the job done was foremost, and that to worry about Willie Jens, or Steadman or Rossler, or any other part of the Plan, was counterproductive.

He tightened the bandoleer of ammunition over his shoulder. Karst continued to drive hard over the twisting gravel road. Dust boiled from under the tires like clouds of gray flour.

"Do you think Alpha 1 will be an easy take, sir?" Karst asked.

"If everyone does their job, Private."

"It happened this morning, and the whole story still isn't clear."

They walked together on Grant's ranch along a fence line, looking out across the open toward the Highwood Mountains. Jane was informing Grant what she'd learned about Steadman's plan to abduct Senator Shelby Barnes, and how something had gone wrong before the attempt had even been made.

"They met at a rundown apartment near the base, and Steadman apparently shot Arlan Rossler through a pillow at point-blank range," she continued. "But so far, Rossler has survived the wound. Lieutenant Hill, on the other hand, was shot and killed just outside the apartment building, by an unknown assailant."

"And Steadman?"

"Disappeared. Without a trace."

"What about Bert Pearson?" Grant asked. "Where is he and the rest of Steadman's men?"

"Nothing is clear on that, either."

"Nothing is clear on anything, then," Grant concluded. "And the biggest part of this whole thing has yet to happen."

"That's why your place is right here," she said, "where no one can implicate you."

IV

Pearson ordered Karst to stop the Jeep under the cover of pine trees. With his binoculars, he studied the field between them and Alpha 1, where the programmed soldiers remained in place, like kids sleeping at a day-care center.

"Ready yourself, Private Karst," he said.

"Yes, sir." Karst stepped out of the Jeep and stood at attention.

Pearson paced back and forth, checking and rechecking his watch. Still no call from Rossler. Something must have gone wrong, somehow. He knew deep inside that having mistaken Steadman for Rossler must have caused problems. Perhaps they called it off. Perhaps something else happened.

But no matter, Pearson knew he must complete his part of the Plan.

And the time had arrived.

The water truck with Densen and Willie Jens was approaching Alpha 1. Things would happen fast, and the soldiers had to be in position for their part in the operation.

"Proceed, Private Karst," Pearson ordered.

"Yes, sir."

Karst removed a flare gun from the floorboards

of the Jeep. With his rifle slung over his shoulder, he marched out into the field toward the row of soldiers waiting under the net.

Pearson knew his end of the operation had few chances to go wrong. Getting inside Alpha 1 was a given. Water had to be hauled there on a regular basis, as the underground aquifer contained massive amounts of salt. The truck generally ran twice a week, and this was the normal second run. If they got in the gates, the rest should almost take care of itself.

Getting the truck hadn't been so easy. A farmer who was the contractor didn't share antigovernment feelings and couldn't be persuaded to loan out his vehicle. In fact, he had threatened to warn the military. So late the day before, Pearson had paid the man a visit. No one would ever find the bachelor's body, thrown down a rock crevice along the slopes of the Highwood Mountains.

During the initial phase of the plan, Pearson had worried that the servicemen on Alpha 1 might wonder at someone other than the regular contractor driving the truck, but Rossler had assured him that there were so many new servicemen that few of them knew any of the contractors, anyway.

Now it was time to see if Rossler was correct in his assumption.

Pearson trained a pair of binoculars on the launch

control facility just over a mile away. He smiled. The gates were opening.

Densen drove the water truck through the Alpha I gate and waved to the guard. Willie twisted in his seat.

"Can't he see Karst coming across the field way out there?"

"Relax, Willie. He's watching us. It's his job."

"Someone's going to see Karst before long."

"Yes, Willie. That's expected."

"Densen, he's looking at me. He knows something's up. I'm going to take him out."

"Willie, that's nuts." He held his arm across Jens's lap to hold him in place. "Do you want General Pearson to court-martial you?"

"General Steadman won't allow anyone to court-martial me."

"General Steadman isn't here, Willie. General Pearson is. And he will do it."

Willie settled back. "Where's General Steadman?"

"Do as you're told, Willie. Don't worry about anything else."

Densen backed the truck up. He got out, and with a tire tool he lifted the heavy metal lid off the cistern, then fitted one end of a heavy plastic pipe to the valve opening on the water tank and shoved the other end into the cistern.

He cranked the valve open and watched the water gush from the pipe into the cistern. He turned and gazed up toward the mountains, focusing on Karst, where he had come to a stop, still a good ways above the hidden soldiers.

Karst was preparing for the next phase of the Plan.

Densen then looked to the LCF main door, where the servicemen on duty inside were going about their day.

He checked his watch. Time to begin.

"Willie, come help me with the tarp."

Jens jumped from the truck and they removed the tarp. Willie held it as a shield for Densen, who struggled with the rabbit cage. The big jack bounced back and forth off the sides until Densen got the latch free and the door open.

The rabbit bounded free. Headed for the open distance, it jumped into the sensitive zone along the perimeter fence. An alarm sounded and in a short time, an alert-response team emerged from the door, looking for signs of encroachment.

Densen looked back up toward the hill. Karst had his arm in the air. A flare gun sounded and a flash of fire rose high into the sky.

The soldiers rose at the signal, yelling, coming out from under the net with their rifles, surging forward like a bad dream. They took position and opened fire on the alert-response team, dispatching them with deadly accuracy. The response team began a systematic return of fire, filling the area with smoke.

Willie dropped the tarp and jumped into the truck. He grabbed his sugar baby and swung it around.

Densen stood at the truck door. "Willie, wait!" he hissed. "Let the Plan work, will you?"

Willie pushed past Densen, ran into the main building, and opened fire on the confused servicemen in the lunchroom. Densen ran after him, yelling for him to stop and to follow the Plan as laid out.

Inside, those who had not been killed or wounded by Willie's murderous fire had dropped to the floor.

Densen grabbed him by the collar. "No more shooting, Willie! Do you understand?"

"I got them good, didn't I?"

"You're not following orders, Willie."

"Okay, okay," Jens said. "I just wanted to be sure we took this place."

"We need hostages, Willie. How many times have I told you?"

"We've got some. Look." Jens pointed to three

survivors trembling on the floor under the tables.

"Keep them covered, Willie. We need all of them."

The burp of an automatic weapon sounded and Densen twisted and fell, bullets having raked his back and left leg. Willie opened fire on the serviceman who had appeared from somewhere outside.

"Damn, I'm hit!" Densen shouted.

Willie dragged him across the room and propped him up against the wall. "I'll get Sam Grant to come for us," he said.

"What?" Densen managed.

"Just keep the hostages covered for me," Willie said.

Pearson watched from the hill. He jumped into the Jeep and moved his position to another hill nearby. He punched numbers into his cell phone and listened to the bleeps. "C'mon, Rossler," he said to himself. "Be there."

He got a recorded message that stated the party he wished to reach was not available and that leaving a message was not an option. Then the connection was broken.

Pearson cursed and looked out into the distance, toward Great Falls. They were yet just dots in the sky, but when he put his binoculars to them he could easily make out three Apache gun ships. The alarm from Alpha 1 had already reached the base and a team was responding.

In less than five minutes the gun ships were circling Alpha 1. One broke off toward the programmed militia soldiers' position. Pearson could see Karst standing with his hands held high as the helicopter approached. Five of the programmed soldiers dropped their rifles and stood with their hands in the air as well.

Five of them had already been killed or wounded. The remaining five stood up in unison and aimed their rifles into the air. They were systematically mowed down by fire from the alert-response team and the gun ship.

Pearson started the Jeep and turned up a hidden road that led back into the mountains behind.

From a fence post a meadowlark sang to the afternoon. The news media had arrived in droves. They hadn't responded in time to view the firefight, or the capture of the five surviving militia soldiers and their subsequent evacuation in one of the helicopters. The bodies had also been removed, taken away by the two other gun ships. So, reporters were focused directly on Alpha 1 and the continued siege inside.

Camped behind FBI and Air Force barricades, their cameras rolled nonstop, gaining valuable footage of three new Apache gun ships arriving from the base.

Willie Jens stood in the control room with his rifle trained on a serviceman manning the radio.

"Tell the choppers to leave," Willie demanded.

"They won't do that, sir," the serviceman told him. "They want you to surrender your arms and come out with your hands on top of your head."

"You know that's not going to happen, soldier," Willie said.

"I don't know why you attacked in the first place," the serviceman said. "You might capture a missile base, but you'll never fire a missile. It doesn't work that way."

"We have a message from General Charles Steadman," Willie responded. "He is building a new nation, and no one is going to stop him. He and Sam Grant are building it together. We are all going to save this nation and our freedoms."

The serviceman stared at him.

"We know where a large compound of terrorists are hiding out, on the Afghan border. One missile will get them all."

The serviceman's mouth dropped open. He noticed that Willie appeared to be mouthing words that were almost recorded within him somehow. His eyes were glassy and his lips dripped saliva.

"Talk into the radio," Willie continued. "Tell them to bring Sam Grant here and I will release the hostages."

"And what if Sam Grant, whoever he is, doesn't come here?" the serviceman asked. "Why would he?"

"I have my orders!" Willie yelled.

The radio operator spoke into the mike to a helicopter pilot and then to an FBI negotiations expert, who wanted to talk to Willie.

"Mr. Jens," the serviceman said, "there is a request that you speak to someone in one of the helicopters."

"I've said all I need to," Willie told him.

"My advice to you, sir, is to surrender immediately," the serviceman pleaded. "That's the best way out of this."

"We'll wait for Sam Grant."

"And if he doesn't come, then what? You know the response teams are already out there."

"We have hostages, can't you see that?"

"And after you've killed them all, then what?"

Willie felt confused. "I don't have orders after that."

He thought a moment and ordered the radio operator ahead of him into the lunchroom. The radio operator complied, his hands behind his head.

"What's this?" Willie said.

Densen lay slumped over in a pool of blood. He didn't respond to Willie's kicks and nudges. The hostages were gone.

"You can end this now, Mr. Jens," the serviceman said. "You can surrender and save your life."

"I can't save anything," Willie said.

The radio operator turned and faced Willie, working on words in his mind, words the FBI negotiator had told him to say if the circumstance presented itself.

"You are supposed to let me go," he said.

"What?" Willie responded.

"Yes, General Steadman said you're supposed to let me go."

Willie frowned deeply. "When did you speak to the General?"

"He's in the helicopter, Willie. He wants you to surrender and come out."

Willie's eyes were even glassier, his mind going in many different directions. "Why didn't you tell me before?"

"I'm going now," the operator said.

"If General Steadman gave the order," Willie said, "then you are free to go."

He ordered the serviceman to run, double time, out of the building onto the LCF grounds. The serviceman did as ordered, churning in a straight line past the water truck toward the open gates, tripping alarms that sounded like loud horns.

Willie Jens gripped his MK-60 and stood at the open doorway. Past the gates, the servicemen had all fallen to their stomachs under cover. Special teams had taken positions all around the area and orders were shouted along the lines.

Willie heard a voice inside his head.

The dark army is coming, Willie. Are you ready for them?

"I'm ready for them," he said.

They don't want our new nation, Willie.

"Our new nation," Willie said. "I'll die for our new nation."

Are you strong enough for that, Willie?

"Yes," Willie said as he started out into the open. "Yes! I'll make all of you proud of me, I promise."

The sun hovered over the tops of the distant mountains, a swirling red ball filtered by waves of heat. The media scrambled for better position as Sam Grant and Jane Connors disembarked a helicopter, along with a number of Air Force and FBI personnel.

"Didn't you get the message?" one of the ground commanders asked. "It's all over."

"Grant wanted to come and take a look anyway," the FBI negotiator said. "Just keep an eye on him."

"Why didn't you let me talk to him?" Grant asked the negotiator.

"It wouldn't have made any difference."

"You don't know that."

"We don't have much time, Mr. Grant," the negotiator said. "And don't go inside. Understood?"

"What am I supposed to see from out here?"

"Just don't go inside."

Grant and Jane talked as they surveyed the area outside the LCF. "I can't believe anyone in their right mind would even attempt this," Grant said. "Makes no sense at all."

"Willie Jens was reported to have told one of the helicopter pilots that you and Steadman organized it. The five captured men said the same thing. All of them." She hesitated. "And that you wanted to send a missile into Afghanistan."

"I know Charlie's off the deep end," Grant commented, "but even he wouldn't attempt to do something like that. Not a chance."

"Are you sure?"

Grant shrugged. "I guess I'm not sure of anything at this point."

"Then what do you think all this was about?" Jane asked.

"If you don't know, I sure don't," Grant replied. "The papers will say that this was an act of terrorism by militia forces, led by Steadman and myself. That will be the official word on the matter."

"They have no solid evidence, Sam."

"It puzzles me that Willie would think I'd come here," Grant said. "I told him repeatedly to take a hike."

"There's a lot that's very strange about this whole thing," Jane said.

They boarded the helicopter, and as they rose up and headed toward Great Falls, Grant peered across the vast countryside and wondered where it would all lead. Nothing about the incident with Steadman early in the morning and this one at the LCF seemed to make any logical sense. He believed, though, that Charles Steadman had been set up and had somehow managed to see it early on.

And the militia soldiers had been told, or somehow forced, to say what they had. No one could believe anyone would try to send a missile somewhere. But in this day and age, almost anything seemed possible.